Eagle's Nest

By

Alexander Presniakov

ISBN: 0-75961-326-5

This book is printed on acid free paper.

1stBooks - rev. 3/12/01

In war truth is such a precious
thing that it must be shielded
by a bodyguard of lies.

— Winston Churchill

About Eagle's Nest

Eagle's Nest is a political thriller set in the most unpredictable period of World War II, the Summer of 1940.

Hitler has Europe in his iron grip and only England stands in his way. Soon England will face the mighty Luftwaffe air raids; Churchill knows Hitler is planning an invasion. He marshals a plan.

Kurt Duran, England's greatest spy, is called upon a mission of the highest order, to penetrate the Nazi high command's inner circle at Hitler's prized retreat called Eagle's Nest, high in the Bavarian mountains. Field marshal Goring will be attending a pre-invasion party and will have with him the secret invasion maps. Kurt Duran is sent to an isolated English coastline to prepare for his mission with the assistance of a beautiful Jewish resistance fighter from France. Soon they fall in love and their destinies become intertwined. Duran and his love race against time to save England before it's too late.

Chapter One

He stood in the only dry spot on the street. The rains pounded the pavement. Kurt Duran lit up a cigarette in cupped hands and took two quick puffs. He waited in the archway of the abbey; the church was centuries old and looked every bit of it. The ship he came off, the *Merry Mariners*, was docked two city blocks down. He wore a reefer coat, trousers, and boots. His furlough had begun and the rains stopped none too soon. He wanted a taste of the nightlife. He was coming back from a dangerous mission, working undercover for the OSS. He was their best operative, recruited during the start of the war.

Right now he needed the pleasing company of the opposite sex. As he brushed his damp, black hair to the side, the lamplight revealed a rugged face full of contradictions. Strong but weary, young yet wiser than his years. He was a burly six foot tall with eyes as dark as coals. He had undone the top button of his reefer coat and began to walk slowly toward the bright lights of the saloon. Inside the music played cheerfully as if all of England had converged within.

To his amazement, as he stepped in, it was nearly empty. A couple of old salts occupied a table to the right, some sailors played poker in the back, and the only decent looking woman was busy sipping a drink at the corner of the bar. One leg crossed over the other, head tilted to the side, she was deep in thought. He ordered himself a Jack Daniels to warm his bones as he sat on the barstool one away from hers. She glanced over. "Are you in the Army?"

"Of sorts," he said. "I'm on furlough, just got in. Say, tell me, is this all the excitement there is in this town?"

She looked him over and took another swallow of her drink. "Depends on what kind of excitement you mean."

He smiled at the mere thought of what that implied and downed half his glass.

He checked his watch. It was nearly 7:30 p.m. There was still plenty of time to have a good evening of fun. His eyes met hers and he asked for her name.

"Rebecca," she replied softly.

"Have you lived here long?"

"Here? Oh no, love, I'm from the south side, been here a whole of two months."

"I see. I myself am from Grosvenor Square, been there all my life until this bloody war started to turn everything upside down."

Her eyes got teary.

"What is it?"

She half turned away. "Oh, my father and brother. They were both killed by the Luftwaffe as they were bringing in their fishing boat. The Germans made quick work of the vessel."

1

"I'm sorry."

"It's all right, it's just—"

The sailors in the back began to fistfight as one of the men claimed the other to be cheating at cards. Chairs were flung through the air, tables overturned. Kurt cupped his drink in hand and smiled at Rebecca. "And I thought I'd come here to relax."

She stood up. "You can still do that, I have a room upstairs. Let's go."

As they exited up a creaking, wooden staircase, the bartender below took out a double-barreled shotgun and demanded a truce.

She led him along the poorly lit corridor with old rugs that barely covered the cracked floors. She stopped by a door and invited him in.

"How do you manage a room in this place?" he said.

She pulled him in by his coat. "I'm the entertainment around here. Lady Rebecca, to be formally introduced. I sing here five nights a week. Tonight is my night off." She closed the door behind her and turned on a radio on her night table. Romantic French love songs filled the air, as Kurt made his way to a quaint burgundy sofa at the end of the room.

He could see the passion in her fiery eyes. She gently kissed his lips as she undid his shirt. His powerful, manly arms at his sides, he just stood there, enjoying the moment.

She slipped out of her blue evening gown, which fell to the floor to reveal to him a most charming figure of a young woman with milky white skin and rosy cheeks. She anxiously removed the rest of his clothes and yanked him into bed with her. The bedsprings creaked as they landed on the mattress top.

The passion that followed was all-consuming in its intensity. She moaned in ecstasy as he kissed her neck and breasts. His eyes were now half closed as he worked his way down to the darkened arrowhead of her pubis. She tingled with excitement. She moved to please him as he lay on his back. She rode him gently at first, leaning forward to kiss his lips. He could not contain himself any longer. He pushed her forward and with a fierce intensity he pounded her. His legs strained, every muscle flexed, as he was about to reach his climax. He took a deep sigh, and suddenly all was still. With his right arm around her shoulder, her head had come to rest on the pillow.

"That was magnificent," she said softly. "Thank you."

"I have you to thank, Rebecca. You and this night."

She turned to him, looking quite solemn. "When do you have to leave?"

He paused for a moment. "When they need me." As an afterthought he added, "And not before."

The rain started up again as the first droplets pounded against the wooden shutters outside. "Kurt, let's just stay here tonight. The nights here are brutal and when it rains it can be merciless."

The rain had turned into an outright downpour. "Whatever you say, my dear, just let me pay for breakfast in the morning."

That night, German wolf packs did much damage to cargo ships in the North Sea, hitting and crippling several destroyers who were out on escort and sinking two of them. The year was 1940 and German high command had demanded total victory at sea. There were to be no supply lines of any kind left available to the British.

Hitler was in his chancellery in Berlin. It was late in the evening, and Nazi SS troops stood guard outside. The Führer was in the final stages of planning Operation Sea Lion—the all-out invasion of England. But certain points of the invasion still bothered him. The RAF, he knew, could be crippled by Stuka dive-bombers, the British Army was a shadow of its former self, yet he had not in his mind worked out all of the possibilities, and it was eating away at him. He knew Churchill was an old warhorse no matter how badly he took a beating. Göring had reassured the Führer that the Luftwaffe would annihilate the British. Hitler reminded him, "Yes, and you said the same thing about Dunkirk, only to have three hundred thousand Britons escape."

He could not rest until he had his guarantee. It had to be there somewhere. He could not risk an all-out invasion of England until he had it.

Winston Churchill had strolled out onto his balcony at Meltham House in his white shirt and trousers, his cigar firmly planted in his mouth, as he read the day's report from British Intelligence. German torpedoes had destroyed all cargo and escort ships at the Devil's Hole in the Black Sea. As the supply line was bending around Norway, German wolf packs had sent the ships down at a quarter past eight in the evening on Thursday, June 19, 1940. Churchill stopped momentarily, lowered the papers, and contemplated. Thousands of lives were lost with several direct hits, he thought to himself.

His valet brought him his usual morning drink, two thirds Scotch and one third seltzer water. He took a quick sip and in his mind tried to find a solution on how to deal with those pirates of the sea. He stared intently out into the fields and hastily disappeared back inside to begin his breakfast.

The morning came, mercifully quiet. Kurt hadn't slept that well in ages, and Rebecca was just waking up. He was staring blankly at the ceiling when she asked him, "Bacon or ham?"

"What?" he muttered.

"For your eggs," she said, "bacon or ham?"

"Oh. Bacon, please."

She went about putting on her dress, and he asked her if she would mind bringing up the morning paper. After a quick breakfast Kurt was all but out the door when Rebecca approached him. "Leaving so soon? And where will you go?"

He shrugged, "Out and about, but I'll be back for lunch. I have a little business to take care of."

Outside the morning air was refreshingly clear after a good night's rain. The sun shined on the old, stony streets as he walked over to the *Merry Mariners*. One of the deckhands saw him approaching and called out to him. "The captain would like to have a word with you in his cabin."

He made his way aboard ship, rushed down below and stepped inside where an old, gruff voice greeted him. "Well, Kurt, I suppose you heard." The man was somewhere in the neighborhood of 50 years of age but looked much older, with gray hair and beard cut short. He was dressed in tacky green trousers and an old, rumpled brown jacket.

Kurt hesitated, "You mean the wolf packs?"

"Yes, third time this week." The captain's voice had a certain bitterness to it. He sank deeper into the wooden armchair behind his desk. His right hand played around with an ivory letter opener, carved to resemble a dagger. He avoided direct eye contact and slammed it on the tabletop. "Do you know what those attacks are doing to the men out there? Do you have any idea?"

Kurt remained quiet. His eyes downcast. What could he say? The captain's face expressed all the rage and despair and hopelessness that he shared.

The captain sighed. "My point is this. We need to find a way to protect ourselves when we go out next time. I thought you'd have an idea or two."

Kurt shook his head. "What I did the last two years was my business. I'll stay with the *Merry Mariners* as long as I'm of service. I'm in charge of operations and you oversee the ship. I will not overstep my parameters, sir."

The captain looked at him calmly, "You will never tell me what happened, what they put you through behind those enemy lines, will you?"

He didn't bother to answer, just turned and walked back outside, keeping quiet and to himself, fixing his coat as he went. The *Merry Mariners* was employed by the OSS, a crack team of special operations agents assigned to various sabotage missions throughout the European theater. Disguised as a fishing ship, she had been on many missions. Tensions ran high at times, too high, but as a team they worked quite well.

Duran was heading down to a local pay phone, checking his pockets for change. He took out two bits and deposited them. As he began dialing a hand gripped his left shoulder and a voice asked, "Duran, come with me." He turned around slowly, a bit apprehensive. It was Ian Richards, the contact for British Intelligence in that part of the country. He had followed Duran since he docked.

"Well," Kurt said, "what the devil do you want? I just got back."

As the men began to walk, Richards steered him past the locals to a deserted factory. "I trust you found your lodgings accommodating?" He grinned.

4

"You saw Rebecca?"

He nodded. "You've got very good taste. Now let me tell you why I'm here. You see, the secretary of state for air defense, Sir Archibald Sinclair, whom Prime Minister Churchill looks upon with the utmost respect . . . This Sinclair is in fact the only person next to the prime minister who knows all the exact data of the RAF. Her strengths, all of her operational procedures, flight commands, as well as her weaknesses. He was on a short vacation with a friend of his from the army, General Hastings, staying at his estate, when we received word that the Nazis have hatched a plan to kidnap him.

"They landed not too long ago. He's trapped on the island off the Cardiff coast of England, at the Devil's Cove. Get him before the Nazis take him back to Germany. The island is small, there's not much to it but some rocks, cliffs, and about three dozen cottages with families and the lighthouse. You'll have to pick up Sir Sinclair tonight under the nose of the Germans. Is that understood?"

Kurt said nothing, just nodded. Just as quickly as he had appeared, Richards left. Duran was silent. He was eager to tangle with the enemy again, he just hadn't thought it would be so soon. He had some time yet before the ship was to set sail. Rebecca was waiting for him back at the saloon. He didn't know if he'd make it back, so he thought, one more tryst won't hurt.

Back in Berlin, Hitler's high command were all but worn out from his frenzied demands to review Operation Sea Lion for the tenth time. He had until now successfully avoided a two-front war. He knew if he didn't conquer Britain quickly it would give her and her allies time to regroup. The Führer had excused himself from the meeting. He had developed an acute headache. All the others had left except for Himmler and Göring, who was sitting in his elaborate field marshal's uniform with the red and white collar, the gray coat unbuttoned. He refused to take it off. He had developed chills from sitting in the damp, cold interior of the oversized living room. Himmler stood up, arched his back a bit, and walked across the vast expanse of the living room and up to the huge window that extended from the ceiling to the floor. He gazed outside. On the table between the two men lay several unfolded maps of Europe, and one specifically of England, enlarged to see every inlet, cliff and roadway surrounding and leading to London itself. Hitler had left his reading glasses on that table in his hurry to have his personal physician, Dr. Brandt, tend to his condition.

Göring was smiling broadly as he arose and walked around the table to look at the map of England. "Well, I will have my Luftwaffe flatten London just enough so when we come to visit there will still be something left to see."

Himmler grinned. "But be careful of the duke of Windsor, he has proven a worthy ally to the Reich."

Göring shrugged, taking up the joke. "But he is nowhere near London these days." Both men laughed.

The room was lit by the light of the noonday sun. One minute after twelve o'clock a young SS officer walked in smartly, dressed all in black, with his ceremonial dagger at his side." Herr Reichführer, the Führer has asked me to inform you and the field marshal he will be available this afternoon at three o'clock. He wishes to resume discussions then."

Himmler waved him on. As the SS officer acknowledged him and spun around leaving the room, Göring leaned over the map, his arms folded across the table. "And so, you are convinced about the duke, are you?"

Himmler nodded. "The duke of Windsor could prove to be quite useful. Von Ribbentrop mentioned to me that he was eating out of his hands at the mere suggestion of him and the duchess being installed as monarchs of England under the guidance of Nazi Germany. He's ready to sell out his own country."

Göring appeared unconvinced. Himmler continued. "The duke has a checkered past. His own people questioned his intentions. He had served as a major general in France. With our army sweeping through, he and the duchess fled into Spain. The duke and duchess from there came to Lisbon and stayed at Estoril. Two British flying boats were there to take them back to England. The duke subsequently refused and sent them away."

"Why?" said Göring.

"Because he wanted a meaningful post. The man is in need of fulfillment. Our glory is his answer."

Göring edged away from the table, checking his watch. "So there is hope in swaying this duke of Windsor. Perhaps some one should do a profile on the man and see how he measures up. If what you say is so, it would be good to have such data. We could play him like a puppet."

Himmler's eyebrows shot up, as they did when he was thinking seriously. "Well the duke is a complex individual, but not wholly unpredictable. One has to be aware of which buttons to press to get the desired results." He looked over to the map of England. "It now will be left to fight alone," he said.

All of Europe was in the iron grip of the Nazi war machine. Even France was out of the picture. Marshal Philippe Pétain succeeded Reynaud, who had resigned. Pétain, the hero of Verdun, as he was known, was not exhibiting any such heroics these days. He had on the morning of June 17 sued for peace with the Germans.

Churchill had tried his dogged best to keep France fighting; he even made numerous trips to France in spite of the recriminations of Reynaud, who had demanded that England provide that which she was incapable of supplying—all of her remaining squadrons of fighter planes.

These Churchill could not gamble away. The prime minister had tried on the 16th of June to create a union. He offered France union with the British Empire.

The union, he stated, would concentrate its whole energy against the power of the enemy, no matter where the battle might be. This offer was brought to an excited Reynaud by de Gaulle himself, but his cabinet rejected it. Reynaud finally fell ill and the following day Pétain replaced him.

Himmler was busy reading over his notes. Göring, consumed by the events of the past several weeks, continued to drift off in a half dream world of reflections that led up to this moment on June 20, 1940. When Pétain sent a delegation for the purpose of negotiating with the Germans, Hitler took that opportunity to mock the French and demanded on holding the meeting in the same railway carriage that was at Compiégne where Marshal Foch had accepted the German surrender in 1918.

When the French arrived on the 21st of June, they were met by the Nazi leaders. All were present, Hitler, Göring, Hess, along with Ribbentrop, Keitel, and Raeder. France was official beaten. Göring was smiling with delight. He clenched his right hand into a fist and slammed it against the map of England. Then he proclaimed that he would squash it like a fly with his Luftwaffe and gain the respect of the Führer again.

Having finished up with Rebecca, Kurt stood at the foot of her bed. She was sorry to see him go. She looked at him soulfully. "They need you so soon? You just got here last night. What kind of a furlough is this?"

"I can't help it, something has come up. It's nothing I can talk about."

She saw the sternness in his face—a good soldier responding to his orders. There was a war on, after all. But somehow she had hoped to make him stay just a bit longer, perhaps a few more hours of selfish pleasure. This couldn't just end, she thought. "I want you to know something. I'm not a one night party girl. What I did with you, I just don't do. Understand?"

He looked on and just listened.

"I don't know a whole lot about you, but what I do know, I like. Promise me you'll look me up when you have your next furlough come along."

He walked up to her and kissed her. "I will," he whispered.

As he stepped back she reached down by her bed and pulled out a basket covered with a blue handkerchief. "This is just a little something for your trip." As he stepped out into the corridor, basket in hand, she leaned back onto her bed and said softly, "Will I ever see you again?"

"Maybe," he said as he turned and walked away. He stepped outside and glanced around. It was bad enough to cut the furlough time, but to give up a woman as fine as Rebecca was even worse. As he walked toward the *Merry Mariners* he heard the sound of airplanes overhead. As he looked up two twin engine Messerschmitts, one flying in front of the sun and the other coming up along the coast, opened up machine gun fire. He rolled on the ground and came to a stop behind a stone dock anchor. Then came the Dornier Do-17s, bombing

7

the edge of the harbor. Bombs fell indiscriminately, some released prematurely. As he stared in horror, one hit the saloon. It was razed to the ground within seconds, flames shooting into the sky. The German aircrafts had flown off. Picking himself up, he looked around. The *Merry Mariners* was still docked, knocked about by the waves a bit but floating nonetheless. People were filling the streets, assessing the damage. He stared in disbelief as the smoke cleared. Where Rebecca had been, all was blown away. He spotted the overturned basket of fruit she had given him. He froze a moment, grew quite pale, and continued on to the boat.

As he climbed up the gangplank the crewmen were just starting to calm down. They knew they were exceedingly lucky. One of them pointed to a merchant ship not more than twenty yards away, smoldering as it went down. He headed straight to his cabin, took out the papers Richards had given him and sat down in his chair to read his instructions carefully.

Then came a knock at the door. "Who is it?" he said irritably.

"The captain."

"Come in." As he stepped inside, Duran told him bluntly, "We've got a mission from high up. A rescue mission at the Devil's Cove."

The captain tossed a piece of pipe on Kurt's lap. "Well, we'll leave, all right. As soon as we fix the engine. That explosion knocked the stuffing out of it." Kurt looked at the pipe, then at the captain. "So we're sitting ducks here?"

"Calm down, it shouldn't take more than fifteen minutes to repair, then we can be on our way. When you get around to telling me the coordinates of where we are going."

"Just make sure we're fueled and ready. I'll get us to where we need to go. Leave me be."

Hansen slammed the door behind him and stormed off. Kurt sank deeper into his chair as he read over the secret instructions. He could be glad of one thing—the islands close proximity. Any further out and they'd be troubled by the German wolf packs. U-boats were knocking out merchant ships as fast as they were appearing on the horizon. Their commanders were even given the title of "aces," like their airborne counterparts in the Luftwaffe. The aces got their fame by attacking ships as they made their way from a convoy at its dispersal points, all going on their own courses.

The invasion of Britain was a real threat, so the Royal Navy was incapable of diverting forces from the areas around the British Isles to protect the farther shipping routes. They simply lacked the resources.

Kurt stood up and removed from under his bed an old, green army chest with rusted hinges. He flipped the top open and there lay an assortment of weapons. Plastic explosives, a Mauser with silencer. There were also several throwing knives, a small commando harpoon gun, and his wetsuit.

He heard the blissful sound of the engines starting up. He folded the paper and tucked it into the back of his trousers then stepped down into the corridor, heading for the engine room. The captain was there with his mates and by the time Kurt walked in, they were all beaming with delight. The engine was running as smoothly as can be, the damage wasn't as bad as anyone thought, but they were half empty on their gasoline supply.

Kurt told the captain to head for Leeds at full speed. At that moment, Captain Hansen requested Kurt to join him in his cabin. Inside, Hansen sat back in his chair and poured himself some coffee. Kurt stood there, arms folded, and waited, wondering what was on the old man's mind.

The captain, in a very low, thoughtful voice, stated serenely, "I just wanted to tell you, my wife gave birth to an eight-and-a-half-pound baby girl last night in Bath, outside London. I just got word of it today."

Kurt's eyes lit up. "Congratulations, captain. That's wonderful." The captain stood up shakily and said, "Look." He took off his leather jacket and pulled out his shirt to reveal a nasty, gaping wound on his side. Shrapnel from the Nazi bombs had hit him topside.

"My God," Kurt said. "Hansen, let me help you." The captain passed out. When he came to he was spread out on his bunk, his side bandaged. Kurt had managed to patch him up as best he could. There were no medics on board so he used a first aid kit, not wanting to alert the others. Both men knew that would be best for morale, especially before a mission. Kurt gave him some Epsom salts that he placed under his nose, bringing him around fairly quickly.

"You're all right for now," Kurt said. "When we get to Leeds, I'll have our boys pick you up and take you back to your wife and daughter."

The captain looked panicky. "But the mission—"

"The mission is none of your concern now. I'm the one who'll be getting Sinclair. I need you well for whatever high command has in mind for us next. Just remember to kiss your little one for me. By the way, you didn't tell me what her name is."

The captain's eyes darted around a bit as he caught his breath. "Melissa. We named her Melissa."

The *Merry Mariners* was fast approaching the docks near Leeds, where the small boats could refuel regularly in relative calm. The Nazis didn't know or care about the few gasoline drums hidden in the area. So small engine seacraft were free to fuel up with minimal risk whenever danger threatened the larger docks and ports along the coast.

Kurt had used his ship-to-shore line to contact his men, informing them to provide fuel and relieve one wounded Mariner back to Bath. "Only don't embellish the story to your wife about how you got that injury," he said to Hansen.

Hansen sat up in his bunk and grinned. "I'll say only the truth, how I saved your bloody ass from the Nazi incoming and was hit from the side in a moment of gallantry."

Kurt smiled. "Remember, discretion is the better part of valor."

The captain had a good laugh, followed by some coughing as his side hurt too much. "What do we say to the crew?"

"I'll tell the others you've been excused from this mission to make ready for a more important one coming up upon our return. Let's just make sure your wound is covered up. Let me help you get a fresh shirt on."

As the ship pulled up, crewmen tossed lines onto the harbor and dockworkers secured them. The crew of the *Merry Mariners* assembled topside. Kurt wanted to send them out for the gas, to have the captain's departure be less dramatic. When they cleared out, a silver Rolls Royce drove up and stopped on the dirt road immediately before the docks. Two OSS agents dressed in dark suits with dull gray overcoats got out. Kurt was quick to signal them to approach the ship.

He helped Hansen down the dock. As they went, Kurt told him to make sure a doctor looked at the wound.

The captain was in considerable pain but mustered enough courage to smile and thank him for his efforts. With the crew still out of view, the captain got into the vehicle, aided by one of the OSS agents, and looked back at Kurt. "Good luck," he said and with that was helped inside. The OSS drove away, kicking up some dirt as they went. Kurt looked on from atop the dock. They'd been through quite a bit together, and the old man was a bastard to the core, but a worthy ally nonetheless.

Douglas, one of the crew hands, began readying the fuel tank for the gasoline that was being brought on board. "Make sure we have spare tanks loaded up," Kurt said.

"Aye, sir."

He checked his watch. It was ten to five. He could get the old boat across to the island by nightfall. Kurt informed the crew of the captain's departure, then ordered full speed ahead and excused himself.

His desk lamp was on and hanging low over some papers. He took out his instructions again to read about the man he was due to rescue. Sir Sinclair it stated, came from Norway. English by birth, he had done research on German aircraft in Oslo. Norway had been neutral from the start of the war, but due to its geographic importance neutrality proved an impossibility, as Germany in the early morning hours of April 9th, 1940, sent ten German destroyers heading toward the north Norwegian port of Navik. The German operation against Norway was masterminded by one man, Grand Admiral Erich Raeder, commander in chief of its navy. It was a daring effort, with their forces outnumbered by the British ten to one. The Germans used almost their entire surface fleet and five assault groups under the command of General Nikolaus

Von Falkenhost, landing at key points with the Luftwaffe providing air support. Paratroopers went on to capture Oslo's airport only moments after Sinclair took off with his daughter for London. The Germans took the city, the royal family fled by train north to Hamas, and a devilish man by the name of Quisling proclaimed himself as acting prime minister in a new pro-German government.

Kurt heard a knock on the door, put aside his paperwork and said, "Come in." It was Wallace, one of the lads from the wheelhouse. He had stopped by to request that Mr. Duran take the wheel. The waters, it seemed, were getting a might choppy and only Duran had the exact coordinates. Both men made a fast line to the wheelhouse where a crew hand was at the helm. Kurt relieved him and set a course dead ahead for the Devil's Cove.

As he was negotiating the final approach, storm clouds grew darker. The ship was pitching in the white-capped waves, and it started to rain.

Chapter Two

In London, in his study at 10 Downing Street, the prime minister was engrossed by dozens of reports about the potential German invasion of England, for the summer or early autumn of 1940. Sitting behind a large oak desk, smoking his ever-present cigar, he had been going over the latest findings by British Intelligence. Emily Windgate, his personal secretary, was there, as he had a long turbulent morning sorting out the data as fast as it came in.

The reports were sketchy at best. Churchill was aware of the threat of invasion as early as 1939. The British War Cabinet had learned from captured archives that the German Admiralty had begun the study of invading England in earnest, and the primary plan was to use the narrow waters of the English Channel. The archives also stressed certain conditions had to be met, such as the total German control of the French, Dutch and Belgium harbors and coasts. Time had fulfilled those demands, and conditions were now as they had planned.

To Churchill the how was just as important as the when. Coastal batteries aside, Churchill was concerned of the need to increase the efficiency of the air defense. The prime minister had scheduled a meeting that afternoon between the First Lord of the Admiralty, representatives for the secretaries of state for war, and representatives of the Air Defense Research Committee. Also, his old and good friend of over twenty years, Frederick Lindemann, a distinguished scientist who had on numerous occasions given Churchill his views on many important issues. Churchill's concern at this stage was radar. For all its progress of '39, June of 1940 found it sorely lacking, and with the onslaught of the Luftwaffe, he found it inconceivable that the technology of radar should be so poor.

The clock on the wall struck 3:00 p.m. He put his paperwork down and stretched his feet a bit. He hadn't budged from his position in the last six and a half hours. His secretary informed him that his guests had arrived. He stood up slowly, meticulously, as he felt circulation flowing back into his feet. He greeted his visitors officially. After exchanging formalities he asked them to be seated. He saw to it that his secretary left the room and closed the door behind her.

He started by stating the facts as they presented themselves to him—his concern for Hitler's aggressive air attacks as well as the rumored invasion—and expressed his thoughts duly. Finally, he got to the heart of the matter. "Gentlemen," he said, "we must brace ourselves for the worst possible scenario which that madman in Berlin is capable of. We need ears across the Channel and mine are too damn old and tired to be of any use. You boys know about the work being done on radar, yet up until now all I've been able to get are bits and pieces from people, and no one can tell me anything substantial."

The representatives of the Air Defense Research Committee were sitting to Churchill's left. One gentleman wearing an unflattering brown suit and circular spectacles leaned close to the prime minister. "Sir, I regret to inform you that as yet there is nothing new."

Churchill looked patient and yet disappointed, for this was the same line he was being fed over and over. He focused on the secretaries of the state for war. The secretaries had confirmed that independent efforts in the area of Churchill's interest had been forthcoming and should be ready shortly. Churchill skipped the Lord of the Admiralty, and looked to his right. His old friend Mr. Lindemann was sitting nearby. Churchill produced a small smile as he began to puff on his cigar.

Clearing his throat, Frederick, who was sitting casually in his armchair, started to relate to the prime minister in great detail all of the developments to date on the subject of radar.

"Prime Minister, there are more sophisticated methods of tracking the movements of the enemy. In fact, a system was devised by a Robert Watson-Watt just last week, and he is currently in the process of working out all of the technical aspects."

Churchill sat motionless as cigar smoke surrounded his head like a scattering halo. Lindemann continued. "The system, Prime Minister, is called the Chainhome Radar System. Now, its format is relatively simple. Radar signals which are sent out from masts bounce quickly back from objects flying through the sky, and they are then picked up by receivers at the radar station. Now, from that point, it will be displayed as blips on cathode-ray tubes in the receiver huts. These blips warn of an impending raid and are able to indicate the aircrafts height, distance, bearing, as well as their strength."

Churchill nodded. "Continue."

"Well, from that point information regarding the raid would be telephoned directly to a filter room, where the invading enemy aircraft could then be tracked with markers on a board, to give a general overall picture of their positions. This filtered information would be passed on to the main fighter command operations room in the area where the raid was expected to take place. The fighter command groups are divided into sectors. They generally have several airfields, each with at least five squadrons, roughly ten to sixteen aircraft each."

Churchill rolled his cigar between finger and thumb. "Interesting. And how could this aid our defenses?"

"Well, sir, in these operation rooms there would be Women's Auxiliary Air Force members who would watch the overall development of the fighting. The controller could alert the RAF pilots to man their aircraft, then they could, in effect, talk the fighter pilots to the correct height and guide the fighter planes to within sight of the enemy aircraft."

The men were all silent, speechless. Churchill himself grinned wryly with the possibilities of such a device. "And how long before they can be installed as working units?"

Lindemann needed no time to respond. "Winston," he said, "they can be put in within weeks. We just need the go-ahead from you."

"You've got it, Frederick." Churchill added, "Now, gentlemen, if at all possible, at this stage of the war, I would find it foolhardy to say the least if we did not take the war against Hitler back to Europe. I have submitted to officials and cabinet ministers a proposal to establish an organization that would control sabotage, subversive activities, as well as propaganda on the enemy forces. What we came up with was the Special Operations Executive, known in initial form as SOE. I hope something good will come of this. Give those Huns some of it back, as it where.

"Now, gentlemen, let me just mention to you. Recently, as you may have heard, I was in dialogue with the Canadian prime minister, Mackenzie King, and what I told him I shall now tell all of you. That being, I cannot envision a future government which, if we were deserted by the United States and beaten by the Nazis, might very easily become a kind of Quisling affair ready to accept German overlordship and protection."

The men in the study all cheered. He continued. "We must find the resourcefulness of mind to withstand the onslaught, no matter how great. Throughout France's trials and tribulations, the United States government maintained a staunch neutrality, and I fear that they will be long in coming to our aid. Our fate will depend solely on victory in the air."

He stood up and nodded Lindemann. "Get on with it, with all due haste." He shook hands with all who were present and led them out of his study. He called to his secretary and as she entered gave her some papers to file. It had been a very long day, and he felt quite drained. He reached into his cabinet drawer and took out a bottle of brandy. As he poured himself a small shot he thought ahead to tomorrow, and the next day, to the struggle he and all of England were to embark upon, one he knew would be very long and hard, and one he knew had to be won at all cost.

It was raining hard over the North Sea, and Kurt was negotiating some sizable waves in his quest to stay on course, but after a few minutes the sea started to calm down. The winds weren't as harsh, the skies not as grim. The storm had blown over toward the British Isles. Breathing easier, Kurt checked his coordinates. There were two crew hands in the wheelhouse with him, one drinking black coffee, the other one chewing on a stick of beef jerky.

The coast of the isle was becoming visible, and from the starboard side he could make out a ship. He reached for his binoculars hanging on the left of the cabin window to get a better fix on it. Sure enough, it was a German U-552, the *Red Devil*, and for the moment it seemed to be heading in the opposite direction. He ordered his crew topside, all hands ready. As the men got busy he kept a watchful eye on the German boat; it was heading due east toward Norway. He did not want a confrontation on the high seas.

The crew was feverishly pulling off camouflaged canopies and fishing nets. The *Merry Mariners* was in reality a captured German gunship taken as a prize of war and recommissioned into the service of the OSS. A flag was raised to fly overhead, and from stern to starboard the crew removed linen wrappings to reveal her guns. Now the battle of nerves was on. The *Red Devil* had sunk nearly one hundred thousand tons of allied shipping single-handedly. It was commanded by Captain Eric Topp, a ruthless, high-seas tactitioner. Kurt hoped to stay at a good distance as Wallace came in to confirm that the guns were now ready. He in turn ordered all the crew, except for Wallace and Jones, to battle stations. The remaining men were to stay with him.

He spotted what appeared to be a Nazi mine floating off the starboard bow. Feverishly, he turned a few degrees to clear it. He saw the *Red Devil* disappear into a low hanging fog in the distance. Kurt guided the *Merry Mariners*, his silencers on; he surveyed the isle with night glasses. His crew were manning the guns fore and aft. The seas pitched, the ship reached the Devil's Cove. And the skies grew darker. Kurt took her into an inlet a quarter mile up the isles' coast, away from several Nazis U-boats docked by a small village. Kurt ordered his men to keep a sharp eye out. The crew were armed with Mausers and Sterlings at the ready. He left to go below to change.

The moon appeared from behind the rows of clouds. The night grew ever colder and foreboding. There was a strange silence aboard as the crew all waited. The Germans could be anywhere on the island. Who knew how many? To risk everything for one secretary of air defense. But they were the OSS and they were there for the worse of it, whatever it took to get the job done.

Kurt disappeared topside in a matter of minutes, dressed as an Anglican priest, with Bible in hand. The men all smiled, some even chuckled, but all grew quiet very quickly. This was his ticket to get on the island. Who would bother a priest? The men wished him luck, and he told them to wait for him until he got back with Sinclair.

He came up the side of the ship as the prow was moved across and the end came to rest on solid rock. He hurriedly made his way up the hillside. He marched along the brow of the hill until he saw the flickering lights of the small village below. To the side of the roadway were some ruins of an ancient British fort. He made his way slowly at first. Soon he saw a group of German soldiers walking. He started to speak in Latin as he thumped on his Bible. Two more soldiers came up the rough terrain. As they passed him, a sergeant stopped and told him to halt. As he stood motionless his face twitched once from nerves.

The German said, "Hey, Englander, say a prayer for the good weather, ja?" Both Germans laughed and walked on. Kurt broke out in a cold sweat. He remembered his orders, six houses down from the well on the left, up the dirt road a hundred yards, and it would be on the right.

As he approached he saw a badly beaten vehicle, white with spots of brownish red rust from exposure to the salty sea air. The vehicle was parked outside and there were two German soldiers, rifles slung over their shoulders, talking to one another. Kurt approached, "I'm Father O'Malley. Good evening, my sons. I'm here to see Mr. Sinclair for a weekly Bible study."

The German on his right told him to wait as he disappeared behind the front door. A moment had passed when a tall, muscular SS officer in full uniform, stepped out. Kurt knew there would be trouble. In perfect English the SS lieutenant asked, "To what do we owe this pleasure, Father?"

Kurt repeated himself and the SS lieutenant gave him a friendly smile. "Well, Father, please come in."

Once inside Kurt found Sinclair tied arms and legs to a wooden chair in the living room. He had been in that position quite a long time and was about to be persuaded by another SS officer, who was clutching a knuckle-duster in his right hand, to reveal certain military data. The SS lieutenant said to Kurt, "It's so good of you to stop by. You see, Mr. Sinclair was just about to tell us of his work. I'm sure you'd like to hear of it, wouldn't you?"

Kurt felt the muscles in the back of his neck tighten. He stared at the older man as he sat there strapped in his chair. His cheeks were hollow, his eyes groggy. He gave the appearance that he had been drugged. "Yes, by all means, gentlemen," Kurt replied.

The SS lieutenant had stopped smiling. "Perhaps you could encourage him to tell us what he knows now. You see, my associate is not in a good mood tonight—his patience has worn thin."

Kurt bent down on one knee next to Sinclair and whispered so only he would hear. "When I give the signal, we'll make a run for it."

As he got back to his spot the lieutenant informed him, "In Germany, our scientists, our most brilliant scientists, have created a wonder drug called Prontocil. You are familiar with it, Father?"

"No, lieutenant, I am not," he said frankly.

"Well, this drug is made from chemicals that are found in regular bricks used in the building of houses. These same chemicals, when diluted into a solution have exceptional healing properties. Gangrene can be prevented, wounds heal much faster. Its only drawback is that it has a tendency to turn urine bright red, but it surely cleans you out. Yes, Father, this is the drug of the age, especially now in the midst of a war. It would be quite useful, wouldn't you agree?"

"Yes," Duran replied nervously, "certainly."

"But, Father, your friend here, the man in charge of the air force for all of England, I...well, if I were to be tough with him, I am afraid that our Prontocil won't help him, no matter how much we give. Far be it for my associate to harm Sinclair in such a manner to retrieve some simple aviation information, wouldn't you agree?"

16

"Yes, by all means."

Sinclair, near collapse, his face downcast and exhausted, just sighed deeply for all to hear. Kurt looked over at the SS officer to his left, and then to the lieutenant on his right. As the lieutenant took a step toward Sinclair, his hand clutched the knuckle-duster, Kurt hastily said, "Gentlemen, you've told me of your work, now perhaps I can mention something about mine."

The lieutenant looked perplexed. Kurt continued. "You see, gentlemen," he said, opening his Bible, "the Lord works in mysterious ways." He looked up for a moment. "That has always been one of my favorite passages. But there is one I enjoy even more."

The lieutenant raised an eyebrow. "Yes, what is it?"

"An eye for an eye." As he said those words he pulled out a small revolver with silencer from the hollow of the book in a hidden compartment, and before the Germans could react he shot the one on his left through the heart, and the lieutenant once between the eyes.

Frantically Kurt untied Sinclair and told him to remain quiet. Even though his gun had a silencer, the heft and girth of both men falling had made a considerable ruckus. The soldiers stationed outside made their way into the living room. As they looked around they saw Sinclair still in his chair, bodies with blood seeping from them were on the floor, and they realized Sinclair had been untied. The front door creaked as a small revolver with silencer extended behind, and two quick shots placed both men on the floor.

Kurt raced to Sinclair, helped him to his feet and toward the front door. "How many Germans are on the island?"

"Twenty, maybe thirty at most. They were going to take me back to Germany with them, you know."

"Well, all that has changed," he said reassuringly. "I am going to take you back to London instead."

As Sinclair stepped out gingerly, Kurt helped him to the vehicle outside. He saw that the keys were still in the ignition and he got in. As they were starting out, he placed one of the dead soldier's hats on Sinclair and put the lieutenant's hat on himself. The headlights were on, and they began to roll down the hill. The fog had cleared and Kurt hoped for a quick run back to the boat.

Driving through the village, loose groups of German soldiers made their way toward the U-boats after stretching their legs a bit. Kurt, eyes fixed straight ahead, raced past. As they headed up an old roadway he looked over at Sinclair, who was coming out of the drug-induced stupor.

"Are we home yet?" he muttered. Kurt grinned wryly.

"Almost, sir, almost there." He had to stop the vehicle at the top of the cliffs and hurriedly made it down with Sinclair on foot the rest of the way. They walked along at angles to avoid slipping as they edged downward.

Wallace spotted them and alerted the others. Three men from the ship raced up to meet them. Kurt told two of them to go and keep an eye out for the Germans. As they negotiated the prow, Sinclair almost fell over after losing his footing. Kurt grabbed him fiercely and helped him into the ship. He told Jones to take him down to his cabin.

A second later all hell broke loose as machine gun fire rained from the top of the hill, killing one lookout. He tumbled hard along the cliffs, fell and plunged into the sea. The other man ran for his life down toward the ship.

"Germans!" he yelled.

Kurt waited until he made it aboard and shouted, "Shove off!"

The crewman was bleeding badly from his right shoulder and grimaced as he touched his wound. "You've been shot quite badly," Kurt said. "Go down below and have it tended to."

The rest of the crew scrambled to get the *Merry Mariners* moving as fast as possible back to England. It could do fifty knots easily, and it started to rattle a bit as it went up to speed. While they were shoving off, several German soldiers fell upon their chests in the firing position along the cliffs and began opening up. With patches of fog appearing sporadically they soon lost aim; a moment later the boat disappeared entirely behind the milky white mist.

Kurt went to the captain's bridge and checked his radar screen. There was nothing picking up. He told his crew to notify him if the screen changed. Upon entering his cabin he found Sinclair laid up in his bunk and reading a book.

"Feeling better, I see?"

Sinclair smiled. "Well, what am I to do? Stare at the ceiling all night?" He tossed the book aside and sat up. "Do you mind telling me who you are? Not to sound ungrateful for the rescue, but I would like to know whom to thank."

Kurt reached out his hand. "Kurt Duran, I'm with OSS. We'll be docking shortly, can I get you anything?"

Sinclair shook his hand and leaned back on the bunk, legs crossed at the ankles. "Well, my boy, I could do with a cup of hot coffee. The SS lieutenant tried to starve me out today. He was about to unleash that monster on me when you showed up."

Kurt got his thermal flask out and poured him a cup. "To your health, and speedy recovery, sir. Is all that true what they said back there, about your work and everything?"

He took a long sip, and smacked his lips. "Right—oh, that's correct." Breathing easier Sinclair proceeded to fill him in. "You see, I cover all of the RAF, all air defense. If I were to spill the beans, as it were, we'd have major problems with the Luftwaffe. Some of our planes aren't running up to par, and we're doing all we can to keep them in the air. The less the Germans know about all that, the better. That's when I got stuck there on Devil's Cove. A friend of mine let me stay on at a property of his for a short sabbatical, and unfortunately the Germans got wind of it and decided to kidnap me instead. They landed just minutes after I arrived and smashed all of our transmitters. We were basically sitting ducks. I just hope my daughter is all right, she tends to fret about me so."

"I'm sure she's fine," Kurt said. "You'll be home soon."

Chapter Three

It was in the early morning of June 23rd that Hitler had left his headquarters at Brûly-de-Pesche and was flown on his private plane to Le Bourget Aerodrome, just outside Paris. He had arrived at a quarter to six. From there he was chauffeured to the most attractive sites. Included was the opera house, which he had admired through pictures he had seen as an art student during his pauper years. Its architecture was breathtaking. From there he stopped off at Napoleon's tomb. After a lengthy tour of its lavish rotunda he turned to his entourage and said, "This is the greatest and finest moment of my life."

After leaving the tomb he gave orders that the remains of Napoleon's son, Duc de Reichstadt, which up until that time rested in Vienna, be moved to Paris to rest next to his father. As he was being driven in a black Rolls Royce limousine, he demanded to be taken to Gestapo headquarters in Paris. The Germans had occupied the most attractive building in the heart of the city, heavily guarded outside by armed SS troops. The building previously had been the city's police station.

Hitler entered its interior with Martin Bormann. They briskly went up the marble stairs to the second floor, where Heinrich Himmler had flown in two nights previously. As the Reichführer of the SS, and chief of both state and secret police, he sought to finalize German control of France from his office in Paris. His officer personnel were working around the clock in twenty four-hour shifts to complete their tasks.

Hitler stepped in; Bormann waited outside. All of the office sprang to attention. Himmler was by his desk reading reports. He turned around and approached the Führer. Hitler pulled him aside and began to explain his presence. After a moment both men became quite animated. Himmler gave the orders for his staff to resume work and excused himself. Both men exited the door in the middle of the room and talked behind closed doors. After a few moments Himmler emerged with Hitler and the Führer wished him well. He was on the last leg of his tour of Paris and as he was leaving he told Himmler, "To have seen the city whose aura has always preoccupied me, I have fate to thank."

As Himmler walked him to his vehicle the Führer asked, "I'll see you in Berlin this week then, correct?"

Himmler nodded. "Yes, *mein* Führer, tomorrow in fact."

In Himmler's office an SS brigadier had been compiling records of all the operations of the last few days. The Gestapo system in France included everything from informers to espionage, terror, and arrest, not to mention routine executions and torture. The Gestapo had agents after a number of people who had been involved in subversive activity, sabotage and espionage. Himmler had required an updated list of the most outstanding cases.

As Himmler reentered his office the SS brigadier placed on his desk in an attractive, leather-bound report chronicling all actions taken against the German occupation of France to date. As Himmler read through it the phone rang on his desk. It was SS Colonel Helmet Knochen, who was calling from a German command post set up in the Hotel Crillon. He informed Himmler that he had found some of the police files on those who were politically active, files previously believed to have been destroyed.

Himmler stood up and told Knochen to bring them to his office at once. Knochen added that the French prefect of the police department, Pierre Laquiert had been interrogated by the Gestapo until he finally broke. He asked Himmler if he should be taken back to his cell. "No," Himmler said, "take him out and shoot him. He wasted two days of my time with his silence already."

Hitler had flown back to his headquarters, thrilled at all he had heard and seen. At Brûly-de-Pesche, Hitler was going over the details with his chief architect, Albert Speer, of a decree returning to full scale construction of proposed public buildings and monuments. These were to be erected in Berlin, designed by Speer, with Hitler overseeing his work, in September 1939. But with the outbreak of the war, all work related to this undertaking had abruptly stopped.

Hitler, inspired by his tour of the French capital, was determined to make Berlin even better. He confided to Speer, "In the past I considered destroying Paris to break the Frenchman's morale, their will to fight and resist. But now, when we complete this monumental work in Berlin, Paris will be nothing more than a mere shadow. So I asked myself why should we destroy it?"

Duran had been making an effort that night not to get within sight of any of his associates at OSS. He needed his free time. He hadn't seen his friend Peter Hawkins in ages and for Hansen, who was recovering back in his home, he prepared a nice surprise. He drove to the country where Hansen had a quaint retreat. He drove down an elegant driveway up to the house, where two youngsters ran down the front stairs shooting toy cap guns. As they raced by he went up to go through the open front door and to the second floor, which was where Hansen was laid up in bed.

Kurt walked in and his friend was by the radio listening to a broadcast of the BBC. His wife, a charming lady of forty, came in from the kitchen with a tray. She stopped when she saw Kurt, and at first didn't recognize him.

"It's all right, Martha, that's Kurt. How are you doing old man?" Hansen coughed a bit and his wife raced over to give him a small cup of hot medication. After drinking it he grimaced. "God, I need something to wash that down with."

She followed up with a cup of hot chicken soup.

"Well, how're you doing, old man?" Kurt asked.

"I've been better."

Kurt pulled out from behind him a small handsomely wrapped present and placed it on the side of the bed. "This is for your birthday that I missed." Hansen smiled.

"That was month's ago."

"Yes, I was on a mission, remember?"

"I forgot, I'm sorry. I'm really glad to see you."

Hansen put the cup down and went about unwrapping his gift. As he undid the package his head pressed upon his pillow and in a low, mellow voice he said, "They operated on that damn wound of mine, and it feels like they've left a scalpel wedged between my ribs. The doctor said it would be a while before I could dance with the missus again, but I should be up and about in a few days." He looked up at Kurt, curious. "So tell me, how'd the mission go? Did you get your man?"

"Yes, I did. He's safe at home now, his daughter is keeping an eye on him. We lost a man on the cliffs of Devil's Cove though. Bradley. He disappeared in the waves, he got hit by German fire."

"I'm sorry to hear that. He was a good man."

"They all are," Kurt said.

"You know, the old boat was due for some fixing up."

"I have her on dry dock being scrapped and tuned, no more barnacles or engine troubles and I've also ordered her to be fitted with a single, four-inch gun on the forecastle, and light anti-aircraft weapons amidship. I want her to have a greater firing range."

Hansen opened his gift, looked inside and gasped in delight. It was a sterling silver copy of the *Merry Mariners*. "How did you manage this?"

Kurt shrugged. "And old silversmith friend of mine in Essex. I ordered a copy of the old hull for your birthday, but was late in picking it up."

Hansen examined it; it was an excellent copy, down to the last details, as she looked when she was in her disguise. The rigging, masting, everything was just right, and on the base was the name "Oliver Hansen, Captain of the Merry Mariners."

His wife came up closer to have a look. "My, it's wonderful."

"I've just the place for it," Hansen said to his wife. "Be a dear and put it on the mantel. That way, I'll be able to see it from my bed."

She walked over and placed it right where he had asked, next to his service medals. Kurt was happy for him. He asked to see the newborn. Hansen's wife led him into the next room. There inside the crib slept a blonde-haired baby girl. Hansen's wife beamed with delight. "She has your complexion," Kurt said quietly.

"And my husband's temperament," she mused.

Kurt returned to his friend's side. "You must be one proud papa."

"That I am."

Kurt checked his watch. "I must be running along, old man. Got a dinner engagement, you know." He wished the Hansens well, left the room and disappeared down the corridor.

He was off to see a banker friend of his, a man of access and wealth, arrogant to the extreme, but nonetheless his friend of many years. He wanted to establish some contact with him while he was still in the city. He had made arrangements for them to dine at Perry's, a supper club catering to socialites in the outskirts of London.

When he arrived, Peter Hawkins and a young woman with a sultry air about her had already been served. Kurt was upset that he hadn't bothered to wait. Peter introduced him. "This is my fiancée, Miss Anna Clemmens." She was a dazzling socialite from Sheffield, where Peter had met her just months before.

Kurt nodded politely and turned to Peter. "Well, you haven't changed a bit Peter, not one bit."

"Neither have you." Both men shook hands firmly and they all sat down at the dining table. The waiter filled Kurt's glass with a red bourdeaux and Peter was quick to apologize. "I hope you don't mind us starting dinner without you but Anna was quite famished."

"That's quite all right. So tell me, how's the banking business these days?"

Peter sighed, then downed some wine. "Well, it has been very hectic, thanks to the war. People are afraid to lose their money and they know the only safe place is the Bank of England."

"Or Switzerland," Kurt said.

"That's true."

Kurt noticed that Anna appeared to grow a bit withdrawn. Peter said, "She happens to be tired from last night's trip."

"I understand." Kurt said nothing further; he could sense his friend was keeping something from him, but he wasn't about to pursue it. Not now, anyway.

Out of the blue the alarm went off signaling an air raid. People started to run for the nearest exits. Peter got up with his fiancée. Kurt yelled for them to stay where they were and to get under the table or they would be trampled.

Bombs started to drop and the restaurant was rocked by thunderous explosions outside. Screams and pandemonium erupted from every corner of the restaurant. Then just as quickly as the bombers came, they left. A strange silence enveloped the interior. The initial shock started to wear off as masses of people waited and listened for more bombers. Thankfully there were no more.

Peter stood up and said in a bitter voice, "Another dry run. Those Luftwaffe do this to soften us up, a little bit at a time."

His fiancée stared down at her dress. Red wine had spilled all over the front of it. She sighed, "It's ruined."

"Be glad it's only wine," Kurt said. "Now let's get out of here, shall we?"

With that they left Perry's and were quick to get back to their automobiles. The streets were still crowded with panic-stricken Londoners, and there were several buildings that had sustained serious damage further up the road. Flames could be seen shooting out from windows and front doors, followed by the horrific sound of a roof collapsing inward as debris and ash shot forth.

"We'll have to do this more often," Kurt said, "but under better circumstances."

"I'm sure," Peter replied. "Why don't you follow me back to my place, spend the night. We could all use some rest." An ambulance roared by. As it came within inches of striking Kurt, he stopped, took in a deep breath, got into his automobile and drove off. It was almost nine p.m.

Kurt was picking up speed and fast approaching his friend's Mercedes Benz. They made their way through the heart of London and onto some clear streets. The route was familiar. His friend's estate was half an hour away. When they arrived, the house looked quite different. It once had belonged to an eighteenth century lord, Sir Wallace Straton.

"How do you like it?" Peter asked. "I had it completely redone, inside and out."

Duran took a good look over. "Must have set you back a bit."

"No, not too much. It was worth every penny, don't you think?"

"To be sure."

Once they stepped inside his French maid, Marie, ran out to the marble foyer nervously. "Thank God, sir, that you are all right. The bombs, the raid, it was just dreadful. And Fifi, I don't know what happened to her. As soon as the bombing stopped I looked but—"

Kurt turned to Peter. "Fifi?"

"That's my pet cat," Peter said. "She doesn't like loud noises. But she'll be back. She's probably hiding in some bookcase somewhere. Would you be a dear and get us a drink?"

As the maid left Peter took Anna and his houseguest into his living room—a grand room with a sumptuous array of antique furniture, exquisite Persian carpeting, a chandelier big enough to swing from hanging overhead, and an array of old master paintings dotting the walls around them. Peter was an avid hunter and the east wall was devoted to his many trophies. Heads of wild boar, deer, and even rhinoceros. He had a previous pet, a Bengal tiger stuffed and sitting in the corner as if on guard, tense and foreboding.

Kurt looked over the kills. "So this is what you do with your time off."

Peter smiled. "One has to keep busy. Besides, the duke of Kent is an avid hunter and a member of my bank. He always invites me to his estate to hunt."

"So he has a rhino on his estate?"

"Don't be foolish. The rhino I got on a safari to Africa back in '38. Come, I'll show you my gun collection."

The maid came back at that point with champagne glasses. Everyone took some champagne and Peter went into his study. His fiancée went up upstairs to change, followed by Marie. Kurt was impressed at the array before him—impeccably crafted hunting rifles and shotguns all on display in a massive glass case. Peter opened the case. "There's the one I fancy most, the Weatherby. Simply the finest hunting rifle in the world, with fitted scope and leather shoulder strap. I bagged the rhino with that one." He handed it to Kurt for a closer inspection.

Kurt brought it up to his face, examining the fine craftsmanship. He looked through the telescopic lens before handing it back. "Nice, I'll take my Sterling any day of the week." Both men laughed.

"Let's go to the next room, shall we? I've got the most charming invitation from the duke."

Peter picked up the invitation from his desk in the formal library. It was another invitation to a hunt. "I shall be there tomorrow and you're welcomed to come along. We can spend a few hours at the hunting lodge together and catch up on some old times."

Kurt was excited by the offer. Having been brought up in an upper class household, well educated and well connected, he even had German cousins whom he often visited in his youth and together they would go hunting.

"And what about your fiancée?"

"I need some space. I've been meaning to get out and about without her for a while now, if you know what I mean."

"I believe so."

"Besides, there will be the most delightful people there. It's not far from the duke's estate. Quiet a large place."

"And will he be hunting wild boar?"

"No. Those are let out on only the most special of occasions. This time a more conservative creature, a fox." He noticed Kurt's deep gaze. "Got something on your mind? What is it?"

"Oh nothing. I just thought about the other day, we had a few rough spots is all."

"That's the idea of the hunt, my boy, takes your mind right off that sort of thing."

"Well then, tell me, Peter, will it take much to make an impression with this duke?"

"Not really. He's quite a likeable fellow, a bit pretentious at times. He tends to live in the past, that one, the Great War, you know. He could tell you stories for hours, so whatever you do don't encourage him to divulge his military history, unless you want to be bored to death."

Kurt took a sip of champagne and lowered his glass. The Swiss clock on the wall chimed ten p.m. Kurt promptly excused himself. "It has been a long day, I think I'll turn in."

Peter picked up a crystal bell on his desk top and rang for Marie. He informed Kurt that breakfast would be at 7:30 a.m. Marie approached and Peter instructed her to show his guest to his room.

Upstairs, Peter entered the master bedroom to find his beloved resting comfortably on top of the bedsheets. She was looking her face over in a handheld mirror.

"You're beautiful," he said.

She glanced at him and smiled. "Oh, well, now tell my worry lines that. All this Luftwaffe business is going to be the death of me."

He undressed and slipped under the sheets. "You know, Duran is an extraordinary fellow. He never ceases to surprise me."

"In what way?" she asked.

"You'll see once you get to know him. It's his personality, as tough as steel. Nothing ever gets to him, nothing. And he is the most reliable of friends. I would trust him with my life."

She put her mirror away and slid under the covers with him. "Really. What does he do, darling?"

He hesitated, "He's in bloody OSS, that's all I can get out of him."

"You mean you don't know?"

"You know how they are, all that top secret hush-hush. It's enough to drive me mad. He asks all he wants about banking but if I ever dare begin to inquire about his affairs, he simply stares me down."

She burst out in laughter. "I rather like that. And he's sleeping in the same house tonight, how exciting."

"Now darling..."

She laughed some more. "I've always wondered what life on that side was like."

"Well keep on wondering because Duran is not about to indulge you with any of his secrets."

She sighed. "I suppose you are right. What I don't know couldn't possibly hurt me."

It was just after seven the following morning when Kurt made his way to the breakfast room. Peter was already sitting with a cup of hot coffee at hand, looking rather tired.

"What's the matter? Didn't get any sleep last night?"

"That's not the half of it. It's those damn fire trucks, I could hear them miles away."

Anna walked in dressed in a white blouse and blue-green skirt. Her hair flowed down over her shoulders. Her face peaceful and rested. "Did you sleep well?"

"Yes, thank you," said Kurt. "By the way, some good news. I found Fifi this morning. She woke me up by walking across my feet."

They all laughed. "Well," Peter said, "thank you for calming my anxieties. I was starting to worry."

Marie served up breakfast, bacon and eggs along with toast and a marmalade. There were also fresh rolls. Kurt smiled. "It all smells so good."

"Coffee?" Marie asked.

"Please."

Peter started to inform Kurt of the day's events. "Just so you know, after our hunt this afternoon we will be getting together with some gentlemen I think you will enjoy meeting. It will all be business talk but the conversation afterwards should prove quite enjoyable. There will be an Egyptian major general, and ambassador from the Spanish Embassy and a nephew of de Gaulle himself, Louis De Vigny, all of whom would like to establish accounts with my bank."

Kurt's eyes lit up. "De Vigny, he was the French minister of foreign affairs until Pétain replaced him with Baudouin. De Vigny never severed his contacts, he is quite active in the French Resistance."

"Interesting. And his nephew is now here?"

"Yes."

"I look forward to today's meeting very much."

"How do you think the French will fair?" said Peter.

"Is there any hope for France?"

"Hope? There's always hope—de Gaulle is the symbol of hope to all of France."

Peter frowned. "But the reality is that France was crushed by the wake of the Nazi war machine. England is next in line. I'll bet our aid to France and Europe will be to hold firm to our rock."

"Do you think there will be an invasion?" Anna asked nervously.

"Well, those Germans aren't bombing us for nothing. But when they'll decide to make an all-out invasion is anyone's guest."

When they finished with breakfast Peter stood up and called for Williams, the house butler and chauffeur, to ready his car. He turned to Kurt and asked him to accompany him to his study. Then walking up to the glass case, he turned and asked his friend, "Which one would you like? I take it you didn't bring a hunting rifle with you last night."

"I'm afraid not."

"Well then, pick one."

Once he had made his selection Peter took it out along with the Weatherby. At the base of the case was a drawer reserved for ammunition. He provided Kurt with several clips, and took a few himself. "There, that should do it. Let's go."

Anna stood by the front door, waiting patiently. "Enjoy yourselves."

"That we shall, my dear." Peter leaned over and kissed her. He whispered, "We'll be back as soon as we can." With that they made for the car.

Williams stood by the open trunk in black suit and hat and packed the rifles away. Both men got in the backseat and sped off.

"Now remember," Peter said, "I want you to meet the duke of Kent. He'll be quite interested in you. OSS has always had a special place in his heart. He was one of the first to support the establishment of the agency's special department of operations, and when the agency was embroiled in that nasty controversy a few years ago he saw to it personally that the newspapers did not get wind of it. That would have jeopardized the lives of many agents out there in the field. The duke is a powerful man, but he is also a good man. You'll do well to win him over."

Kurt listened intently. He pulled out his cigarette case and fixed himself a smoke. He stared out into the distance as the Mercedes wound its way along a quiet country road. There were some sheep populating the fields on either side and an old man was driving a truck filled with hay in the opposite direction. He honked twice as they passed. They were nearing the lodge.

"Do you really love her?" Kurt asked.

"Anna? Of course."

"Well, I've never known you to be the marrying kind. Is she..."

"Is she rich? Dreadfully so. She's got more money than all of our lodge members put together, and that's one of the reasons I love her." He laughed and took out a photo from his wallet and showed it to Kurt. "There, see that?" The photograph showed Anna in a group of people in front of a large mansion. "This is her family." He pointed to the man in the middle. "That's her father, Trevor Clemmens."

Kurt thought a moment. "I have heard the name before."

"As well you should. He is one of the richest men in all England. He owns the Newcastle Shipping Company, third generation. He hasn't done an honest day's work in his life and Anna, bless her heart, has managed to remain unspoiled."

Kurt was impressed. "You've got yourself quite a catch there."

With that Peter looked offended. "That's what she had said about me."

As they drove up, Peter saw the duke receiving guests at the steps of the lodge and pointed him out. Williams opened the side door and the men exited. Peter was quick to make his way to the duke of Kent, hand outstretched. "Wallace Straton, sir, how are you? There's someone I wish to introduce to you, Mr. Kurt Duran. Kurt, Sir Wallace Straton, duke of Kent."

Duran shook his hand. The duke was a man of seventy, quite tall in stature with graying hair. His face was tough yet amiable; he had a certain coarseness to him, and his right leg dragged slightly due to a wound suffered in the trenches in 1918.

"How do you do, Mr. Duran. Welcome to Remington Lodge. We have scheduled a fox hunt this morning, I hope you'll join us."

"Yes, but of course."

"Very well. Peter, why don't you show our guest to the locker rooms. We'll all meet out in the back at 9:15. We'll finish up by, say, 12:30, in time for lunch."

The men headed to the front door.

"He likes you," Peter said.

"How could you tell?"

"Believe me, I know the man. Now let's change before the hunt starts."

When they finally got there Peter asked, "Are you a large?"

"No. Extra large."

"Fine then, this should fit you, official red." He handed him a large hunting jacket. "Don't worry about your pants, but you will need riding boots. What size?"

"Eleven."

"Here's a ten and a half."

In the corner a portly gentleman was stripping to his waist. As he was negotiating to pull on his undershirt Peter stepped over and slapped him on the back. "Theodore! Good morning to you."

The man gasped and looked up, startled. "Oh, my God, it's you. Well, what are you all about today?"

"Here for the hunt, of course. By the way, this is my good friend, Kurt Duran. Theodore here has been a lodge member for the better part of twenty-five years and he hasn't bagged a fox yet."

"I heard that," the older man grumbled. Peter and Kurt burst out in laughter.

Out in the field the duke was already mounted, rifle in hand. The other members of the hunting party started to emerge, all dressed in traditional hunting attire. After Kurt and Peter mounted the duke said a few words and wrapped it up by adding, "Let's have a good morning, shall we? I wish you all well. And after I bag the fox today we'll retire for drinks in the club."

The fox was brought out in a small cage by a keeper and released. As it darted into the brush someone fired a cap gun and the hunt was on.

Back in London Churchill was finishing up a letter he was dictating to one of his secretaries when another of his secretaries informed the prime minister he was due to inspect the opening of the new ops room that he had ordered built. His chauffeur was parked outside as the prime minister told his secretary to have the letter dated and mailed out promptly as Churchill got into his limousine. He had a young officer accompany him. The route would take them to fighter command headquarters in Stanmore. As they went, Churchill was reeling, his heart heavy. He had been disappointed by the events of the last week.

While arriving in the limousine Major Tieger had asked the prime minister to look over a field report from the RAF. Churchill gasped as he read it through. That morning a large convoy of cargo ships in the English Channel were targeted by German aircraft which had assembled behind Calais. A flight of Hurricane Fighters and Spitfires took off to protect the convoy. As he read on, he removed his smoldering cigar, his eyes deepened, he sat stunned.

The RAF had been met by a hundred and twenty German aircraft. This, Churchill knew full well, was far more than the Luftwaffe had ever used before against British targets. The RAF was badly beaten; the convoy sustained heavy losses. Churchill closed the report and handed it back to the major. He sat back in his seat. "Those devils. They've started it up, their Kanalkampf." That was Field Marshal Hermann Göring's expression, meaning "Channel Battle."

He tapped his hands impatiently against the leather upholstery of the limousine. This, the prime minister knew, was the beginning of operation Sea Lion. As his Rolls Royce limousine approached fighter command headquarters he could see that incoming RAF wounded and dead were being driven away by field ambulances. Churchill ordered his driver to stop. He got out and approached an injured young pilot on a stretcher as he was about to be lifted up into the rear of an ambulance. Dazed, the young man looked at him and realized who he was. "Prime Minister, is that you, sir?"

"Yes, dear boy, I wanted to thank you for your courage and bravery. I know what you and your friends did for us today and I will see to it that you are all honored for your efforts." He put his hand gently on the young man's shoulder then went away. Looking over to the other men, saluting them, he got back into the limousine and arrived at the main gates of fighter command headquarters.

A soldier of the guard, with a rifle slung over his shoulder, approached the driver, who stated that the prime minister was there to inspect fighter command. The soldier promptly walked toward the end of the vehicle, the window was rolled down, and Churchill sat bolt upright, wearing his hat and a scowling stare, challenging the guard. "Well, don't just stand there, let us through."

The guard went numb, dashed to the gate and let them pass.

Chapter Four

Churchill was taken to the main room of operations in the circular gallery of fighter command's ops room. From a balcony he was able to look down on the WAFs, who had covered the battle overview at the ops room with long-handled plotting rods, with which they could mark the targets of both the raiders and defenders. Currently, they were at the end of the table compiling their latest data.

Churchill was absolutely livid. He could not comprehend the damage the Luftwaffe had inflicted. A strange-looking man, bespectacled with a receding hairline and small beard approached him. "And who might you be?" Churchill snapped.

"Sir, my name is Robert Watson-Watt. I understand you have some questions. I'm the senior scientist who created Chainhome radar."

Churchill looked surprised. "Well, then, tell me, Mr. Watt, how is it that a hundred and twenty German planes were able to fly in and utterly destroy our RAF squadrons, not to mention the convoy of ships they were supposed to be guarding? I have been told by a trusted advisor that this would be a foolproof system of early detection."

"Yes, well, Mr. Prime Minister, you must be referring to Mr. Lindemann. He is correct. You see, the system my team of scientists and I put in does work. The problem, Mr. Prime Minister, was not the system, it was the one hundred and twenty German aircraft."

Churchill looked perplexed. "What are you talking about?"

"Well, you see, they came down on a handful of English pilots. The system worked. Our radar stations along the southeast coast detected German aircraft to be sure and their controllers at sector operations alerted the RAF. The pilots knew ships were being bombed. What we need, Mr. Prime Minister, are more planes."

Churchill was silent. He realized the man was right. He'd let his emotions get the better of him. The RAF was overwhelmed and he would be wise to beef up the number of Spitfires and Hurricanes stationed at the vital airfields at Biggin Hill, Manston, Kent, and Croydon bases. Churchill turned to go down to the main level where the Women's Auxiliary Airforce members plotted the incoming moves. He thanked the scientist and left.

Walking along the railing he told Major Tieger, "RAF command headquarters must double the planes at all airfield positions by tomorrow morning at the very latest, by my orders."

In the main room Churchill reviewed the huge table holding the map of Europe and carefully studied it. The WAFs all stood silent. He shuffled a bit to the side to get a better look at that part of the map that covered Germany. He stood there pondering a moment, not saying a word, then turned and thanked all in the room and went back to his limousine.

As they drove off the major said, "Mr. Prime Minister, the scientist, his—"

Churchill cut him off. "I know, Tieger, he was right. The idea in war is not to sit back and wait to be pounded but to be just as cunning, just as aggressive and just as relentless as the enemy. Defense is of secondary importance. We must rip the heart out of the Nazis in Germany."

"It sounds like you have a plan, Prime Minister."

Churchill lit a fresh cigar and simply sat there in his seat. He had a plan, to be sure.

After a quick shower and change of clothing, Kurt followed closely behind Peter as they made their way to the hunting lodge for drinks. The hunt itself was over, and Kurt was content to relax in the comfort of some good company. Peter came to the table reserved for them on the balcony overlooking the expansive estate. He spotted the Egyptian major general and raised his right hand in a friendly manner. The Egyptian, dressed in full uniform, walked up.

"Gentlemen, good afternoon."

Peter introduced Kurt. The Egyptian smiled amiably. "A pleasure, Mr. Duran. What charming countryside you have."

"First time in London?" Kurt said.

"First time in England," the Egyptian replied.

The other members of the group showed up. "Hawkins!" cried the Spanish ambassador in a loud, booming voice.

Peter turned. The ambassador was a middle-aged man with thick, black hair and a moustache. He was walking with Louis De Vigny. "Good day," said the ambassador, beaming. He had just flown back from Barcelona and had met up with De Vigny that morning.

Kurt shook hands with both men and in a distinct French accent the young De Vigny went right into it. "Mr. Hawkins, I want to thank you for your services. My countrymen, as you well know, have been ravished. I think France needs to have her assets redistributed in banks such as yours. I have Mr. Kafir from Egypt, and Mr. Silvano, who are eager to secure their private investments as well. We have faith in your institution, as well as in Churchill."

Peter graciously thanked De Vigny for his good words and wasted no time in taking out some papers. He handed the documents to each of them to review, and as they looked them over he continued. "The Bank of England will stand firm, and your money will be safe. Now, if you will just sign on the line below I can complete the transaction this afternoon."

The transaction he was referring to was considerable. Their monies would be converted into English pounds and deposited into three separate accounts. After each man signed De Vigny insisted they have a toast. Peter asked the lounge boy to bring them drinks.

Kurt asked de Gaulle's nephew some questions of interest. "Sir, I have been an admirer of your uncle for quite some time." De Vigny listened intently. "I have a concern. After his evacuation form Bordeaux he has been very quiet."

"That's correct." De Vigny leaned back in his chair, crossing his legs. "My uncle is aware of the dangers the Pétain government has placed him and all of France in. He hopes the war will turn and he can lead free France to victory, but until that glorious day comes, he feels it wise to regroup and plan his strategies." He changed the subject.

"Now, tell me, what is it that you do, banking?"

"No," Kurt said. "I'm with the military."

The men took notice. "Ah, yes." The Egyptian major general smiled. "You take an active part in the war. We in Egypt only watch and wait to see how far Hitler will go."

"He'll go farther than you think," Kurt said. "That's why we must all be on the ready."

The waiter brought in the house wine and served them. De Vigny raised his glass and made a toast. "To us, gentlemen, and our money, as well as the Bank of England."

Glasses clinked. "You must miss Paris," Kurt said.

De Vigny's face turned somber. "Yes, very much. It pains me to know what is taking place back there." Kurt could see the sorrow and anguish in his eyes.

"Remember, you are not alone."

"Yes, Mr. Duran, you are right."

While the Spanish ambassador became engrossed in a debate with the Egyptian, Kurt whispered to Peter, "de Gaulle's nephew is the spitting image of the old man."

Peter nodded. "And just as stubborn. I worked a whole month to secure this transaction with him, but he still put the bulk of his money in Swiss' accounts."

The Führer was in the final minutes of a meeting with his commanders in chief: Göring for the Luftwaffe, Raeder for the Navy, and von Brauchitsch for the Army. With them were Himmler and von Ribbentrop and his generals, Keitel, Halder, and Jodl. They had all assembled in Hitler's underground headquarters, known as Wolf's Lair, which was found deep in the forest of East Prussia, near Rastenburg.

Hitler was in a joyful mood. He had a wicked smile on his face as he paced in the map room. All present were silent. He was to divulge his plans for the all-out invasion of England. The German command for months had argued over the details of such an invasion. The Führer was to gather up all the points and work them out into a final version all his own. He began by referring to a map of Europe hanging on the wall directly behind him.

"I have decided to prepare a landing operation against England. The aim of this operation will be to eliminate the English homeland as a base for the prosecution of the war against Germany, and to occupy it. The successful execution of Operation Sea Lion will be the most effective means of bringing about a rapid conclusion of the war."

He informed the German high command of the facts. "For this, the Army operations will require forty divisions. They will require no less than 2,500 seafaring transporters to cross the Channel."

The commanders in chief and the generals all sat in quiet apprehension. Hitler smiled widely. "Gentlemen, I give you thirty days."

The men all gasped. The generals grumbled. Von Ribbentrop stood. "Mein Führer, forgive me, but I must ask on what you base that decision. Thirty days to prepare is a very short period of time."

Hitler laughed. His eyes sparkled. "My dear von Ribbentrop. Sit down and relax, all of you. Thirty days is all we need. The Army is ready."

He looked at von Brauchitsch, who nodded to confirm. Hitler looked at Göring and Raeder. "The Luftwaffe, the Kriegsmarine?" Both men nodded.

Hitler took his pen, signed a piece of paper on the table in front of him and ordered Admiral Raeder to get it. Apprehensively, Raeder approached the Führer who handed it to the man. "I have just issued Directive 17," he said. "This for the official conduct for the air and sea warfare against England." He turned, facing the large map before him, his arms folded across his chest, his eyes fixed on the English coastline. He went on to say that a successful German air offensive was a prerequisite for an all-out seaborne invasion. So he had given the orders for the Day of the Eagle, the intensification of the air war against England in which Hitler would have a huge, German armada of aircraft flying in search of English air stations, aircraft facilities and radar, targeting them all for destruction.

Hitler turned abruptly and slammed his hands on the table. His slick, black hair slid slightly forward on his forehead over his left brow. He looked confidently at the men assembled and said, "Meeting adjourned." Only Hitler would know the exact date for Sea Lion, and he would wait until the last possible moment to announce it. Thirty days was all the German commanders in chief had time for, as they rose rather uneasily they offered one another with reassuring glances, and all headed out of the room.

Chapter Five

The sea was raging, the *Merry Mariners* pitched. The wind blew fiercely across her bow. The night sky was ablaze in automatic gunfire from the German night fighter that descended a third time, opened up both barrels, hit one crewman in the chest, knocked him over the side into the white froth between the waves, then disappeared. There was an explosion on the starboard side, a near miss from a German U-boat.

Kurt had ordered the ships guns to be trained on the U-boat while the light, anti-aircraft guns amidship pounded the night sky. The German night flyer crisscrossed and attacked once more, this time hitting the main battery of the ship's guns, killing its two crewmen instantly. As Kurt looked up, the German guns hit his shoulder. He went down, flung against the wheelhouse wall. His right side was bleeding badly. Dazed, he staggered to his feet only to spot the U-boat coming straight for them. From her came a blurry, white line that rapidly approached under the water. Then suddenly an explosion, and after a moment of confusion Kurt was floating in his life jacket. Bodies were floating all around. The ship was on fire, engulfed in glowing flames. An explosion ripped through her, her stern lifted, and she vanished.

Kurt was pulled down by a wave, half choking him. He thrashed wildly for air and came up gasping. He drifted farther out and was lifted higher on another wave. He coughed up the seawater that seemed to have filled his lungs, when out of the darkness a line was tossed to him. He grabbed one end. His eyes were half blinded by the salt. He looked up. It was a German captain in uniform aboard the U-boat. He said nothing. Kurt could see the German was smiling. He pulled out his Luger from his holster and took aim. Kurt let go of the rope, frantically trying to swim away. The officer pulled the trigger.

Kurt felt an intense pain in his upper body. His eyes blurred, he cried out in agony. As he screamed, he sat bolt upright in bed, saturated in sweat. He looked around his room, his heart beating wildly. It was a nightmare that seemed all too real. Taking a deep breath, he swung himself to the side of the bed wearing only black pajama pants. He didn't bother to try to put on his slippers. He got up and headed for the kitchen. The clock on the wall showed it to be 7:00 p.m. He had dozed off soon after getting home from his luncheon with Peter and his friends. Not being particularly hungry he poured himself a Scotch. His right hand trembled as he reached for the glass.

There was a knock at the door. He said, "Just a moment." He headed back into his bedroom and put on his robe. He looked through the spy hole. He could make out Ian Richards, and there was some stranger next to him. He opened the door and next to Richards was a man of fifty with graying hair and a stocky build.

35

Richards said, "Well, may we come in?"

"Certainly." He opened the door fully and both men strode by. "Well, what brings you to me this hour of the evening? Let me guess—you've got another mission for me."

"Very good, Kurt."

Kurt turned and went back to the kitchen to get his drink. "It wasn't really hard, old man. I only see you when you have another job for me."

"This is Mr. Hardwick," Richards said.

"Well, sir, may I get you something to drink?"

"No, thank you, I'm all right."

Kurt walked over to his chair and sat down. "Well get on with it Ian, I haven't got all night. What could possibly drag you to my apartment?"

Richards and Hardwick both looked at each other then smiled. Kurt was quick to react. "I don't like that look, Ian. You're up to something."

Richards laughed loudly. "Nothing could be further from the truth. Really, Kurt, is that all you ever think about, that I will be your angel of death?"

With a sarcastic grin Kurt cocked back his head. "You took the words right out of my mouth. Before you go on, remember one thing, Ian. I was promised a full week of relaxation. I need my time to rest in order to be at peak performance."

"I remember what I promised. But duty calls. Hardwick and I need to take you to OSS headquarters tomorrow and brief you on an assignment that was tailor-made for your particular skills. And this comes directly from the top."

Kurt looked tired and detached. He focused a bit.

"Who? The head of OSS?"

"No, the prime minister himself."

Kurt was stunned. "Churchill?"

Ian looked over at Hardwick. "Yes. Nothing I can talk about here. You will be fully informed tomorrow." Hardwick took out a small cigarette and lit it.

"Is it all right to smoke in here?"

Kurt didn't answer, just stared at Ian, "So you don't call me and ask me to come in."

Hardwick looked at him. "There is a reason for everything we do," Ian said sternly. "You should know that by now." Kurt was uncomfortable. Hardwick was still staring at him quite intensely.

"I think he'll do just fine," Hardwick said.

Richards glanced at Hardwick then back over to Kurt.

"Yes, I agree."

"Agree to what?" Kurt said. "What the devil are you talking about?"

Richards laughed again. "Relax. You'll know by tomorrow. In the meantime, I suggest you get some shuteye, Kurt, you look terrible."

As they all got up Kurt asked, "What time?"

"Eight a.m. sharp. Have your bags packed."

Both men stepped out and he closed and locked the door behind them. This would be no ordinary mission, he thought. Something was up.

On the way to Richards' car, Hardwick tossed his cigarette on the pavement. As both men got in Hardwick said, "This is better than I hoped. Where did you find this one?"

"Best of the best," Richards replied.

Next morning at headquarters Kurt was met by the head of operations, William Denhurst and his assistant Victor Langford. Denhurst sat behind an ornate, mahogany desk in a cluttered office with files in the corners and bookshelves filled beyond reasonable capacity. It had the smell of an old library. Kurt was sitting in the chair immediately in front of Denhurst's desk, with Richards to his left and Hardwick on his right.

All the men were quiet except for Denhurst, who was reading over a letter from the prime minister. When he finished it, he leaned back into his chair, placed the letter on his desk and clasped his hands on his stomach. Head tilted back, he stared at Duran, as did Langford.

Richards and Hardwick stared as well. Finally Kurt spoke up. "Well, gentlemen, you sure know how to make a man feel welcome. It's not like I've got the plague."

"Calm down, young man," said Denhurst, "you're here because we need you. You have an advantage over a number of other agents in our employ. Your special skills set you apart." He got up, "But there is more, much more." He pulled out an 8 x 10 black and white photograph from the desk drawer. It was a head shot. He handed it to Kurt, who was stunned.

He said nothing because he was not sure what to say. The picture was of a man who looked much like Kurt, wearing a German officer's uniform. He shifted a bit in his chair. "Is this a joke?"

"Hardly," Denhurst snapped. "That man you see before you is Heinrich Kruger, and he happens to be Field Marshal Hermann Göring's most trusted aid. Kruger is a major in the Waffen SS. He is highly decorated, a confidant of Göring as well as Hitler and Himmler. He and Skorzeny, the young SS lieutenant, both did missions together in the Netherlands and Greece. Later he soloed in Belgium and France. He is presently recuperating from a bullet fired from a member of the Czech resistance. He is due to be fully recovered and released in two weeks time."

Denhurst leaned on the side of his desk and sat up on it slightly, left leg dangling over the edge, his arms folded across his chest. "The resemblance he has to you is uncanny, except for the hairstyle and eye color. That and the fact that he is six feet two inches tall and you're only six feet. Minor obstacles that can be overcome."

Kurt's eyes widened. Denhurst nodded. "Yes, Kurt, we want you to take Kruger's place. You see, it has come to our attention that Hitler is finally up to something definite in his plans for the invasion of England. Due to the immediacy of this situation we are in a very difficult position, because all we have to go on is the place and date of Göring's next meeting with the Nazi high command.

"There is a chance for you to be slipped in and uncover the necessary information for invasion, and to relay it back to us. If we know the full strength, the how and when they will strike, we will stand a chance to delay an invasion."

Kurt put the photograph back on the table. "But, sir, I must say that I know nothing of this man or his career, nor do I pretend to believe I look exactly like him."

Denhurst shook his head. "You, Mr. Duran, will be placed in a special training program run by our best and most talented SOE personnel. They will not only educate you in everything Heinrich Kruger ever did, said, or thought, but also his personal life, and you will be taught all he knows about the peculiar habits of Göring and his morphine addiction, and everything else that will make you the living replica of Kruger. And as far as your appearance, a change of hairstyle, dark contact lenses, and some elevator shoes should do the trick nicely. Kruger is scheduled to be with Göring at the high command meeting in fifteen days."

"But, sir, that's ridiculous. You can't expect me to—"

Langford cut him off. "You will have a special contact assigned to you while you are in Europe. We will monitor you from headquarters and you will be given full backup."

"You're our only chance," Denhurst said. "You and you alone can make this work. We know the risks involved. We will see to every precaution. The nation needs you—we need you. You have a chance as an individual to do that what no army or legion of spies can do for us."

Kurt sat there, fists clenched. He stared at the commander, at Richards and the rest. He lowered his head slightly; he could feel the weight of the whole world upon his shoulders now. He looked at Denhurst. "How will this be done?"

Denhurst smiled with delight. "We have an agent—two of them in fact—who will help you. One is Frantz Schmidt. He was born in November of 1900 and lived in Germany all his life until Hitler came to power in the 1930s. When the Nazi party started to become a serious threat, Schmidt contacted British Intelligence and, after a careful screening, he was recruited as an agent in the field and has worked for OSS ever since. He has been an aide to Keitel and Ribbentrop, but was summarily omitted from all high profile meetings, unlike Kruger, who is the darling of the Nazi inner circle. Yet Schmidt has enough going for him to provide vital overviews on various high command activities.

But his access is very limited. He can get you half way, but the rest will be up to you."

Kurt leaned forward a bit in his chair. "And the other agent?"

Denhurst pulled out a file and Kurt looked it over. There were pictures of both operatives, Schmidt and a beautiful brunette with long, silky hair. "Her name is Jacqueline Pabon," Denhurst said. "Our finest Resistance fighter in Paris."

Kurt was apprehensive. "A woman?"

"I'll have you know women agents have been found to operate far better under stressful situations then men, and Pabon has incentive to drive the Germans right back into Germany. Jacqueline Pabon is a Jew who comes from Burgundy. Her parents were picked up by the Gestapo in Paris last month and she hasn't seen or heard from them since. Recently she was contacted by some of her friends in the Resistance who claim that her parents were sent to a concentration camp in Germany, but it is not clear if they are still alive. She fears the worse. She has converted her parents' house into a base for the French Underground. Dozens of agents meet their regularly to pass on information as well as to receive instructions from us here in London. She will be quite useful to you."

"And where exactly do I go to fulfill this objective?"

Denhurst stood up. "Ah, yes, I was getting to that. Why don't all of you follow me?" He opened the door, and they stepped into the corridor and entered a large, cold room with lamps hanging overhead. There was a low table in the middle, as sections of maps occupied the walls on all sides. With everyone assembled, Denhurst began by pointing at the table before him. "This, gentlemen, is a scale model of Bavaria."

Kurt looked it over. Its minute detailing impressed him. Every village, every town, every last house was depicted. Kurt positioned himself immediately next to Denhurst as the man began to elaborate.

"Hitler recently celebrated his fiftieth birthday there. The German high command built it for the Führer as a retreat, high in the Bavarian Mountains." He used a long pointer to show the location on the map. "The retreat is called Eagle's Nest. Its primary function is as a place for receptions and conferences. It's located six thousand feet above sea level and it's accessible only by a tunnel leading to an elevator. This is where Göring, Keitel and Ribbentrop will meet."

"Göring will have his invasion plans with him and this, Kurt, is where you will be also, mingling amongst the power elite, listening to every word spoken. We need you to photograph the plans. Once you've discovered the time and place of the actual invasion, you will contact us immediately." Denhurst looked over and studied the geography of Eagle's Nest. He turned to Kurt and smiled. "This should be just the ticket for you. Rescuing the head of RAF was your warm-up."

"Warm-up?" Kurt said. "Listen, this mission is nothing short of suicide." The men around him all laughed. He looked at the model of Bavaria once again, hands at his side and said nothing. Denhurst held the pointer under his arm as if it were a riding crop.

"My boy, when Kruger was shot, he was alone, unguarded momentarily. He was on a trip to the European countryside. The Czechs set an ambush for him that backfired. The original objective was to kidnap Kruger and use him as a bargaining tool in trying to get the Gestapo to release guerillas rounded up by storm troopers. But Kruger put up a struggle and by the time help arrived he suffered a broken nose, blackened eye, bruises to the face, neck and torso, as well as a bullet in the chest. He is now recuperating in a Bavarian hospital with bandages all over his face, head and upper body. He is nothing short of a mummy. When he is released it will be you they're letting go. We'll make the slip at night with the aid of the Resistance in Paris. Dispose of Kruger, and you step into his shoes. He already lost some of his distinct features in the attack. Once we groom you, no one will know the difference when the bandages come off."

Kurt looked perplexed. This was an outrageous scheme. He stepped back and said thoughtfully, "Let's suppose I manage to fool the German high command and get past the heavy security, and even find the plans for invasion. How will I get them out, and where will I go? The Nazis would chauffeur Göring and me into the meeting in a limousine, but I doubt they'd extend the same courtesy to me once they knew I'd stolen the plans for invasion."

Denhurst took in a deep sigh, gestured to Langford, who pulled out a small cigarette case from his pocket and handed it to Kurt. There was a camera inside with eighteen exposures. "This is our latest gadget from SOE and it is foolproof, not to mention waterproof. The end that you would normally open to get a cigarette has a lens. The back has a button designed as an ornament on the case itself. Press it, and it will take pictures. It automatically goes from one frame to the next."

Kurt looked at it a bit. Finally he said, "All right, that answers how I bring the data back, now how do I get back?"

Denhurst used his pointer to indicate the back of Eagle's Nest. "Here is the den. Inside will be a safe on the north wall. It is behind a painting Field Marshal Hermann Göring himself gave to Hitler as a birthday present, by Holbein, a gift from his private art collection. Inside that safe will be the invasion plans. Once you have photographed them you will merely slip over the side, using a rope. The first hundred feet is a sheer drop. From there, the terrain becomes manageable and the mountainside more forgiving. You will be able to make it down in time before anybody notices you're gone.

"Members of the Resistance will be waiting for you at the bend in the mountain road here. Then you will be driven to a field with a plane waiting for you and you will be flown back to London."

Kurt was still unconvinced. "Sir, I'm not Kruger. It's just that simple. The whole plan rests on me being passed off as this Nazi major. Even if I do look like him, I still need someone guiding me with information along the way."

Denhurst put the pointer down. Walked back to a desk by the wall and told everyone to sit down. He turned off the light switch, stepped up to the far wall in front and pulled down the projector screen. As the men sat silently behind him, Denhurst turned on the slide projector. On the screen was a slide of Pabon in the arms of Kruger.

Kurt gasped. "Jacqueline doesn't only run around blowing up bridges or shooting at motorcades," Denhurst said. "She has all the makings of a fine field agent as well. This is her and Kruger six months ago in Berlin. She was his mistress at the time and all the high command knew it. They were inseparable. She never told him she was Jewish."

"What about her parents?" Kurt asked.

"She used a different name so when her family was rounded up by the Gestapo the Germans couldn't trace them to her. But with Kruger's injury we put her to work in the more coarse assignments with the French Underground. She is not on any Gestapo list and as far as any of them are concerned she is nonexistent. When Göring goes up to his retreat he will have the Fräuleins lining up. His lust for the ladies is almost equal to that for morphine."

"You mean her and me?"

Denhurst didn't bother to answer, he just changed slides. This one was a full-length picture of Jacqueline in the Bavarian countryside dressed as a native in traditional costume. "She will fill you in on all the particulars of the personality of Kruger." He took out a long, black cigarette holder from his suit pocket and loaded it with a small cigarette. "She's been with Kruger for the better part of a year. And she is being permanently removed from the field to guarantee your success in this mission. She knows him better than he knows himself and she happens to be in the next room."

Kurt was taken by surprise. "Really? But I thought she was a contact."

Denhurst smiled. "I said she will be useful to you for the next two weeks. You will meet on a daily basis, and she will give you all of the information on Kruger you will need to make that transformation complete. She was flown in earlier this morning after Hardwick and Richards told me how much you and Kruger looked alike. We need to get things moving as fast as possible."

Kurt stood up. "May I see her?"

"Certainly."

Ian Richards opened the back door. Kurt stepped through. The room was a small study filled with books, a desk crammed with papers, a lamp glowing brightly on the left, in front of a large bookcase. Jacqueline sat in the armchair next to the desk. Her head turned toward the open door; she stood up.

The pictures did not do her justice. She was simply gorgeous, dressed in a long, flowing black dress and a short fur jacket. Her hair was tied back. He felt an immediate attraction to her.

Denhurst closed the door behind him. "Miss Pabon, this is the gentleman I was telling you about."

She looked him over in amazement. As he walked up closer to her in the light, she studied his features. "Remarkable," she said at last. Her full, sensual lips formed the words quietly to herself a second time.

Kurt extended his hand. "Mademoiselle Pabon, it is a pleasure to meet you."

She smiled and couldn't help laughing out loud, "I'm sorry, but you look so much like Kruger...I mean, it's incredible."

"To his misfortune and to my gain, I suppose," he said. Denhurst sat down behind the desk and took a long drag on his cigarette. He checked his watch.

Jacqueline asked if she could sit down. "The trip last night was dreadfully unpleasant," she said. "The Messerschmitts were out and we had a couple of close calls. I slept all of three hours. But anyway, tell me, Mr. Duran—"

"Please, call me Kurt."

"Very well then, Kurt, tell me, how long have you been in SOE?"

"Actually I'm not. I'm in OSS. Denhurst here filled me in only this morning on the mission." He started to look for some clues in her face, her expression. She knew Kruger, and her immediate reaction to seeing him was so sincere it was reassuring to a certain extent, but unnerving just the same, as if he had found out he had a long lost twin brother.

He wanted to work his way back a little bit. "Jacqueline, you know the plan. What is expected of me?"

She smiled, her eyes widened. "Yes, I was informed about the mission in its entirety."

"Then you realize the role I'll be playing. Do you think I can actually pull it off, I mean now that you've seen me in the flesh?"

She didn't answer right away, just looked at him. She nodded, reaching out to touch his hand. "The resemblance is incredible."

Denhurst stood and excused himself. "I'd like a few words with Victor. I'll have Ian come back for the two of you momentarily."

As he left the room Kurt shot up out of his armchair. "Damn it, not you too."

She was taken aback. "What did I say?"

"It is what you didn't say—this whole business, the mission to Eagle's Nest, it is insane. It couldn't possibly work. So I resemble a major in the SS. After the bandages come off half of the Nazi command is going to be staring me down. Face it, as soon as I open my mouth and speak—"

She switched to German. "And they told me you were their best operative."

Forgetting himself, he spoke back in fluent German, reaffirming his distinguished career with OSS.

She laughed again. "You see, you speak the language without any accent. If I were to close my eyes I would swear I was talking to Heinrich in person."

He leaned back into his armchair, took a deep breath, broke out in a broad grin. She smiled delightfully, and he was starting to relax a bit.

That afternoon Denhurst gave the orders to move out.

Chapter Six

Station Five was covered in a thick mist. It was drizzling. This was SOE Training Center for Special Operations. Northeast of Chester by the coast, in an isolated wooded area, the rough terrain provided ideal training conditions. The main building was to the immediate left of the grounds, the other two structures housed living quarters and training center facilities. There was not a soul in sight. The only sound was that of the wind howling as it rose up from the sea, through the trees along the cliffs. A small town thirty miles away was the station's nearest neighbor.

On a grassy road leading down toward the grounds, leaves flying across it, came a gray-green military jeep, speeding ahead. The driver was Frank Lloyds, a young pilot with a cleft in his chin and steely eyes. He wore RAF blue and highly polished boots. His flying jacket was undone. He slowed to clear a dip in the roadway. Next to him was Ian Richards, smoking a cigarette. He had checked some papers in his briefcase and was closing it back up. His assistant, Hardwick, was in the back seat with Kurt, who sighed with discontent as the rain picked up. "Doesn't it ever stop raining?" he said.

Hardwick looked out into the growing torrents of rainfall. "Not too hospitable a climate."

They had flown in to start preparing Kurt for his mission. The driver parked close to the front entrance and the men set out to make their way inside. Duran looked the place over. In all his years with OSS he never once had need to be here. He felt strange. The interior was roomy and there were two people there waiting for them in the rotunda, Captain Davis of SOE, a man of sixty in a distinguished uniform, and Lieutenant Granger, in his mid-forties though he looked much younger, with a fair moustache.

After they made their formal introductions Richards said, "It is cold enough to freeze to death."

The lieutenant suggested they head to the kitchen. The men arranged themselves around a large breakfast table, and the lieutenant went to the stove to pour each man a mug of piping hot tea. Richards said to Kurt, "Lloyds will be flying you out over the Channel to Normandy. He's done this kind of thing before."

Lloyds raised his mug. "Not much to it, just need to stay away from Jerry and the night fighters." He took a swig of his tea. "Have you done much flying?"

Kurt looked indifferent. "When needed."

Said Richards, his cigarette dangling in the corner of his mouth, "We've put together a flight plan, you'll be flown by Liberator low under German radar. The night fighters are looking for bomber formations, so by staying below their usual line of flight you should not have too much trouble. You will be landing in a field in Normandy."

Kurt asked, "Why Normandy?"

"Because it is the least patrolled area in France. Members of the French Underground will guide you in by lamplight. Your recognition code will be Bay-1. If they don't confirm, you don't land." He removed the cigarette and put it out on an ashtray.

"Who'll be my contact?" Kurt said.

Denhurst cleared his throat slightly. "Maurice—that's all he goes by. He is the leader in the group. We've had some bad luck with the Germans knocking out our planes the last few weeks. So once Lloyds drops you off he is out of there. You want to make a quick line to the woods and hope the Germans don't see you."

Kurt placed his hand around his mug of hot tea for warmth. He stared into it, sighed and looked over at Richards. "How many will be waiting?"

"A total of ten."

"Why so many?"

"The first moments after landing are critical. If you're spotted, the Germans will come down on you like lightning. You'll need all the cover fire you can get to make it to Brussels. The woods will be crawling with soldiers on patrol. The underground is there strictly as your backup."

Kurt stretched his legs a bit. "That's reassuring, but I prefer working alone."

Hardwick shook his head. "The Germans are very cruel to prisoners of war, as you well know. If the Gestapo caught up with you there wouldn't be enough of you left to send home."

Richards looked out the window. "We had one of our very best counter-intelligence officers picked up just last week in Le Mans. He was with SOE a very long time. The Gestapo found papers on him that he had stolen from a general in the SS. They contained all of their troop strength, their armament, as well as a list of Nazi sympathizers for the region of Le Mans. Do you know what they did with him?"

Kurt sat back. "No, what?"

"First they detained him and ordered the execution of his companion, a young female from Marseilles. Then they interrogated him for three days until he finally died from severe beatings, but in the end he told them nothing. I know you are used to working alone but trust me on this one—it's too big a mission."

Kurt smiled. "Fine, all right. Then what?"

Richards took over. "The next thing will be for you to safely arrive into Brussels. That's your departure point into Bavaria, a train runs into Germany from there. You will get on it. Just blend in with the Germans."

"I see, so I take a civilized route into the heart of Nazi Germany. Quite original—I like it."

Richards frowned. "Cut the sarcasm and listen. Once you've arrived at the station there will be a contact waiting for you on the arrival deck, Frantz Schmidt."

Through the briefing Kurt remained analytical, coolly weighing in all the facts as a seasoned professional. He had learned long ago to discard any emotional attachment to his work. He did not say anything. Properly trained, he could do anything. But he had to convince himself about this particular mission. It was just too outlandish, too absurd not to work. He reasoned, therefore, that it would.

Ian sat back, finishing up his tea and checking his watch. It was one fifteen in the afternoon. The rains had stopped and from the kitchen window they could see the countryside clearing up, the heavy mist fading away. Richards got up, lit another cigarette and turned, looking out across the rolling hills. "I met with Churchill personally. It was late last night after we left your apartment. He ordered Denhurst, Langford and myself to Windsor Castle." He turned and looked squarely at Kurt. "The prime minister was very pleased with your record. He was particularly interested in that little adventure of yours at Devil's Cove. Sir Archibald Sinclair has recovered from his ordeal and has taken the helm of RAF defense plans again. Churchill wanted me to thank you personally for your great work."

Kurt was astonished. "I'm genuinely touched, Ian."

Richards cracked a smile. "As well you should be. There will be a medal in it for you, but you need to take care of this other business first."

Kurt stood up. He was tense. He went over to fix himself another mug of tea. Richards told Lloyds to fly back and pick up Pabon and Kiel Holmby. "They should be ready."

Kurt looked puzzled. "Who is Holmby?"

"You'll know soon enough."

SOE had arranged for Jacqueline and Holmby to be waiting at the airfield when Lloyds flew in. She had only met Holmby a few moments before. There was something about the man she didn't particularly like—perhaps his eyes were set too close together, or the fact that his skin was so aged by exposure to the sun, but she tried to do her best with him. His personality was extremely unpleasant, a very irritable man to say the least, but since they were all to be at the same place for some time it would make sense not to be too judgmental.

As the plane taxied down the runway Pabon was dressed in a spiffy field uniform with boots, while Holmby was in his training fatigues. She was told she would remain dressed in formal military attire during the duration of her stay at the training facility. "How long is the flying time?" Pabon asked Lloyds.

Lloyds was rather taken aback. "Are you in a particular hurry, Madam?"

She pouted. Looked at the sky. "I prefer not to fly in a rainstorm."

"About twenty minutes, ma'am."

The plane was spartan in design, seating no more than eight at a time, one in the cockpit and seven in the back. Holmby took his gear and offered Pabon to carry hers. She refused.

"No, thank you, I'm all right."

Lloyds helped her up into the rear of the cabin. Holmby took the window seat. Jacqueline preferred to sit opposite him. Suddenly she realized Lloyds had disappeared. The engine started up and she hurried to strap herself in. At that moment there was a sudden shift as they lifted off.

"The flight was not particularly exhilarating; the roar of the engine made conversation difficult and all she could do was sit there and watch outside as the sky grew ever darker. The rain beat against the windows until all things visible outside were awash in the blur. The plane would bounce erratically whenever it hit an air pocket. She glanced at Holmby, who was content to shut his eyes and try to rest.

She thought about herself, her life, why she was even on this plane. Then she remembered her mother and father, and the life they had shared in France, and how the Gestapo had destroyed all that. If it was too late to save her own family perhaps by fighting the Nazis she could help save the lives of others. She was strong. She was a Jew. Her people had suffered and struggled much in their history and had always managed to survive. She would teach Kurt all she could about Kruger, the Germans, and perhaps about life.

The plane came down roughly. The landing strip at the training center was too wet. The plane skidded a few times before it came to a complete stop. Richards was in his jeep waiting to greet them. As he drove up, Jacqueline jumped out of the plane's cabin and ran for the vehicle. Inside, her hair dripping wet, she wiped raindrops from her face and asked anxiously, "Where is Kurt?"

"He's here, back at the base," Ian said. When Hardwick and Lloyds loaded in, Richards drove off.

Kurt was now in his assigned room, a cramped place with a simple desk, a chair, a bookcase, a bunk, and room for one chest of his belongings. He heard the jeep and saw them drive up through the window. He exited the room and went down into the kitchen to fix himself some tea and wait for them. His quarters were not only cramped but chilly. The heating system in the station was medieval.

He sat himself down at the dinner table. When the pilot came in Kurt gave him a quick glance. A strange looking man followed. No more than five feet four inches in height, he was dressed in gray trousers and army boots. His leather flying jacket was removed and slung over his left forearm revealing broad shoulders and powerfully developed arms. He had the physique of a boxer.

Jacqueline walked in and smiled at Kurt. "Thank God, you've made tea." She hurried herself over and poured a cup.

The new face came up to Kurt and introduced himself. His right hand extended. He said, "Kiel Holmby, at your service."

"Hello," said Kurt as he shook his hand. Holmby sat down opposite Kurt. "I'm with SOE, from Department D. I'll be your trainer for this particular mission of yours."

Kurt hesitated. "Department D—ah, yes, the dirty tricks department. How charming."

Holmby's face grew serious. "That's not all we do. I'll be training you for every aspect of your mission. Have you done any mountain climbing?"

Kurt stood up and headed toward the window. "A bit, now and again."

Holmby turned in his chair to follow Kurt's movements. "Well, a bit won't work here. Starting tomorrow I begin to prepare you."

Kurt nodded in approval. "Thanks, I'll be looking forward to it." He turned to Pabon. "How was your flight?"

She didn't look at him. Her eyes were fixed on the kettle as she poured herself the tea. Mixing in a teaspoon of honey she said in a quiet voice, almost whispering, "It started to rain hard and got very cold. Only when we approached the camp here did the weather improve." She looked up at him shyly, as if waiting for a word of sympathy. But he didn't need to say it, his eyes told her what she wanted to hear.

He tried to get closer when Ian Richards walked in. "Well, did you all get properly introduced?" As he was removing his raincoat he glanced over at Holmby and Kurt.

"Yes, sir," said Holmby.

"Good. I suppose you men are anxious to get started."

Holmby nodded. "Tomorrow morning is our appointed date to begin. I need to ready a few things first, and the weather should clear up by then."

"Good. Now, what say we have supper?"

Jacqueline offered to make some soup when Lieutenant Granger stepped in and announced, "I will have dinner ready by five thirty." She blushed. She was use to kitchen duties while housing the underground.

Kurt asked Jacqueline to follow him into the reading room. Tea in hand they made their way through the growing congestion of bodies filling the kitchen. Adding to those already there, Hardwick and Captain Davis came in. Jacqueline sighed with relief as they exited into the foyer. He led her to the comfort of a couch.

The reading room was simple. A rug on the floor, a clock on the wall, and some chairs. There was also a flame in the fireplace. She positioned herself close to him on the couch and placed her tea on the coffee table. "I suppose we should begin what we came here for," Kurt said.

She pulled herself up toward her tea and stared far out into space as if in a trance, her mind fixed on the swirling array of imagery flashing in her mind all at once. Kruger was a complex man, no doubt about it. A war hero at twenty-nine, his characteristics could not be explained away with a few phrases. She drew a blank, not knowing where to begin.

Kurt sensed her anxiety. "Could you start from the beginning?"

She smiled and laughed. She didn't know what made her so nervous so she laughed again. Kurt smiled reassuringly.

She leaned closer to him. "Well, Kruger is first and foremost a professional soldier. His uniform is altogether immaculate, he walks like a storm trooper on parade. He has a nasty habit of picking fights with men at least his size or larger, and he always keeps his Luger under his pillow at night when he goes to sleep. I met him in Amsterdam—of all places in a bakery. I was on my way home to Paris and wanted fresh bread for my trip. He was dressed as a civilian, he was handsome, and I was attracted to him. We had lunch at a bistro and he just left. Only later, when SOE recruited me to the French Underground, did I find out the man I met was a Nazi. I felt bad," she said bitterly. "You understand."

Kurt saw the dark circles under her eyes. She had spent many months at work against the occupiers of Vichy. He knew reliving certain parts of her past would be hard for her but it had to be done. "What was it about Kruger that most struck you? How does he talk, what does he say?"

She took a quick sip of her tea. "His voice and yours are almost the same, except of course you speak English. But in German you shouldn't have problems convincing his friends you are Kruger. You might want to talk a little bit deeper at times, and a bit slower."

She crossed her legs. She was still quite cold. "Kruger, when very upset by something, curses passionately, over and over, repeating the word 'swine'. Everything is swine when he is angry."

"Swine?"

"Yes," she said. Kurt stood up and walked over to the fireplace, leaning up against the mantel, his left hand squeezing the back of his neck. He raised his eyes towards the ceiling.

"Are you married?" she asked.

He was quiet, with a look of surprise on his face.

"Well, are you?"

He stared back at her. "No, of course not. I've always been a bachelor. That's the way I like it. A man needs to have his freedom."

She perked up on the couch. "I see." He walked back over and sat down.

"What about you, Miss Pabon?"

She took another sip of her tea, placed it on the saucer, then turned to him. "Yes, but it was some time ago, to an American. We had no children but we did spend three and a half years together."

"Where?"

"Why, in France, of course. First we lived in Monte Carlo. He was a manager at one of the casinos. It was called The Golden Palace. It was a magnificent place to be sure, only the very rich went their to gamble and most would lose terribly. My husband always said it was just luck, but I knew better. Claudette LaBell, one of the hostesses, she told me the tables were all rigged. Anyway, we lived in an apartment five minutes away for one year. It was a nice life and they paid him well. We always had money."

She paused. "He got greedy and stole from the casino. When they found out, he relocated us to a beautiful house by the ocean. But he didn't stop there. He spent the next two years with the French mafia—he was into diamond smuggling. One day a policeman came to my house and told me my husband was dead. Of course, I didn't believe it until he took me to the mortuary to identify the body. He was shot many times." She looked pale and withdrawn. "I discovered then his secrets, all of them. His taking money from the casino, his smuggling." Her eyes got teary as if still in disbelief. "That's how the mafia handled their people."

He was speechless.

"And you see I needed to support myself, my family. Being a minority in a country like France was very difficult. The American was good to me." She looked at him and her eyes lit up. "I'm so sorry, I didn't even tell you his name. It was Anthony Douglas, he was from the Midwest."

"Well, what happened to you then?"

She smiled sweetly, raised her saucer and cup with her right hand. "I worked in restaurants. When the war came, I needed to do something positive to help. You know the rest."

He cleared his throat and changed subjects. "Now, about Kruger."

The men in the kitchen were huddling around the dinner table as Granger finished preparing dinner. Richards conversed heatedly with Holmby. "Duran's the best man I've got for this mission. The French Underground has informed our office Kruger has been recuperating from his wounds and he will be released in ten days, not the original time table we had hoped for. Now, with less time to prepare I need you to concentrate on the essential elements of this mission. Make sure he knows how to get in, take the pictures of the data, and the escape route out."

Holmby sat patiently observing Richards' demands. He would have to accelerate the program in due course. First thing in the morning he would have Kurt versed in the fine art of counterespionage.

Hardwick entered the reading room. The fireplace crackled. Pabon was finishing up her conversation. Hardwick announced, "Dinner is ready. Shall we?"

Kurt got up and escorted Jacqueline to the dining room. A spectacular crystal chandelier hung from the ceiling, which was carved wood. The walls were paneled and there was antique furniture all around. A portrait of Churchill looked down from the far end, greeting the guests as they sat down to dine. The table was set, and steak was the main dish for the evening, with roasted vegetables and Yorkshire pudding. There was also a bottle of red wine.

Kurt pulled out a chair for Jacqueline and sat down next to her. The others had waited for them. Kurt beamed with delight and said, "If I didn't know any better, I'd swear we were sitting down to eat at Catherine's," which was his favorite restaurant in London.

Amidst chuckles from the other men, Richards, who was sitting directly across from him, said, "By the way, old man, we upped the ante—you've got ten days to ready yourself, starting tomorrow."

Kurt's smile faded. "So what happened now?"

"Oh, everything is just fine. Kruger is making a remarkable recovery, that's all, and the hospital doesn't want to keep him any longer than is necessary. It's a blessing in disguise really, the weather will be more favorable to get you across to Normandy. Now relax and enjoy your dinner."

Chapter Seven

It was morning and the sky was clear. The grounds had a salty smell to them as the winds blew cold air in from the sea. Kurt was staring into the mirror that hung on the wall of his bedroom. He studied his face thoughtfully and looked over at the photograph of Kruger wedged at the side of the mirror, between the mirror and reflective glass. He thought it inconceivable that there could be such a strong resemblance, but there it was. There was no reason for it, they were not even related. No explanation whatsoever, other than dumb luck. He noticed Kruger's eyes. They were in deep thought when the picture was taken. Kruger was a man of quick temper, as Kurt had learned in his private talks with Jacqueline. He looked at himself as he raised his hand and, in a sarcastic voice said, "Heil Hitler!" He cracked a smile. He had been killing Germans almost two years. Now he would be socializing with some of the biggest names in the Nazi high command. War has a certain irony to it, he thought.

There was a knock at his door. It was Kiel Holmby. "Hello in there." Kurt fixed his shirt promptly. Dressed in green pants and combat boots he walked over and opened the door.

"Morning."

Holmby nodded in greeting. "Breakfast is in five minutes, then the rest of the morning you're mine."

As he finished pulling his shirt sleeves up, shrugging his shoulders, Jacqueline walked by and smiled. "So there you are."

He just looked at her. "Yes, it's me all right."

She came up closer. "They gave you this to stay in? Oh my..."

He looked confused. "And your surroundings?"

"Are larger and prettier to say the least. If I were you I'd complain to management."

"Ah, but with free meals I think I'll bear it. Will you join me for breakfast?"

"Why, yes," she said delightedly. "Lead the way."

The lieutenant had prepared the first meal of the day for them. In stark contrast to last night's dinner, breakfast was a simple bowl of oatmeal with a glass of orange juice. Reality had set in. This was a training camp. As they both sat down they were pleasantly surprised to see no one else at the table with them. The lieutenant had cleared off the stove and exited the room with a passing, "good day."

There was a strange kind of quiet now. "Did you sleep well?" Kurt said.

"Yes, as well as can be expected under the circumstances I suppose. And yourself?"

"All right. By the way, I meant to warn you about Ian. He is a bit of a flirt with the ladies. If he ever gets out of hand let me know."

She looked amused. "Oh, hardly Ian?" They both laughed. She developed a serious expression on her face. She fumbled with her spoon and Kurt noticed the mood change.

"What's the matter?" he said. She looked away with teary eyes. "What is it, what's wrong, Jacqueline?"

She looked at him longingly. "I need to tell you, just so you're aware of the facts, that Kruger is a marked man with several powerful Nazis. They are envious of his position within the high command. His own hostility towards them doesn't help matters. On several occasions I overheard some unpleasant things."

"Who are these men?"

"General von Brauchitsch, General Halder, and Martin Bormann."

He realized her concern for him. He reached out, placed his hand on hers. "You need not worry. None of those men will be anywhere near me, and if I see any of them I'll make a point to avoid conversation at all costs."

She revealed the faint traces of a smile and released a deep sigh. She was compelled to lean towards him, her eyes half closed, and placed a delicate kiss on his lips. As she pulled away they heard footsteps approaching.

There was Kiel Holmby in full tactical field dress: a colored, short-sleeved shirt and summer pants that came down to the knees, along with dark brown boots. In his right hand he held a coil of rope. Without saying a word, Kurt got up and followed him outside. They left through a corridor down to the rear of the building. As they went out, Holmby said, "Eagle's Nest is a treacherous place. You'll need to master your way about it if you want to get out alive."

They walked through the open country. The sun shined brightly and it was starting to warm up. Fifty yards from the camp was a peculiar rock formation not far from the cliffs. Holmby motioned and Kurt followed. As they approached it, Kurt saw a strange structure on top of the rocks. "This is an exact replica of Eagle's Nest's east wing," Holmby said, "the site with a balcony for your escape. Now you've got the picture, and also what you're going to do with the remaining morning hours."

Kurt observed the steep incline of rocks. He heard a laugh from behind. As he turned, Ian Richards lit up a cigarette. He exhaled and said, "Well, well, my boy, by all accounts this will be the quickest and simplest way out for you. Kiel here has studied the building from aerial reconnaissance photos. This reproduction, or a third of it anyway, will give you something to go on." As he talked he stepped up, taking another drag on his smoke. He gazed upward. "You will be inundated with the flirtatious charms of dozens of ladies that day. The place will be one large, non-stop party. All you need to do is separate yourself for a moment and take the pictures. The rest will be fairly simple. Just toss the secure line over the balcony and climb down. Our people will be waiting for you down the road."

He lowered his cigarette. "It's all in the timing. You need to find the right moment, the opening, for it to work. My suggestion is to wait until things lighten up a bit. Let the generals have their fill of champagne and such before you venture off."

Holmby called out from the side of the rocks. There were wooden steps attached, leading up to the top. "Come on, man."

Kurt tugged at his pants and ran up the stairs. "Kurt, remember, once you're outside the balcony stay focused on the east wing. There will be guards walking around the terrace routinely at five-minute intervals."

From the top there was a surrealistic feeling to things. Holmby reached the final step that landed him in the main quarters where the wall safe would be. The replica was perfect down to the last details. He opened the door and saw that the room inside was a flawless reproduction.

Kurt walked in and looked to his left—there hung the Holbein reproduction. It was a fair copy, a photographic enlargement on canvas in a museum quality frame. He gingerly pulled it aside, and it swung out on hinges and the circular safe was revealed.

Holmby walked to the center of the room with sunlight filtering in through the windows. The walls were all painted an off-white and the ceiling was wood paneled with draperies at the sides of the French windows. Simple furniture filled the interior: a table with cups and saucers, a desk, pictures of Hitler's mistress Eva Braun. "The only way up to it is for the guests to use an elevator," Holmby said, "which would be several rooms down from this one. It's studded with mirrors and brass fittings to alleviate Hitler's claustrophobia. Once you arrive in it, you will exit to the main reception room. That will be where they start up the celebrations."

Kurt looked the room over, turned and walked to the terrace, where he started to open the French doors. "That part comes later," Holmby said. "Now you open up the safe."

Kurt spun around without saying a word. Rubbing the fingers of his right hand together and placing them over the safe immediately in front of him, he began to work. He listened to the tumbles inside as he worked the safe. His ear closer, he started to move the dials one last time. Finally the safe popped open. Kurt straightened up but a smile soon disappeared as he noticed the way Holmby looked at him. "Well, what's wrong?"

"Well, for starters, it won't be that easy, but I suppose you did all right."

Kurt laughed, walked back to the window, swung it open and stepped out into the terrace. He rested his hands on the railing and the wind blew firmly across his face. He squinted, gazing out to sea, and turned his attention to Ian below as he strolled along the grassy base, puffing on his cigarette. Kurt called out, "A piece of cake, Ian."

Richards stopped and looked up. "It should be for sticky fingers, now let's see what you're really made of."

Holmby informed Kurt that he had thirty seconds to secure the line on the railing and heave over the side. "It will take a full three minutes to climb down, with a minute and a half to spare once you reach the bottom. "That last minute and a half is your running time, until the guards swing around again."

Kurt looked sternly at the sheer drop from the balcony.

"I'm ready."

Holmby checked his stopwatch and said, "Go."

Kurt began to tie the rope around, securing it firmly, using a mountain climber's belt, fitting it around his waist and closing it up at the midsection, he leaned over the edge and lowered himself down. His feet straight with the rope between his boots. He hooked the rope around his back and began to descend. The rocks and branches made it awkward as he scaled down. It would take almost all of three minutes just to clear the obstacles, he thought. Suddenly he swung over, pushing off from the rocks with his feet, and propelling himself along in a zigzag against the cliff, rappelling down to the ground below.

Ian broke open a satisfied grin as Kurt dusted himself off, removed the belt and walked over.

"Incredible!" Holmby shouted. "You have two minutes to spare."

Kurt grinned at Ian. "Got an extra smoke?"

Ian reached into his jacket pocket and pulled out a pack. Kurt looked up and over at the balcony, his eyes following the twisted terrain down. "I've always liked a fast exit."

Ian smiled. "You never cease to amaze me. You handled that as though it were a cakewalk, but remember the real thing is going to be deadly. For now I'm satisfied. There will be more for you to do later. In the meantime, get back to camp and have a drink or two and relax."

These were orders Kurt could hardly resist. "Yes, sir, and thank you."

As he went away Holmby ran down the wooden steps exasperated. "Where is he off to? We just got here."

Ian shook his head. "Remember what he is here for—to train for a mission, to know how to execute his orders. Why push things now? We know that he can make his escape, it's time to make sure he's able to get into the place. I want you to make him look like Kruger. His hair, eyes, everything...you've had time to study him. Use your cosmetic skills and make sure when the time comes you can whip him into Herr Kruger himself without any problems."

Holmby smiled widely. "Understood, sir."

At lunch time Jacqueline prepared something nice for Kurt. They relaxed under a large oak tree away from camp, laying comfortably on the white cloth spread on the ground with an open picnic basket containing sandwiches, salad, and a bottle of white wine. He thanked her and said, "The last time I ate outdoors like this I was in my senior year in college, with an old girlfriend of mine, and I had a little picnic at lunch break before I had to take my geometry exam that afternoon."

"And how did it go?"

He leaned on his elbow, holding his wine glass. "The picnic or the exam? Oh, I failed. I hate geometry, it's my worse subject. I never felt there was a need for it, all those meaningless computations."

She laughed as she took a sip of her wine. "I know what you mean. I was the same way with history. What happened was in the past. I prefer the here and now." She had worked all morning on papers she'd brought along with her, background notes he could refer to again and again until he had absorbed all the facts and knew Kruger inside and out.

He set down his glass. "Did you mean it—that kiss you gave me back there?"

Jacqueline looked up at the sky and said, "In what way?"

"You know what I mean."

"Oh, I suppose. I hate the thought of spending my time teaching someone only to have them..." She stopped short of saying it. She looked him squarely in his eyes. "Be careful when you go."

"Of course." He began to flip through the pages. "Interesting," he said to himself as he read over the data. "So Kruger was on a secret mission in the harbor of Dakar, the chief French naval station in Africa?"

"That's correct," she said.

As he continued reading Jacqueline elaborated. "During the summer of 1938, Hitler was increasingly preoccupied by the idea of a war with the other western powers. Kruger told me that Himmler, after long discussions with Hitler, in turn talked to Heydrich. Hitler believed once war started Germany would be victorious, but he was concerned about the possibility of the Americans uniting with England and trying a counterattack against Nazi-occupied Europe from North Africa."

Kurt listened intently. "Go on."

She sat up and extended her feet to the side, her body resting closer to his. "Hitler decided to give the orders to have the West African coastal region and its harbors surveyed, so that autumn of 1938 Heydrich instructed a Nazi spy by the name of Walter Schellenberg to be flown to the harbor by Kruger, who happens to be a very good pilot. Kruger didn't tell me anything of the mission, he was sworn to secrecy about that part. So the details of the trip, what he said..." She just shook her head.

"So you spent all your time with them?"

She brushed her long hair off the side of her face. "Most of it, those were my instructions. But I did manage to help some Jews fleeing the Gestapo by putting small groups in touch with the French Underground in Paris. Many were smuggled out to London, others went as far as the United States."

He embraced her and said affectionately, whispering into her ear, "That's very noble." He pushed the papers aside and kissed her passionately. Jacqueline raised her hand and stroked his face. He kissed her neck and she tingled deliciously at every caress of his lips against her flesh. She ran her hands down through his thick, black hair. Then for a moment they lay quiet.

He relaxed his eyes. As they closed, her head rested on his chest. He said tenderly, "I'm sorry, that wasn't suppose to happen."

She pulled herself up, sitting next to him, looking at him seriously. "Why not?"

He smiled smugly. "I mean, I was supposed to be studying and here I was seducing my instructor."

She placed a finger on his lips and said, "Have another glass of wine, it's good for you."

They rested there, seemingly cut off from the war if only for a moment. "Are you involved with anybody?"

She smiled. "No," she said, "unless you count yourself."

"I just don't want either of us to get hurt."

She placed her hands on her lap as she sat on the blanket, gazing at the rolling clouds overhead. The sun streaming down on her face, warming her from head to toe. "When I was a little girl I was afraid of the dark, so my mother would always come to my bedroom and tell me a bedtime tale. I had one that was my favorite." As she spoke, her eyes got moist. "Whenever Mama finished telling me the story she would hug and kiss me afterward and tell me that love will always survive. Love..." she sighed. "So no matter how scared I got I knew that in the end love will always wait for me. Love has a lot of meaning to it, when you love someone nothing else really matters. And I'll never forget Mama and the time she told me each night to make sure I went to bed feeling loved and secure."

He embraced her. "Your mother was very wise."

She nodded in agreement; afterward they kissed.

That afternoon went by fairly quickly and after dinner the men chose to head out to town for some nightlife. Only Ian, Kurt and Jacqueline remained behind. Ian had retired for the rest of the evening. Jacqueline was smoking a cigarette by the window of the lounge, while Kurt sat in an armchair finishing reading up on all the information she had supplied him that afternoon. He closed up the folder and placed it on the coffee table in front of him. "They should have given you a medal for putting up with this man."

She lowered her cigarette. "Hardly, I've had worse."

"Worse than Kruger?"

"Two or three times."

"You kept busy."

"Yes, but I didn't want you to know that."

He crossed his leg over and rubbed it. It had fallen asleep on him. As he stomped his foot he thought out loud. "It had occurred to me, if Göring was going to the party with his boys at high command he'd get pretty intimate in conversation. Is there anything besides what I covered in the notes that I should say, or perhaps know how to answer?"

She turned from the window and briskly walked over. Her eyes moved from side to side as she thought. "The only thing that comes to mind in that area is Göring's two favorite girls, Gretchen and Hilga. They usually go to every party with him. He gets bored with only one, you see, so he takes two to have company. And from what I've seen, they tend to be very flirtatious with Kruger as well. Göring never seems to mind. By the time that occurs he is too plastered to care."

Kurt was taken aback. "That's it?"

She thought about it and said, "I believe so."

He stood up and walked over to the fireplace to warm his hands. He rubbed them together a few times. "By the way, Ian mentioned to me some top brass was due in this week to observe my progress. On special instructions from Churchill himself."

She looked bedazzled. "My goodness, that's wonderful. And when do we meet the prime minister?"

"That I don't know, if at all. But this will be nerve-rattling enough." He made a straight line for the record player and after making his selection, set it to play. She looked on with a sparkle in her eye as he strode up and nonchalantly asked her, "May I have this dance?" He took her in his arms, leading her around the room. With gaiety and laughter they twirled.

After a few spins Jacqueline giggled and spun herself over into a corner, sitting on the couch, all the while holding on to his hand. She took in a deep breath and said, "That was wonderful. Where did you learn to dance like that?"

He grinned. "By watching Tyrone Power movies."

They both laughed and Kurt sat closer to her. She gazed into his eyes. His face did not betray so much as a flicker of emotion as he said, "It's raining." She looked out the window and sure enough it was. "The men will be taking their time getting back," he added.

"Why don't you shut off the record and come to my room?" She leaned up and kissed him. She headed for her bedroom, which in reality was the captain's room. It was the only room on the base with a decent-sized bed. It was lavishly designed, boasting an ornate backboard and floral curtains covering the windows, and there was antique furniture all about. Not at all in keeping with military regulations but then again this station was officially, non existent to begin with, so it mattered little.

As she got in she stripped out of her formal attire and slipped on a black lace nightgown. She turned off the lights and there was a knock at the door. Kurt came in. It would be a few more hours before the drunken men came swaggering back. Neither of them knew if they would ever get this chance again.

He started by smothering her with kisses as they stood in a lover's embrace, his right hand on her lower back pressing her closer to him. Her scent all but intoxicating him, he began by kissing down her neck and her breasts. Her skin was of an olive complexion, the kind he found irresistible. She was five foot seven inches tall, so he towered over her. Her long, black hair, flowed like a stream over her shoulders. He pulled her up tightly, placing his hand down between her tender, soft thighs. She moaned, her eyes half closed.

She pulled away, saying, "Silly. You don't make love like that." She unbuttoned his shirt. "When you're ready, let me know."

He hastened to remove his garments and lay down next to her on top of the covers. She had slipped out of her nightgown altogether and he watched her gorgeous form undulating on top of him as the moonlight filtered in through the half-drawn window curtains. Her breasts were full and large, her nipples hardened. She lowered herself just enough for him to get his mouth on them. Her divinely sculpted abdomen tightened at his touch. It was all he could do to control himself. He was falling into sweet surrender as she rode him into total ecstasy. She let out a moan of satisfaction, her eyes glowing in the heat of the passion as she dug her fingers into his masculine shoulders. He had rotated positions with her, and she was on her back as he suspended himself above her.

His thrusting increased. "More, more," she cried out. "Faster...that's good. There..." She inhaled deeply. His firm buttock flexed rhythmically and she coiled her long legs around his back, bringing him in closer. Her eyes rolled back as she smiled. She was reaching total satisfaction. "Oh, Kurt," she sighed suddenly, her legs lowered. She was limp, her muscles relaxed, her body restful. He rolled over to the side. They were both out of breath and quite content. "That was incredible," she said.

Wiping some perspiration off his face, he said playfully, "I'll second that." She cuddled next to him, inhaling the fragrance of his flesh. She raised her left leg, resting it on his side, her hand playing with his earlobe. She sighed contently and said, "Tonight I will always remember as my night of nights."

The weather outside had not dampened their spirits. The whole world seemed to be revolving around that bedroom.

Chapter Eight

She had slept well and when she awoke called out his name. Her eyes opened hesitantly. He was gone. She let herself forget momentarily where she was. He had been up for hours training with Holmby. Her clock said nine fifteen but there was no sunshine. The mist had rolled back in and the morning was as bleak as last night had been spectacular.

She laid there for a moment composing herself, awash in the afterglow of Kurt's time with her. She still felt a tingling sensation throughout her body which was inescapable and delightful. Then just outside she heard the sound of a plane landing.

Kurt and Holmby looked on as Lloyds taxied down the strip. When they came to a halt Ian Richards got out with two distinguished looking gentlemen well into their sixties, dressed dapperly, trenchcoats down to the knees and Derbies on their heads. One carried a walking stick. As everyone disembarked Ian called Kurt over. He hurried front and center along the moist grass as one of the men pulled up his collar. Ian made the introductions.

"Kurt, these gentlemen are here as observers on behalf of the prime minister himself. His eyes and ears. They will be observing your progress and reporting it to the prime minister."

Kurt was low-key. He didn't know whether to shake hands or salute and wound up doing neither. Ian did not reveal their rank, or their titles, nor for that matter, their names. All Kurt could do was wish them a good morning. Ian dismissed him and led the men inside. Up until then Kurt had handled the whole affair as if it were just another mission. Now he started to feel some unwanted pressure.

Kurt was finishing up an obstacle course when Lloyds came along to observe, wearing a leather pilot's jacket and chewing on a stick of beef jerky. He leaned up against a branch of a tree to watch Kurt's work in progress. After completing fifty grueling sit-ups, followed by push-ups, and crawling on his belly under ten yards of the barbed wire that lined the open field between the rows of trees, Kurt was ready for a break.

The silence of the morning was shattered by the sounds of gunfire out in the distance, over the ocean. There was a fierce dogfight being waged between two Spitfires and a Luftwaffe fighter plane that seemingly had flown off course. As the action intensified, the men outside walked over closer to the cliffs to observe. The Spitfires were still at a marginal distance behind the German aircraft, their guns not having much effect.

Ian came out smoking a cigarette. "Blast it all, those Germans—how in the devil did they get out here?" Suddenly the German fighter dived inexplicably straight down. The Spitfires followed, blasting at the enemy plane with all their might. Kurt looked on with anticipation. The Luftwaffe aircraft was plunging like a fallen stone with the Spitfires racing behind it in blind pursuit. Quickly at the last moment the German pilot pulled up as he neared the water, like the Stuka dive-bombers did in air raids over Europe. With it came an awesome sound, like rockets exploding, the earth shattering.

The Spitfires followed suit. Both pilots tried to pull up but one of the aircraft did not respond fast enough. The first plane flew back up in the nick of time, but the second continued on a downward trajectory and then it was all over. The waves churned with debris from the wreckage. Parts of the aircraft floated on the waves, engulfed in flames. There was no pilot to be seen.

The German knew exactly what he was doing, Kurt thought to himself. At that moment he went up into some clouds. The Spitfire was at a loss, plodding along the blue skies in search of the missing enemy plane. When finally the German fighter burst out of the cover of windswept clouds and opened fire, the Spitfire was hit, rotated and moved around, appearing directly behind the German, at which point the British pilot struck the enemy in the fuselage and the aircraft ignited into a fireball. The pilot didn't have time to eject and it sailed erratically through the air until it hit the side of the cliffs and exploded. The wreckage fell into a heap at the base of the shore.

Lloyds and Ian cheered while Kurt kept an eye on the Spitfire, which had started to develop engine trouble. It rattled along with a churning sound. Ian took notice as well. The pilot was attempting to come down on land, and he spun around and headed in their direction.

By now, Jacqueline was outside, fully dressed and accompanied by the two observers. Captain Davis and Lieutenant Granger ran for the jeep and began to follow the Spitfire as it glided overhead, descending in a smoky line.

All was quiet now as it disappeared behind a tree-covered hill. There was no explosion and Ian told the observers, "It's a good thing you got here when you did. Had you come here a tad later..." He didn't bother to finish his remark.

Hardwick ran out of the front door and approached Richards. "Sir, London called and said the city is being bombed again and that several German raiders have driven deeper inland."

Ian looked at his observers. "I suggest we go back inside." With that, they all walked to the main entrance.

Jacqueline was keeping in step next to Kurt and said to him very quietly, "I missed you this morning."

"And I you." He looked lovingly at her and she smiled.

"Thank you," she said.

Ian, in a robust voice, bellowed for all to hear upon entering the foyer, "Until this all dies down, let's spend the afternoons indoors. There is plenty to be done today." He led them all into the lounge. The observers took the couch, the rest all grabbed chairs, except for Ian, who was diligently puffing away on his cigarette by the window.

One of the observers remarked, "This was exactly what the prime minister told us about, his concern for the escalating air war over England."

His associate nodded. "Things will get worse before they get better. As long as they don't wander out here very often." He turned to Ian. "So where did you find such a lovely guest as Jacqueline?"

"I was just about to introduce you when the fighting started outside," he said, walking over to her. "This is Miss Jacqueline Pabon, a special agent of ours from France. She is helping Kurt Duran prepare for his mission."

"I see. Well, very good."

There was on the coffee table a black briefcase, which one of the observers opened. He removed a manila envelope and took out aerial photographs of the European coastline.

"What's this all about?" Ian said.

The observer glanced up from the photos. "Before full-scale military action against the British Isles can begin there will be a gathering of the storm, as it were, and these photographs are proof positive. Troop movements, heavy artillery, convoys, things of that sort, all beginning to stir up over there and assemble along the coast. These air raids are meant to weaken our resolve before they come in full force."

As he continued to talk, his voice became more aggressive. As he spoke he looked directly at Kurt. "Churchill looks upon this mission of yours as pivotal in what we do next in our defense strategy. There is of course only so much time before all hell breaks loose and we need to know where and when. These latest photos are secret and not all of them are actual deployments. Some are bluffs to full our reconnaissance, but nonetheless things are stirring up."

He sat forward, dropping the photographs on top of his brief case. "Field Marshal Göring is in the Reich Chancellery today with Hitler. Our intelligence tells us they've been holding secret meetings for the last few days. We sincerely hope, Mr. Duran, that your trip to Eagle's Nest will help us with our efforts. Time is of the essence."

Kurt sat in his chair unflinching. Davis and the lieutenant entered the lounge, a bit short of breath. They reported to Richards in front of the others. "We've found the pilot," Davis said.

Ian's expression was blank. "So where is he?"

"The pilot is dead, sir. His neck was broken upon impact."

There was a moment of silence. Richards directed the lieutenant to notify the RAF and have an ambulance sent out to retrieve the body. Kurt got up and looked at the observer. "I will do all I can at Eagle's Nest." The lieutenant mentioned it was lunchtime and for everyone to head to the kitchen.

Ian thanked him and said they will be right over. "Eight days, gentlemen, we have all of eight days, then we will know what the future and the Nazi high command have in store for us."

Over lunch there were numerous heated exchanges amongst the men. Opinions were aired as to the Nazis next moves. Jacqueline opted to remain quiet and after a quick meal excused herself back to her room. She'd had her fill of politics and debates for one day. She went through her belongings and removed some old letters from her purse. Placing them on the edge of the bed she laid down, not feeling well. She decided to have a quick nap.

It had started to rain again as the men finished up their lunch and headed for the den. Richards turned on the BBC. Reports were coming in over the airwaves of fatalities after the last German bombing raid. There was also a speech by Churchill.

As the others listened intently Kurt approached the observers, who stood by the archway leading to the corridor. He was curious about something and wanted to hear it from the top. "Excuse me, but if the Germans decide to land sooner than expected, what then?"

Both men said nothing. Their faces as stony as marble busts. There was his answer. He told Ian he had to study up on Kruger and left the room.

As he entered his room he fell down on his bed. Report in hand, he heard Jacqueline by the door. She opened it and stepped inside. In her hand were those letters. He looked puzzled. "What are you up to?"

She sat down next to him and took out the first letter from its crumpled envelope. "Here, some more information on Kruger. He wrote me a dozen times when he was away on trips. There might be something in there of importance."

As he poured over them he noticed some intimate dialogue. He looked up at her. "How close were you?"

She placed her hand on his leg gently, tenderly. "It was an assignment, it is all behind me now." She could not have said it more thoughtfully or delicately, and he left it at that.

Now there was only the matter of Holmby doing him up for the observers. Richards insisted that morning they see first-hand his transformation. Holmby was in his room, the door was closed and he had a briefcase open on top of his desk. From it, he removed plastics, hair colorings, molds, and arranged them all neatly in front of him. He closed up his briefcase and said to himself, "Herr Kruger, whenever you're ready." Holmby was an irritating man whom Kurt found just as displeasing as Jacqueline had, but he was a consummate professional, quite thorough in all details, and it was his skill in that regard that made Holmby at least tolerable in Kurt's mind.

That evening Kurt was placed on center stage. Holmby had made him over to perfection and he was put in a room with the observers and Richards only.

They spoke at great length. Ian occasionally glanced down at his clipboard for more questions to put to Kurt. The questions covered all the possible angles of Kruger's life. Without ever having to think, Kurt meticulously answered each question.

Ian stopped a moment and said, "Herr Kruger, how long have you been in the army?"

"Five and a half years," he said. Kurt's performance impressed the observers, shrewd men who had kept fine notes throughout. Nothing could be left to chance.

Richards went on. "In February of '39 you did work for the Führer."

Kurt sat straining in his chair. He raised his hand to scratch his chin, his eyes half closed. "I was on assignment in Spain, aided Franco. Revolutionary guards had attempted to assassinate the general and I was called in to oversee security and strengthen it by coordinating a German parachute regiment to act as a backup against any further insurgence."

"And what happened to you in January of 1940?"

Kurt changed positions in his chair, leaning to one side and clearing his throat. "I was flown on a night mission to Tunisia. Allied ships were docked at Cape Bon. My orders were to assassinate several admirals of the Royal Navy." Richards looked on unflinchingly. Kurt continued. "I made my way through rocky, Tunisian terrain with the help of an Arab scout who was familiar with the region."

"And were you successful?"

"I tossed one hand grenade in the hotel lobby where they were assembled, killing all of the admirals and a handful of guards."

The observers looked at each other approvingly. Richards stared at his list some more, smiling. "Herr Kruger, I thank you for a very enjoyable evening. Have a nice trip back to Vienna." Kurt smiled and corrected him. "Berlin."

Ian nodded, quite pleased. "Of course, how foolish of me." As the men exited the room Ian turned off the overhead lights and pulled Kurt over. "You've scored some points today with those two, just so you know. Why don't you take the rest of tonight off. Head into town or something."

Kurt liked the idea. "Could I take Jacqueline with me? She isn't feeling well, all cooped up like this."

"I don't see why not, just remember you have to be up tomorrow by seven a.m."

Ian departed, and Kurt looked for Jacqueline with the others, but she was nowhere to be found. He checked her room. She answered his knock and invited him in. "How about you and I go out on the town tonight?" he said.

She grinned. "That would be marvelous. Is such a thing possible?"

"Well, don't just stand there, go get changed while I fetch us some transportation." He paused. "Oh, one more thing, where is the bathroom?"

She led him to it in the next room and said, "You can wash up here." He removed his colored contact lenses, rinsed out the dye from his hair and splashed the makeup off his face.

Ian led his guests to the den where they lounged by the bookcase. One of the observers took out a copy of *War and Peace* by Leo Tolstoy. "He knew how to write, that one," the man said. "Not just about war but about people. I've read every book he has ever written and this one twice. My favorite part was when the French entered Moscow, only to find it deserted and on fire. The Russians would not surrender." He put the book back, walked over to an empty leather chair, and sat down. "Churchill's that same way, you know—never surrender. The man certainly knows how to inspire passion."

Ian shrugged. "Then again he has all those years of practice."

Finally Kurt came out of the bathroom, putting on his jacket. Jacqueline was a step behind him as they hurried past Lloyds and Davis, who were in the kitchen. "You're off?" Davis grinned.

"Oh, you know it." As Kurt said that he opened the front door and let her out. He helped her to the jeep, jumped inside and they drove off.

The evening was inviting. For a change the moon was completely visible, there was no rain, and the stars were out in force. They could even see the Milky Way.

"I was getting claustrophobic back there," Jacqueline said. "Too many people in one place." She brushed her long hair back over her shoulders. "By the way, where are you taking me?"

"The Cavalier. I understand it is the best supper club in town and as far as I know the only one in town. We should be there soon."

They arrived in the quaint little town and passed an ice cream parlor with ten flavors advertised on the sign outside, a movie theater that played Hollywood's less impressive films, and a dance hall for sailors and lonely townsfolk. The rest of the town was an average-looking juxtaposition of shops, flophouses and residences, with a red-light district on the east side of town.

The lamplight glowed brightly as they drove up to the Cavalier. Some hoots and hollers shot across the street from a not too shy group of young men. He held the door for her. "I hope you like French cuisine, English style."

The interior was surprisingly ornate given its location. Jacqueline delighted in the setting and whispered to him, "Can we get a table in the corner please? Force of habit with me. I like to see everyone who walks in." The host came up, he led them to a nice spot. The lights were dim and the candles burned on the table between them. What was happening between them was just as exciting as the prospect of the mission itself. She wasn't ready to call it love, but deep down she felt that word. He was handsome, courageous, and he could be dead within the week. She had faith in him and wanted therefore to do her utmost to help him in whatever way she could to make sure he returned. She had been hurt too many times in this war to have her feelings be crushed again.

She felt his hand on her knee. He stroked it tenderly. She couldn't help but smile. "Everything will be just fine," he said.

The entertainment was a middle-aged man in a three-piece suit playing a piano on stage with multicolored lights shining overhead. He sang a melody familiar only to the locals in these parts about the beauty of Chester and her sea, and what he lacked in voice he made up in his mastery of the piano keyboard.

The waiter brought in a bottle of red wine and told them the main course would be ready within ten minutes. Kurt poured her a glass and one for himself. "And to what do we drink to?" she asked.

He smiled. "Well, to a successful mission and a long furlough." His eyes grew fiery with delight.

She whispered across the table, "Do you think there is a chance I could go with you to Normandy?"

His back straightened. "What? You want to go where?" He tried to settle down, to think rationally. "You know what all this entails. It is not the sort of thing you should get into. Anyway, you couldn't go to..." He lowered his voice, "That place."

"I won't need to be there," she said, "but I could be with the people who will be waiting for you when you're done. The French Resistance knows me better than anyone. On your way back you'll need all the help you can get." Her face was strained with nervous tension. "Don't you see, when you head back they'll be on to you. If anything were to go wrong, you'd be dead. With me there I could muster all of my contacts and guarantee you a safe trip home."

His mouth was slightly ajar. It hit him. She was totally serious. She threw more fire on the flame. "Besides, I don't trust those bastards back at the training camp. What about those two fat old men, those so-called observers? They don't even bother to tell us their names. Sounds like you are deemed disposable if something were to go wrong. All they want is a little data, you pass it down to the French Underground and right away you are history. They relay it to London."

He told her to keep it down. She softened her voice but continued in the same aggressive manner. "Don't you see you'll be expendable? Don't be blinded by their brainwashing."

He was genuinely surprised. In all his years he had never met a woman so concerned for his well-being. "All right, Jacqueline, look. Let me talk to Ian tomorrow about this and see what he says."

Her eyes locked with his. "You promise?"

"Yes."

The waiter brought in the dinners on a serving tray and they began to dine.

Chapter Nine

The deer was in full sight. He pressed his finger against the trigger for what was to be a clean shot when suddenly a flock of birds took off from their perch along the trees in the thick forest of Rominterheide, East Prussia, scaring off what was to be Reichsmarschall Hermann Göring's latest hunting trophy. His face puckered in an unrelenting scowl. Frustrated, he let out a deep sigh. Dressed in traditional German hunting attire, he lowered his rifle down and told his hunting companion, "I believe I'll call it a day."

One of his friends, Hamptmann Hahn quipped, "I think the birds are with the English, Herr Reichsmarschall."

That was enough to make Göring break out in laughter. "Ah, yes, could be." He was at his prized hunting lodge and Sea Lion was much on his mind. It was an ever increasing anxiety amongst the high command, and Göring was no exception. His Luftwaffe was to lead the way over the Channel and on to victory. He needed an escape. The last few months of the war had finally caught up with him. The hunt was a way of replenishing himself, a retreat into his beloved Germanic countryside.

When he returned back to his lodge he wanted nothing more than to relax. He raised his boots onto his desk, folded his arms and closed his eyes. He instructed his valet, Robert Kopp, who always accompanied him to the lodge, to slip on a favorite gramophone record on the turntable, "The March of the Heroes," which was from Götterdämmerung. Listening to it always helped to restore Göring's humor and calm his nerves. As it started up he opened his eyes and hummed along to the music. He lit himself a Virginia cigarette and continued to listen to the soothing sounds when the phone rang.

It was the Führer himself, beset by the latest developments. He wanted to see Göring that very evening. Without thinking, the Reichsmarschall sprang up as if in attention and acknowledged the Führer's orders. Flying time was an hour and fifteen minutes. Göring was driven hastily to the Chancellery. Inside, Hitler was brow beaten. His eyes were glued to a map of England and the Channel. He traced with his finger a line between France and London. He saw Göring walking in, greeted him informally and asked the Reichsmarschall to join them.

With the Führer was Major Hennig Strümpell, a seasoned pilot and already an established ace over England, as well as a thirty-year-old man by the name of Walter Rubensdörffer, a tall man of Swiss descent who held a unique command in the Luftwaffe. He was leader of Test Group 210. Hitler had summoned him from the Luftwaffe's experimental station at Rechlin on the Baltic. He had spent long weeks of trial and error there proving that fighters not only could carry bombs but also were capable of hitting their targets, a notion that a number of

Luftwaffe chiefs had mocked. Rubensdörffer, who himself was a former Stuka ace, was the originator of this idea and had the pleasure of seeing it play off.

As Göring positioned himself behind the others overlooking the map on the table, Hitler beamed with delight. His speech was highly excited and passionate. "Just this morning Test Group 210, on my instructions, swooped on a British convoy, letting loose salvoes of 250-kilo bombs. They successfully scored mortal hits on half a dozen large ships." Göring was visibly impressed.

Hitler grinned. "Then those foolish Englishmen and their Spitfires commenced to engage. Our men resumed their role as pure fighters. The result was that twelve British fighters were annihilated over the English coast."

Göring was ecstatic. Hitler went on. "When our glorious air force launches its all-out attack on the British Isles I want to have the confidence knowing that nothing can stand in our way. Therefore, I have issued the order for Test Group 210 to fly on the most crucial mission—to eliminate four key radar stations on the Sussex and Kent coast."

Göring knew what that meant. If Rubensdörffer succeeded then the way would lay open for Oberst Johannes Fink's massed airfield attacks. There was a wicked sparkle in their eyes as Hitler and Göring conferred on the final details of the plan. The targets themselves were a vital defense hidden in the Kentish apple orchards and flat salt marshes. They were brick radar stations guarded by barbed wire and a complete mystery to all except those who were living and working in them. Steel aerials rising over three hundred feet added to the sinister appearance. "Gentlemen," Hitler said, "attack time is tomorrow at 07:00."

The morning brought a particular exhilaration for the German pilots who flew over the icy waters of the English Channel. The formidable force glided effortlessly across the sky.

On the ground below the first station to spot trouble was at Rye, which was near the old Kentish seaport. Sergeant Morris Dreyfuss was on the morning watch and had just come over to a screen after fetching his morning coffee when suddenly he was alerted to a V-shaped blip of light that registered off Northern France. Then it went from detector station to fighter command's filter room. Then to Air Vice Marshall Keith Park's headquarters. Eleven fighter groups were protecting all of Southern England.

When asked about the height of the incoming Dreyfuss confirmed about twenty thousand feet but as he studied the V-shaped blip of light on the convex glass screen in the station's receiver block he added, quite anxiously, that range was fast decreasing. The plotter at the other end of the line asked if he could make identification but Dreyfuss could not.

The filter room, apparently unruffled, had marked the course with an "X" which in their terminology signified "doubtful." One of Dreyfuss' group came running in with a tin hat on yelling, "Dive-bombers! Two dive-bombers, coming down, clear out!" The filter room only heard the explosion. It was all over for the station at Rye. With split-second precision, Test Group 210, now divided into squadrons of four, attacked in early dawn all along the coastline.

Oberlieutenant Lutz and his men raced for Pevensey by Eastbourne. Oberlieutenant Hintze flew straight for the Dover radar station while Rubensdörffer was attacking the mess at Dunkirk, near Canterbury. The stations wooden shutters were falling to the wayside, tables and chairs splintered against the walls and chunks of earth heaved hundreds of feet up to splatter the steel aerials. As Rubensdörffer flew back up, distancing himself from the destruction, he could see all along the coast stations breaking up and black smoke rising high into the clouds.

Rubensdörffer notified his team by radio and said, "Return to base, mission complete." But it didn't end there. Inland there was chaos as well. In the fighter commands filter room, Officer Wingate overheard the frantic commentary of a detector station on the Isle of Wight which was being ravaged by a dozen Junkers 88 dive-bombers. The station was engulfed in flames. With the silencing of the radar stations, the coastal airfields lay open. The Luftwaffe took the opportunity in haste. By then, Rubensdörffer's Test Group 210 had regrouped over Kent's east coast.

Rubensdörffer got on the radio and ordered thirty bomb-laden ME-109's and 110's to dive at four hundred miles an hour on Manston, a five-hundred acre base code named "Charlie 3." When it was over Manston was leveled, pockmarked with over one hundred craters. Rubensdörffer called out to Oberlieutenant Hintze and instructed him to hit Squadron Number 65. As they flew he said, "I want it done right the first time."

The squadron was caught before it had a chance to take off. From a height of four thousand feet Oberlieutenant Hintze spotted the Spitfires as they lined up in V-shaped formations of three, engines running. Rubensdörffer came down hard, bombs released. A hangar shot upward in a dark gray cloud. The planes disappeared from sight. After reappearing from under the heavy blanket of smoke, the planes continued to taxi down the runway, at which point Rubensdörffer and Hintze dropped down and sprayed them with enough machine gun fire to blow them to pieces.

As the morning progressed, the blinding speed and efficiency of Test Group 210 echoed throughout England. A fierce cloud of Junkers 88 dive-bombers headed for Hawkinge Airfield. From the ground, hundreds of bewildered Englishmen saw the sinister black fleet approaching, then felt the whole earth shaking as planes dove and pounded the airfield with dozens of bombs. The hangars were broke in two. The sky overhead was a blinding red wall of flames leaping indiscriminately, several workers below catching on fire while others were felled by shrapnel.

Rubensdörffer let out a hearty laugh as he looked down and surveyed the damage. Their work was done for now. He ordered his pilots home. As the armada drifted back across the sky he thanked them all for a job well done. Upon receiving confirmation Göring was delighted with the outcome and complimented the commander of the squadron on behalf of the Führer.

Ian Richards had been in his office all afternoon waiting impatiently for word on the results of the Nazi attacks. Station 5 was more than surprised at these revelations. In fact, Richards was in deep discussion behind closed doors on his private line with Air Vice Marshal Keith Parks.

In the meantime Kurt was out taking a walk with the observers. He was going over the data he had learned to date and they wanted to hear all of it. There was a sense of urgency now and Kurt felt it. Outside in front of the jeep he came to a stop and as they spoke Hardwick called out to Kurt from Ian's open office window.

Kurt excused himself. Upon entering Ian's office Kurt saw sadness and shock on Ian's face, his eyes deep within himself. "That was a good friend of mine," Ian said. "The situation is bad. The Germans did quite a number on us today, weakening our defenses. Airfield bombings. I could go on and on. I want you ready and able this Friday." Ian looked at his calendar. "We need to stay on schedule or we'll never get this chance again. Kiel tells me you've mastered the obstacles of Eagle's Nest and then some. Jacqueline reports you can tell me Kruger's life story backwards. All I have to do now is get you out and back in one piece. Be ready tomorrow night at 06:00."

"Yes, sir," Kurt said coolly, did an about face, and exited the room.

At that precise moment Jacqueline headed for the front door to get some fresh air. He caught up with her and began to fill her in on the events of the day. He stopped, his hands placed in his pockets, looking over the compound. "I need to get away a bit. Will you go with me for a drive?"

"Yes," she said eagerly. They left in the jeep.

He spotted a dirt road leading off the main drive and turned abruptly.

"Where are we going?" she asked.

"As far away from Richards and his kind as possible. There's a nice park-like area by the cliffs just ahead. I'll take you to it."

The coast was particularly spectacular in this part of the country and beyond the curve of the mountain lay waiting an area as breathtaking as it was secluded, with rocks and shrubbery on three sides. The grassy area was sprinkled with flowers and trees, some of them had been bent with the winds.

He picked a spot and pulled up. He looked out anxiously over the sea, trying to make himself comfortable. "I was told I leave end of this week." She looked surprised; she had lost track of time. "When I was a little boy I'd go to the coast just like this to reflect, or maybe even daydream." He cleared his throat.

Jacqueline smiled, "Didn't you have a happy childhood?" Her question sent a stabbing sensation into his flesh and he looked away miserably. "You don't have to tell me," she said.

"No, no, I want to. It's just that my family put me into a boarding school, which is common enough, but I got the worse teachers, the worse classmates, and the worse location. So whenever I had a chance to escape I headed to the beauty of the sea with its rolling waves and ever-changing persona. I felt there was a greater power there than my schoolmaster. If I wanted to run naked on the beach no one could chase after me telling me it wasn't proper. I had a sense of freedom and it helped to keep things in perspective."

Jacqueline was silent as he turned to her and they started kissing. In her mind came a sequence of thoughts. Her heart lay open for him but she dare not press it until after the mission. She felt it best. If things went as planned and they both returned, then Paradise would be a place on earth, something both of them could enjoy. The drama of life was never as poignant in peace as in wartime. All thoughts and feelings inadvertently were drawn to it, no matter how strong the desire to shy away from it might be.

Kurt surprised her. "When this is all over I'll take you to Stratford..." He paused and her eyes widened. He continued. "I have a place left to me there by my late uncle. Up until now I never had much use for it, was just too busy one way or the other. That's of course if you don't mind sharing it with me."

She was beside herself with joy. "Whatever will make you happy." A tear ran down her cheek. She had waited for such a proposal each time they were together. He wanted to say more on the matter but didn't, not until it was all over with Eagle's Nest.

Kurt got out of the vehicle and walked around to Jacqueline's side to help her out. Hand in hand they walked in companionable silence on the grass. The sun warmed them. The wind blew her silky hair in the breeze that picked up sporadically. They stopped some yards from the cliffs; the waves were beating against the rocks, the gulls were flying overhead, and the smell of summer was still in the air. This was the perfect picture to keep in their minds in the days ahead.

Back at Station 5 Richards was in the rotunda with Kiel Holmby and Lloyds. All three men were finishing the stages before take off, and all three knew what was at stake. The observers had been flown back to London that morning. Captain Davis and his aide were at Whitechapel. The place had been whittled down to the final few.

Hardwick was busy with a call from London when Kurt and Jacqueline came in and saw the office door open. "Where is everybody?" Kurt said.

Hardwick covered the receiver with his hand and said, "Go to the lounge room, I'll be there momentarily."

Five minutes had passed as they patiently waited, when finally he stepped in and was quite direct. "Kurt, I wish to let you know that you will be flown by Lloyds tomorrow evening to Normandy. The weather outlook is mediocre but he should have no problems in getting you there. We will have a meeting tomorrow at 07:00 hours at the map room." He said no more, just headed back to the office. Jacqueline looked withdrawn. The atmosphere was so final, so foreboding to her. "What did Ian tell you? Can I go?"

He lowered his head and in a small voice said, "No, Jacqueline, you can't."

She was heart broken. "But I—"

"It's for the best, don't you see? If something happened to me and you were there, things would just get complicated. I'll be all right, and when we get to Stratford, I'll spend every possible moment with you that I can."

She was understanding but disappointed nonetheless. There was nothing further to discuss on that issue. They were both silent and suddenly she said in an upbeat tone, "Remember that when you're at Eagle's Nest and are about to go to the safe, make sure you lock the door. Those generals have a bad habit of chasing the ladies, and tend to hide in the most out of the way places for their love trysts." She stood there innocently, her eyes transfixed on him as if in a dream, and he kissed her.

"Thank you," he said, whispering into her ear as he pulled away.

She got nervous. He noticed. "What's the matter?"

"Oh, nothing." She turned her face to the side.

"Tell me."

She sighed, walked over to a chair and sat down. Her eyes half closed, she raised her hand to her face. "Kruger liked to cheat on me whenever the big German brass was partying. He left me to go on his adventures. I should have told you sooner, I suppose, but I was afraid.

I mean..."

He smiled and said, "I understand."

She continued. "Kruger couldn't' help himself, like a little boy in a candy store he needed to sample all of the delicacies before they ran out, and if you are not as aggressive with them, they might suspect."

He ran his hand through his hair and folded his arms over his chest. "Is there anything else I should know?"

She crossed her legs and looked to the side. "No."

"All right then, I think I'm all set. Now all I need to do is..."

Hardwick marched in that moment. "It's Ian, he's on the line."

Kurt followed him into the office and picked up the receiver. As he listened Richards let him know to expect them within the hour. He was at RAF headquarters miles away. He sounded a bit too anxious, Kurt thought. He hung up the phone and headed back to Jacqueline. She was outside now on the terrace, the glass doors wide open.

He joined her there and leaned against the parapet. "You did a good job preparing me, you know."

She smiled. "Thank you."

"You know, strange how things work out, I mean meeting you like this under these circumstances. If it weren't for the mission..." He stopped mid-sentence, and she turned around and kissed him. There was a long, passionate embrace. He pulled away gently and finished. "I never would have met you."

When Richards arrived with the others they all hurried to the map room, a cramped place with desks and chairs, a chalkboard on the side wall, a projector and a pull-down screen in the middle. Kurt was sitting patiently at the side of the table, Lloyds was at the corner of the room, as was Hardwick. Jacqueline was present but sat down in the back. Ian was finishing up sorting through some papers on the desk before him. As everyone settled in he began.

"Congratulations, Mr. Duran, you have passed the training and are now set to embark on the most important assignment our department has ever had the opportunity to prepare—to steal the plans for Operation Sea Lion." He took a piece of chalk and scribbled some numbers on the board. He looked at his audience. "At exactly 06:00 tomorrow night you will be flown by Lloyds to Normandy, where you will land and meet up with the French Resistance. From the moment you set foot on French soil you will be Kruger. You will think and talk only in German and you will take his position at Göring's party."

There was a heavy silence. Expectations were great and so was the challenge. Everything rested on clock-like precision. Kurt asked what the figures on the board represented. "Troop strength," Ian said. "German troop strength to be exact. It will be a sea of Nazis over there and you will have to swim very carefully at all times." After a lengthy recap of his objectives Ian wrapped things up in a hurry. "We're in for a full day tomorrow," he said, "I wish you all the best."

The next evening was somber. Jacqueline had said her good-byes and stood outside by the landing strip with Ian as Kurt boarded the plane. He smiled to her affectionately and waved. Lloyds started up the engine. The propellers cut into the evening breeze, spinning faster and faster. "He is a brave one," Ian said to her. He called out, "Wait a moment!" Kurt turned around, half way up the stepladder. Richards produced a thermal flask and poured him a drink. "Here's something to get you by on a cold night like tonight." Kurt polished it off and it hit him going down. "It was whiskey," Ian smiled. "Your favorite kind." He sealed up the thermal flask and handed it to Kurt. "Save the rest for later."

"Will do." Kurt climbed aboard, the door was closed shut and the plane started to taxi down the strip.

As Kurt put on his life jacket, he looked back behind and saw Jacqueline disappear in a blur. The plane started to take off and Kurt yawned. He was tired and he fell asleep in his window seat. All was quiet.

When he awoke the plane was still. Lloyds walked in and shook Kurt by his shoulders. "Get up man, we're here."

Anxious, he opened his eyes, cleared his head, and picked up his gear. He was armed with a Luger on his side and stretched to fix his hat. As he stood up he removed the life jacket and walked toward the door dressed in full Nazi regalia. Lloyds warned him, "Remember, keep low and out of sight as you move across the field."

Kurt waited a moment as he saw the signal lights in the distance. The night air was cold. It pierced his lungs. He jumped down on the ground and cleared the plane as it took off. Kurt looked up just momentarily as it departed back to England. The sky was dark with the moon disappearing periodically behind windswept clouds. The stars shone sporadically as far as the eye could see, and the sound of crashing waves in the distance along the shore had a haunting effect.

He set out for the lights, then something happened. They went off inexplicably and a second or two later sounds could be heard in the distance like branches breaking. He heard a stern, German voice shouting, "Halt! Halt!" All at once automatic gunfire ripped through the night and he could do nothing but dive. He fell face down in the dirt and was motionless. His heart racing. Were the Germans there all along, waiting? Or did they just cut in front of the French Resistance?

He waited a moment before moving. No more shots were fired. The Resistance must have been captured. He was all alone now in hostile enemy territory. He undid the catch on his holster and took out his gun. He readied it to fire as he laid there panning the woods before him. Not a sign of life, yet there were Germans there waiting to pick him off. He heard engine sounds, headlights started to make their way toward him.

Jumping up, he ran for a rock formation past the clearing. More shots rang out. He positioned himself and fired off several rounds. He looked around for an escape route. Up ahead to his left was what seemed to be a roadway. He sprang for it. Up the incline he spotted an old abandoned farmhouse to his immediate right. He bolted inside through the open doorway, breathing heavily. He looked back and all he could see were those headlights following. He noticed a ladder leading up to the hayloft. He climbed it in haste and waited. The army truck braked to a halt outside. He heard orders being given in German, followed by the sound of boots beating against the hard, dry land, fanning out in all directions. It sounded like a least a dozen men out there. As he pushed himself into a corner of the loft, Luger pointed at the doorway, the Germans were coming in. "Mach schnell!" said the SS sergeant major, and SS troops in black stormed in.

Kurt let out five shots point blank, hitting the first two that entered. The rest retreated behind the stone wall of the farmhouse. For a moment there was silence, and Kurt looked for a way out. Behind him there was an open window with rope from a dangled and rusted hay hook that was used to hoist and stack loads up to the main loft. He tested the line and it was still tight. He looked over the edge and fired one more round. After an intense volley back from the Germans he exited, lowered himself on the rope, which came up short. He jumped the last ten feet.

As he got up he felt the cold barrel of a Schmeisser machine pistol pressed against the back of his neck. The SS sergeant major grinned. "Guten abend. Hand me your gun." Kurt did so but slowly as the metal of the German's gun ate at his flesh. "Now come with me." He led him back past the dead Germans into the farmhouse, which was at least a hundred years old. Kurt saw ten grim-looking SS men in front of him, half on one side, half on the other. In the middle was a crate. He was pushed down onto it as one of the German's came up and tied his hands together from behind. He struggled as the cords stung his flesh. The SS sergeant major said, "Do not resist, you'll only make it worse." He shined the bright light into Kurt's face. As he strained to look up, Kurt only saw the dark silhouette of a German in uniform. "So tell me, what were you doing out there, Herr—"

"Kruger. My name is Heinrich Kruger, I'm a major in the Waffen SS." He twisted in his unzipped, heavy leather jacket until it finally parted open, revealing his insignias.

"So why is a major in the Waffen SS parading in the dark on the Normandy coast? Did you lose your girlfriend?" The SS sergeant major stepped closer.

"No, I was just—"

"You were out for a walk? Yes, and the plane that flew away had nothing to do with you being here?"

Kurt got angry. "Listen, damn it, I'm Major Kruger of the Waffen SS. Call headquarters, ask for Colonel Heinz Gerhardt, he will verify who I am. I was out because my car broke down. I was hoping to get to a house and call for help." His eyes grew fiery with rage. He looked at his surroundings more carefully but could only seeing hulking figures with no faces, mere shadows on the walls.

"Just one moment," said the SS sergeant. He stepped outside. A minute had passed and the sergeant came back. "Untie him." As the SS guard loosened the ropes Kurt struggled free. His wrists felt as if they were on fire from the tightness of the binds. "I radioed in and the Colonel said you were recently released from a hospital, is that correct?"

Kurt placed his arm forward on his person and then answered thoughtfully, "Yes."

"I see. And what hospital was it, bitte?"

"St. Michael's. I was released just last night. I came to Normandy to see a friend and on my way back my vehicle had difficulties." Blinded by the intensity of the light, Kurt said wearily, "Must you continue to shine that thing in my face?"

He didn't answer. "And where do you live?"

"What?"

"Answer the question."

"In Bavaria. Schwabing to be exact. Around Münchener Freiheit."

"You like the nightlife do you?" the sergeant said sarcastically.

Kurt got defensive and remembered he had to react as if he were Kruger. "I am a bachelor."

"And what was your supervisor's name?"

"I've told you twice already."

There was the sound of laughter. Kurt felt uneasy. The SS sergeant was laughing, so were the SS troops all around him. He thought, this is it, it's over, they're going to shoot me where I sit. The lights came on all around and Ian Richards stood before him in full SS sergeant major uniform. He lowered the interrogation light to his side, with the two observers directly behind him and Hardwick on his right. The rest were all SOE special agents. Ian lit up a cigarette and grinned.

Kurt stood up, stunned. "What the devil is going on around here, Ian. How?"

Ian smiled as he puffed on his cigarette. "You did quite well, my boy, quite well indeed."

The observers stepped forward, listening intently. Kurt looked at the others as some took off their helmets and lowered their firearms. "Blast it! This was a rehearsal, is that it?"

"Right-o," Ian said, "for you."

"What about the men I shot." They stepped in at that point smiling.

"Blanks of course," Ian said.

Kurt was still unclear. "But where are we really?"

"North England, of course. I slipped you a mickey so you'd be asleep for the trip. Lloyds flew you up the coast, we came in and waited until you started to come around. I suspect I gave you too much."

Chapter Ten

It was just after ten the following morning when Kurt entered Jacqueline's room. She sat on the edge of the bed, quiet and aloof. He looked at her, noticing her bags were packed. "And where are you off to?" he asked.

"With all this phony mission business out of the way, and you leaving tonight for real, I saw no point in staying."

Kurt crossed his arms and leaned against the doorway. "Is that so?"

She looked up from her packing. "Don't misunderstand. It's my sister, she's arrived in London. I haven't seen her since the start of the war. We are very close, she needs me."

Kurt walked up to her. "I see. And how long will you be gone?"

She straightened up, looking out through the window. "I really can't say for sure, several days, a week maybe."

Kurt stepped up next to her, his arm against the window pane and gazed out with her. After a moment of silence he asked, "How do I contact you?"

She took out a piece of paper and wrote something down on it and handed it to him. "I'll be at Katie's on Nelson Street. Call me when you get back, won't you?"

"Of course."

There were tears in her eyes but she tried not to show it as she hastily got her bags and went over, kissing him good-bye. After their embrace, she softened in his arms for a moment and seemed to relax.

"I love you, Jacqueline."

She looked up at him and reached toward his lips. All at once she pulled away and, without saying a word, left the room. He wanted to follow but felt it best not to.

Outside Lloyds was waiting with the plane at the ready. Kurt went to the lounge and poured himself a drink from the bar. He felt a strange feeling inside, one he didn't want to deal with. Holmby walked in, sweating profusely. Along with him came Hardwick and Granger. They had dismantled the fake Eagle's Nest training tower. Holmby stood there a moment; finally he spoke. "I could use one of those."

Kurt poured him a glass and left it on the bar. He walked over to the couch and sat down looking quite world-weary. After taking a swallow of his drink, he said, "So this is it. Tonight's the night."

Holmby eased up on the barstool. "Any rough spots?"

Kurt didn't bother to answer. "Did you hear the weather report?"

Holmby shrugged. "I was under the impression that it might rain."

Ian came in. "Well, well, tonight we are off and running. I've been on the phone to London just to confirm everything is set to go and on schedule. The

Underground will be there waiting for you in Normandy. From there they'll take you to Brussels were you will catch the Berlin Express."

Kurt finished up his drink and placed it on the couch, jerking his neck around a bit to relieve the tension. "And what about my makeover?"

"Kiel will start up on you this afternoon," Ian said. "After he is through you'll board the plane and hightail it to Europe. I suggest in the meantime you check your gear."

Kurt shook his head. "Did that this morning. I suppose I just don't like the idea of waiting like this."

Ian walked over, sat down across from him and smiled sincerely. "Well, then why don't you and I stretch our legs outside a bit."

Once outside Kurt seemed to relax. Ian was in good spirits and said, "Sorry about last night, old boy. It wasn't my call, the higher-ups asked me to arrange it to test you. They needed to be sure."

Kurt laughed it off. "Mine is not to reason why..."

They headed to the open field and heard a plane fast approaching overhead. It flew by dangerously low and as it passed it made quite a sound. Because they were in direct sunlight Ian wasn't sure if it was theirs or the enemies. Kurt looked on as it started to climb and the insignia of the Spitfire became apparent. "Ours," he said with confidence.

They continued their walk. Ian was a man of great complexity, at times exceedingly generous but capable of severe discipline. A man with a single-minded purpose, with a sense of humor, he was like a father to Kurt. Neither would have admitted it, but they felt it just the same.

"Just so you know," Ian said, "as far as I'm concerned we have the best man going off tonight."

Kurt smiled. "If I didn't know any better Ian, I'd say you were getting sentimental."

Ian tightened up. "Damn you, man, be serious. This isn't a game. If the Germans get the slightest suspicions about you, you're a dead man. You know that."

Kurt said nothing, his expression was answer enough. Ian added, "Doing your best here isn't enough. You have to out do yourself. Don't think of the war, or Churchill, or me for that matter, only what's in the safe at Eagle's Nest."

The wind blew a refreshing gust of air from the sea. "I understand, Ian."

At that moment Göring was in his dress uniform. He had been presiding at a ceremony honoring German heroes during the fall of France. Medals were pinned, hands shaken, sentiments exchanged gratuitously. Just a day away would be a spectacular adventure waiting for Göring and he had arranged for some of the finest looking women in Bavaria to be waiting for him and his crowd. He even stayed away from his morphine to have his senses heightened naturally. His papers were in his briefcase and he was to make two more stops that afternoon before setting off for the party.

The following day he was chauffeured in a black limousine. He gazed passionately as he passed a crowd of adoring German youth. This was the pride and joy of the Aryan nation and far be it for him to deny them this pleasure. He made sure the chauffeur progressed slowly through the crowds.

Keitel and Ribbentrop were both tied up with commitments of their own. That afternoon the propaganda minister, Joseph Goebbels, engaged in a heated debate with Ribbentrop about matters of foreign diplomacy at Goebbels' office in Berlin, and Keitel was tying up loose ends at the meeting of generals deliberating the fate of French and English spies. There was a question about whether to use rope or the firing squad. Keitel always preferred the latter. That afternoon Göring made his appointed stop and picked up both men respectively at their locations. Then it would be one more stop in Bavaria the next evening.

As they were driven the field marshal sat robustly on one side facing his companions when Keitel stated, somewhat casually, "Today thirty spies were executed, twenty French and ten Britons."

Göring smiled gleefully. "Did it take long?"

Keitel laughed. "All of two minutes."

Göring was taking them to his office where he had to stop and make an official phone call. As the limousine drove along the stone paved streets Ribbentrop said, "Perhaps next time we have a party we will do well to invite the duke of Windsor along."

Göring's eyes lit up. "The duke, you say."

"The man is a total puppet," said Ribbentrop. "I've met him enough times to know, and in my discussions with him he has always been decidedly pro-Nazi."

"Well tell me something I don't know," Göring said.

There was a silence. Then Ribbentrop added, "The Führer had mentioned to me in the most positive manner that when England is invaded and the present monarchy disposed of, the duke and duchess of Windsor will be assuming the throne of England."

Göring frowned. "The only problem with that is that the duke is not an Aryan." He stiffened in his seat. "You decide those details amongst yourselves. My job is to oversee the air force." Ribbentrop was pleased, recalling Göring's views on matter of state being for diplomats and politicians.

The limousine pulled in, and Göring made a quick walk to his office.

Now that the laborious task of applying colored eye contacts had been completed, he braced himself for the transformation. After that came the hair coloring and the minute details around the face. The platform shoes were on, and he was in full uniform. While Holmby put the finishing touches on his hair, Ian finalized the assignment. Ian mentioned a slight change. "Kruger was taken out this afternoon, officially released from the recovery unit of the hospital."

Kurt stiffened. "Where is he now?"

"He's dead," Ian replied. "Killed by the Underground. He was heading to his residence in Bavaria. When you get into town, go there. Göring is due to make a stop and pick Kruger up there tomorrow, late afternoon. He knows not to come any sooner. The women won't be there until 09:00."

As Kurt sat under the hot lamplight he stared at himself in the mirror. The transformation was just as haunting as ever. Ian reiterated his concern for Kurt's safety and emphasized the need for speed. Everything was planned out on paper to the last minute. Kurt felt that reality would prove somewhat different. Kurt blinked and moaned. "Damn it, Kiel, these contacts are starting to hurt..."

Holmby took out a small, plastic bottle from the side of his white apron pocket and pushed Kurt's head back a tad, keeping his eyes wide open. Kurt felt some soothing droplets moisturizing and lubricating his excessively dry eyes. After a moment it felt normal again. Holmby shoved the bottle in Kurt's hand. "Here, keep it with you."

Ian checked his watch. "All right, it's time to get moving." Kurt sprang to his feet. With his briefcase at his side he looked smartly at Ian. He cut a dashing figure.

Lloyds was at the front door in pilot garb and with parachute at the ready. The weather was getting cloudy, but no rain fell. "No tricks this time, old boy," said Ian. "Make it a good trip." He saluted. Kurt returned it, if somewhat awkwardly, turned and headed to the Liberator, a plane perfectly suited for crossing the Channel under the most extreme conditions. Simple in design, yet heavy in performance.

Lloyds started her up as Kurt climbed on aboard. Kurt looked out at Ian, who stared smugly from a distance. Kurt gave him a thumbs-up. In a moment they were airborne. The plane flew toward the English Channel. There was nothing but darkness all around.

Kurt kept his briefcase at his feet. All seemed quiet. Not another plane in the sky and only calm waters below. The pilot was watching the airspace ahead and the Normandy coast had started to become visible due to the surf. The white waves in the dark of the night pounded relentlessly against the rocks and shore. Kurt noticed something to his immediate left. He spotted a flash of light and then another. The French Underground had started to guide them in with electric torches.

The Liberator started a gradual descent. When from nowhere came machine gun fire. It ripped into the cockpit and Kurt saw blood splatter the windshield in front. Lloyds' head hung down, motionless. Kurt called out his name. There was no response. To his right, he saw a German night fighter zeroing in for a second time, and this time he could hear the plane coming. More bullets pounded the side of the aircraft and gasoline began to escape from the fuselage. The plane began to dive.

In haste, Kurt pulled back the glass roof frame and grabbed his briefcase. The Liberator began to burn its oil and flames started to shoot out around the area of the propellers. Kurt held his breath, then jumped. He free-fell, dropping like a stone down toward the North Sea, then pulled the parachute's release cord. The white canopy mushroomed out and his body jerked several times as he leveled off. The Liberator by now was only a few hundred feet above water. Then it smashed into the sea, bobbing up for a moment, only to disappear quickly under the waves.

Kurt cursed to himself. The night fighter mysteriously had vanished. Kurt looked out to see where the lights had been, but they had all stopped signaling. He quickly got his bearings, and the sea grew ever louder as he descended. It roared with a ferocity as it crashed into the shore. He felt the sting of the icy, cold North Sea envelop his body as he went under, the chute falling to the wayside. He unbuckled it under the waves and after what seemed an eternity came up through the murky blue-green water. When he finally broke surface he gulped deep lungfulls of air. Suddenly out of the darkness came a seven-footer. The wave was heading straight for him, and Kurt thought it was his time. It turned out to be a blessing as it carried him over the rocks and onto the shore. No sooner had the wave gone down, exposing his wet body on the beach, that he staggered to his feet. Miraculously, his briefcase had washed up several yards away.

He heard a voice from behind the rocks.

"Maurice?" he said.

In a deep, thick French accent a man gave the code name, "Bay-One."

The moon had found an awkward time to come out of its hiding place behind the clouds and started to shine brightly.

"The beach is not safe, Monsieur," the man said. "Come quickly."

Kurt scrambled to pick up his briefcase and raced behind the rocks. Three men stood silently with Sterling machine guns slung around their shoulders. Finally the man called Maurice extended his hand. His face was coarse, hardened by combat. He was a man of forty five, but appeared quite older, with deep-set eyes and a fine beard that was graying.

"Welcome to France," he said.

Kurt thanked him and observed that the other men were much younger and all dressed in similar clothing. Simple blue-gray, a fitting camouflage. "Where are the rest of you?"

Maurice pointed back into the woods by a truck. "Let us now depart."

The brush was so thick in places that walking a straight line was all but impossible. As they plowed on Kurt looked back and saw the beachhead.

The truck was closer now and Kurt could see figures silhouetted on it, toting guns. Finally they reached the dirt road. Now they were running directly for the vehicle. The men in the truck were stony silent. Maurice gave the orders to move out, and Kurt felt a hand grabbing him on his shoulder while another pulled him up by his arm. He was lifted into the truck and covered with straw. The Frenchmen, heads out, their firearms pulled in tightly, were all covered with straw as well. The driver stepped on the gas and the vehicle churned a few times and started up.

As it picked up speed a voice barely audible said, "Don't move, Monsieur, there are Germans up ahead." The truck was making quick time to a roadblock. SS patrols had been dispatched to check the area for the downed pilot. The driver started to brake and the truck came to a halt.

Kurt could hear German's approaching and what sounded like the cocking of a gun. The SS lieutenant marched coolly up to the driver with his Luger drawn and began to ask him questions. Maurice gave a friendly smile. "Sir, please forgive me but we are in a hurry. My wife, she is expecting. It is my first you see. I have to get home to take her to the doctor, she's in labor. I was out late getting straw for my farm when I was told of her situation."

The lieutenant looked the truck over, all the while pointing the Luger at the driver. "Get out."

The door opened and as he stepped down the lieutenant said coldly, "Did you see any planes here tonight?"

The driver shook his head. "No, sir. No planes, nein, no."

The German walked back along the length of the truck. Kurt listened intently. The German called out to his men and ordered five armed soldiers to search the vehicle.

The soldiers, their rifles at their side, positioned themselves at the rear. The lieutenant took calculated steps closer to the vehicle, his black, polished boots coming ever near until Kurt could see them through the straw below. There was a pause and all at once members of the Underground sprang to life. Jumping up and opening fire on the Germans. Before they knew what hit them, they were all cut down except those left by the blockade. Maurice and the driver took them out quickly with their Sterlings thundering, releasing a barrage of bullets. The Frenchmen on top of the vehicle joined in until there was a heap of Germans dead. The shooting stopped.

Maurice wiped his face. A bullet had nipped the tip of his forehead, slicing his skin like a razor. He placed his fingers on it and pressed firmly. "Pigs," he said. "Those Nazi pigs." He spat on the ground and went back around the truck. "Any hurt?" The men all smiled, it was a clean strike. There were no casualties on their side.

Maurice ordered Kurt to come up front. Putting his firearm away Kurt jumped out and walked up, slightly bewildered. Maurice put his hand on his back and said, "From now on, we stop for nothing."

The trucks smashed through the barricade. There was a certain amount of tension now that the men all felt. Kurt and the Frenchmen knew the Germans would be on them like vultures sooner or later. "I thought the Normandy coast was the least defended of areas," Kurt said.

Maurice smiled. "Monsieur, compared to the rest of France, it is, but the Germans are everywhere. Remember that."

When the SS lieutenant didn't report back in, security was put on alert. The Germans wasted no time in sending out a patrol unit to canvas the area. Dark troop trucks moved down the dirt roads searching the woods until the sergeant in charge saw the dead. "Halt!" he said, his voice gruff and irritated. He marched out and looked them over. None were alive.

"There is a fast road leading all the way to Belgium," Maurice said. "We will stay on it until we get you to Brussels."

Kurt checked his revolver. It was empty. He set about reloading it. "How are we on time?"

"We're right on schedule." His cut had stopped bleeding. He looked into his rear-view mirror, "It won't be long now."

"For what?"

"The Germans, of course. They'll be catching up soon. Unfortunately my truck is not as good as the Nazi's." He pounded the back of the vehicle wall with his fist. This was a signal. The Frenchmen began to spring up from the straw, several of them took out cans of lighter fluid and soaked the bundles of hay, lifting one at a time up to the edge of the truck and lighting it, then dropping it on the road behind them.

Kurt could see the flames shooting up in the side truck mirror.

"What the devil is happening?"

Maurice smiled. "Relax, monsieur, it is all under control."

As the flaming bundles continued to fall over one at a time Kurt spotted a second road up ahead. The Frenchmen tossed a spare tire out and also parts of an old front fender and door. The vehicle changed roads.

Kurt smiled slyly. "So you've got it all planned out, I see."

"But of course, monsieur. But of course."

The new road led into a desolated place of high hills and endless brush, with no sign of the Germans. The wind was kicking up and the mist was starting to roll in from the sea, at times appearing to glow with the kind of phosphorescence between the dark trees. It was a strange and eerie sight.

"How long have you been with the Underground?" Kurt said.

"Too long," Maurice replied bitterly. "And with no end in sight. At first the Germans were only a threat to our soil, now they own it. But not for too much longer, I assure you." His eyes looked out far beyond him into the darkness. His lips pressed firmly together, and what appeared to be small tears welled up in his eyes. He casually blinked them away.

Just up ahead was an old stone bridge. The driver stopped. Maurice waited a moment, then asked him to drive on. Going over it at the reduced speed, the bumps didn't seem as severe. "The Germans like to booby trap these bridges," Maurice said. "I've lost six good men last month alone because of it."

The German troop truck came to a stop by the burning straw. The sergeant surveyed the scene and called out to his men, "Look for bodies." After a few moments the soldiers all came back empty-handed. The sergeant frowned a bit. "This was a trick." He turned toward the truck and stared down the road, pointing to the left. "We go that way."

Kurt held his gun comfortably on his lap. The road ahead seemed more drivable now. "This old road," Maurice said, nodding. "It was a Roman road. Also the stone bridge that we crossed. They knew how to build back then, yes?"

"That they did."

The driver was picking up speed, doing at least sixty miles per hour. The Frenchmen in the rear were quiet, hiding under the remaining batches of straw. Out of nowhere the sound of automatic gunfire shattered the calm. Bullets tore into the truck. The volleys ripped into the driver, jerking his head back, his face bloodied.

Kurt dove downward below the dash. More gunfire came and a round struck Maurice. The truck lost control and came to an abrupt stop in a ditch at the side of the road. Kurt immediately jumped from the vehicle and crawled to the truck's front right tire, his eyes searching the countryside for the attackers. Only rolling mist and darkness greeted him. Just briefly to his left he saw metal catching some moonlight. He fired two shots and a hail of gunfire answered, hitting the vehicle head-on, knocking out one of its lights, glass falling around. Kurt ducked for cover.

The guns had stopped. There was the sound of an engine and after a moment it ceased. The Frenchmen had exited the truck and spread themselves out along the roadside behind trees and rocks. Kurt crept beside the brush closer to where the last rounds of gunfire were coming from. A grenade exploded, killing two of the Frenchmen instantly as they advanced around the ditch. The tortured moans of injured men lingered in the air around them.

Kurt dove on his stomach and pushed along under the continuous gunfire until he got to a fallen tree that blocked his advance. Another grenade was tossed by the Germans and one more Frenchman was killed outright. The bullets kept flying, pounding into the trees and hillside, buzzing over the Frenchmen's heads.

Kurt was up and over and rolled down into the wet, moist grass as he continued his advance. Through the mist he saw two German's in the jeep with a heavy machine gun mounted on the swivel in the rear. He had to get in closer if he wanted to finish them off. Kurt made it to a tree stump to the immediate right of them, ten yards out. He took another look to make sure they were alone. There was the German driver and the gunner positioning himself to toss another grenade. Kurt took aim and fired, hitting him in the chest. He fell over dead, and the grenade disappeared under the vehicle. The second German panicked and tried to dismount but was too slow. The explosion lifted him sky high.

When it was all over there was nothing left but smoldering machine parts. Kurt called out, "It's all right now, get back to the truck."

He made his way back, only to find the driver spread out on the roadside, dead, with a gaping hole in his head. Maurice was wounded but standing, head lowered in grief. As Kurt walked up Maurice said somberly, "It was his birthday today, all of twenty-one years."

The Frenchman carried off his body and explained, "This way at least the Germans won't use him for target practice."

"Let me see your arm," Kurt said. It was bleeding profusely, and he had loss quite a bit of blood. Kurt tore off some of the older man's shirtsleeve and used it as a tourniquet to stop the bleeding. Kurt said, "I'll drive, you tell me where to go."

"That's fine by me," he replied.

Once aboard they drove off as fast as they could. Kurt glanced behind him through the rearview mirror and it seemed clear for now. He said, "I give the Germans about five minutes."

Maurice groaned, then said, "The road will be unbroken from here on. It's little used, being overgrown by the forest like this. Just stay on course, I need to close my eyes a bit and rest."

Kurt looked over at the Frenchman, his held tilted to the side. He was fast asleep.

Chapter Eleven

The truck accelerated down the roadway as Kurt gave it all it had. He drove intensely until he heard over the rumbling of the engine someone knocking at his window. A hand was pointing to the rear. The Frenchman was trying to warn him. Kurt rolled down the window, the cold night air hitting his face forcefully as he stuck his head out. He spotted a German troop truck following him on a road parallel to theirs, only closer to the beach. It was no more than thirty yards away. Their guns were silent for the moment.

With all of the truck lights knocked out Kurt wasn't sure if they had been seen yet. He shook Maurice until he awoke, all the while flooring the gas pedal. As Maurice came around Kurt said, "We've got company," and gestured to the side.

"Those animals," Maurice said angrily, his eyes wild with rage. "They're using the dirt roadway."

"How far ahead does it go?"

Maurice didn't need to think about answering. He had used both roads many a time in the past. "For miles, my boy, for miles."

The Germans came to an open stretch of roadway and opened fire. Bullets scored direct hits, killing two Frenchmen right off. A third fell back onto the hay clutching his upper chest, severely wounded. With only five men left Maurice pounded twice on the wall of the truck. This was the signal. The men removed a canopy cover and exposed the mounted machine gun and commenced firing, splintering trees and branches, they hit everything but the Germans, who had disappeared into a fold in the ground.

"Dam it to hell," Kurt muttered.

"Relax," Maurice said, "this is just the start of things. The roadways are a nightmare of parallels. They'll pop up again in a few miles or so."

Kurt got an idea. "Do you have anything more powerful than that mounted machine gun in back?"

"Of course I do. We have an anti-tank launcher and four rocket heads that go along with it. But to use it properly we have to be in full range and on target. It would be difficult under these circumstances."

Kurt stuffed his pistol into his belt and gripped the wheel with both hands. He accelerated to over seventy miles per hour. The darkness of the roadway was anything but inviting. The rain began and the grounds became increasingly difficult to negotiate. After a mile or so Kurt noticed something to his left. Maurice moaned, his wound giving him trouble. He turned to Kurt and said, "What's going on? Are the Germans gaining on us?"

Kurt shook his head calmly. "No."

Lightening flashed, illuminated the road ahead. There was a tunnel entrance that became visible for a few seconds. It was no more than a quarter of a mile away. Kurt cracked a smile. "Hold on, Maurice, I think our luck is about to change." There were rows upon rows of trees lining the way on either side of the road. Old and weather-beaten, they stood like giants swaying in the increasing winds. Thunder roared in the distance.

The rain was pouring now and Kurt had no choice but to slow down. Just then came a burst of machine gun fire, bullets plowed into the road ahead, but Kurt kept going. On his left, back twenty yards, was a Nazi troop truck. More volleys came their way but none hit home. The rain was starting to fall so hard that even the largest of targets became obscured in the distance. Kurt headed straight for the tunnel opening.

He glanced over at Maurice. "They're probably in touch by radio to their base, giving a detailed account along the way."

Maurice fumed. "And you are due in Belgium in just a few hours."

Kurt nodded reassuringly. "Let me worry about that. You just sit back and enjoy the ride."

He stepped on the gas, the truck skidded a bit and straightened back out. Maurice pounded on the truck wall again and the Frenchmen began to open up on the Germans in the rear. Then the Germans stopped. Their vehicle sat quietly as the rains pounded. It disappeared all together from view as Kurt drove into a defile between high rocks and came up on the other side. The rains pounded harder; Kurt started to slow as he entered the dark mouth of the tunnel a few moments later.

He stopped all at once and told Maurice to sit still. He got out and went around the back. The Frenchmen all looked half dead but could still function as a fighting unit. He instructed one man to stay with the mounted gun and the rest to go with him. He walked back to the entrance of the tunnel. There was still no sign of the Germans. He positioned two men at either side of the opening. He waited a moment; there was nothing. A cold draft blew into the tube of the tunnel and he glanced around him to the other end, which was quite a walk down.

He ordered the remaining two Frenchmen to run its length and wait for him. As he stepped lively back to the truck there was a hissing sound and steam was coming from under the hood. "Just my luck," he said to himself. "Not now, please." As he approached the rear of the vehicle he smelled gasoline. It was leaking from the tank, marked by four bullet holes. He ordered the Frenchman on top to get down and set up the grenade launcher. From there, he went for Maurice. "Out," he said.

"You told me to stay here."

"That's right, now I'm telling you to get out," he said firmly as he forcibly led him out of the vehicle.

Maurice was on the edge of his nerves. He saw the state of the vehicle. "My God, how do we get you to Belgium now?"

"Don't worry, I'll find us another truck."

Maurice stopped in his tracks. "You don't mean—"

Kurt grabbed his arm and said nothing. He called for the front point man to help get the gun off the vehicle and position it in the center of the opening. Kurt waited. A few minutes had passed when out of no where headlights were racing straight for them. The Germans had somehow managed to cross the rough terrain and get on the other roadway.

Shots rang out and two bullets ripped into one of the Underground fighters, sending him flying backward into the darkness of the tunnel. Kurt opened, aiming for the driver. He unleased a steady volley until finally the truck swerved off the road and came to a stop. Germans were shouting angrily and as the front headlights shined through the muddy base of the hill a tremendous amount of gunfire erupted. The Germans were giving them all they had.

Kurt hit the ground, as did the others. The truck behind them burst into flames. Kurt sprayed the road and the shrieks of dying men filled the night. He called to his backup man. "Are you all right?" There was no answer. The firing stopped. Kurt took out his pistol and crawled toward the German vehicle. He paused a moment. Dead German soldiers littered the roadway. There was no movement. He stood up and walked over to the open door of the truck. The body of a corporal fell out, sprawling across the ground.

He got into the driver's seat and started to get the vehicle back on the road. He went in reverse to clear the ditch, straightened out and drove ahead past the burning truck. He looked down at his fallen comrades. He accelerated and behind him came a great explosion as the fuel tank erupted. He stopped and Maurice got aboard with the others in the rear. Maurice looked solemn.

As they drove the rain seemed to let up to a drizzle. "Wait," said Maurice. "What's that ahead?" There was a checkpoint. Kurt stopped the truck. Just fifty yards ahead was Belgium. It all seemed simple enough. He was in German uniform, his papers were in order, he would get out and walk across, the Frenchman could turn around and go home.

Then a German supply truck pulled up immediately behind them. "Well, Kurt, what do we do now?"

"Nothing to panic over. Get down, I don't want you to be seen."

Maurice did his best to crouch under the dash as Kurt started the vehicle up and drove for the checkpoint. His heart was beating like a drum as he slowed up and stopped. The sentry approached him. "Papiers?" Kurt slowly pulled out a folded wad and handed it over, all the while keeping his right hand on his gun. The sentry went back to look at the documents under the lamplight when the phone rang inside.

"What's happening?" Maurice whispered.

Kurt frowned. "Be quiet."

A moment later the German reappeared and rather cheerfully returned the papers to Kurt. "Did you see anything unusual on the trip over tonight, Herr Major?"

"Unusual?" Kurt replied.

The sentry nodded back the way they'd come. "It appears the French Underground attacked a troop truck of ours earlier this evening. I thought you might know something."

Kurt leaned out the open window and stared the sentry down. "If I had seen anything do you not think I would have alerted base command?"

The sentry turned a quick pale gray, stepped back, and raised his hand in salute. "Heil Hitler!"

Kurt saluted and drove off. He said to Maurice, "You can get up now."

Maurice was visibly shaken. He made the sign of the cross and kissed his hand. Kurt smiled. "You can relax, we're just entering Belgium."

He made his way to Brussels. After what seemed an eternity of endless streets and boulevards he reached his destination. The city was aglow in nightlife. The occasional Nazi soldier strolled by and coolly ignored one another on their way to the city. Kurt pulled the vehicle over in an alley between darkened apartment buildings. The main city square was several more blocks away and there was a train station near it.

Kurt shook Maurice's hand and thanked him profusely. Overcome with emotion the Frenchman leaned over and hugged him saying, "Good luck to you." Kurt got out and, with his gun stashed in his jacket and his briefcase in hand, headed for the nearest hotel. Registering as Heinrich Kruger he got a suite for the night. The manager handed him his keys. "Second floor, room two ten."

He found the one-bedroom suite with bathroom and walk-in closet. The view was a decent one, and no sooner than he thought that than a Gestapo car drove by. He immediately pulled down the curtains and turned off the lights. He headed for the bathroom. The night was one he would not soon forget. It had left him soiled, to say the least. He flipped on the switch and drew his bath. The water slowly began to fill into a tub that seemed a relic from the Victorian era. He began to undress, leaving a shirt and jacket on a chair. He was about to place his revolver nearby when he heard a knock at the door.

"Who is it?"

A seductive voice politely answered him on the other side. "My name is Paulette, I'm here to serve you."

He opened up and a voluptuous temptress in high heels, fishnet stockings, and a black leather coat stood casually in the hallway. "Aren't you going to invite me in?" she said.

His face drew up sternly. "I don't think so."

She couldn't help but laugh. "Darling, all the German boys want a fräulein for their furloughs." She took a drag on her cigarette.

"Yes, but I am not on furlough, I am here on business."

She smiled politely. "Yes, I see. No pleasure before business?"

He hesitated a moment. "I'm afraid not."

He closed the door and locked it. The water by now was filled a third of the way in the bath. He removed the last of his clothes and placed his towel on the stool next to the bath with his revolver on top. He got in slowly as the water was quite hot now. He finally eased in all the way and took a deep breath. His thoughts were of Jacqueline and how she was faring, and if she had ever met her sister in London. Every muscle in his body ached. He knew a hot bath would ease his tension.

He tried to relax, closing his eyes. After about fifteen minutes he felt halfway human. After finishing his bath he rested somewhat comfortably on top of his bed, with his towel around his midsection. He was due at Eagle's Nest the following evening and he was unable to sleep. He was going over in his mind all that he and Jacqueline had discussed.

In the quiet of the early dawn Kurt finally managed to sleep soundly and awoke when shots rang out. More followed. He heard voices outside. He sprang out of bed and looked out the window. The Gestapo was rounding up Belgian youths. Three young men with their hands tied behind their backs stood solemnly, heads cast downward. Two more lay dead on the sidewalk in front of them. A van drove up and stopped. Several Gestapo agents got out and approached the youths.

Kurt could not hear what was being said. One of the agents slapped a youth hard across his face. He gestured and the other Germans pushed him along with the other boys into the van. Saboteurs, he thought, resistance fighters perhaps.

Kurt finished dressing. He had readied his gear and spotted himself in the mirror. One of his colored contact lenses was missing. "Blasted," he muttered. He fumbled around in his jacket pocket and produced a small container holding a second, reserve set. He flipped it open, took out an identical contact and carefully placed it on his eye. He combed his hair a bit and pulled down his jacket. "Today's the day," he said to himself, and with that went downstairs.

Outside, the Gestapo had departed and the lobby was congested with guests. He asked the hotel clerk, "Where is a good place to eat?"

"They serve breakfast here at seven o'clock, sir, down the hall to your left," the man said passively as he flipped through his registration book.

He had half an hour to kill. Lighting up a cigarette, he headed for the lobby and rested on a sofa. Next to him sat an elderly Moroccan in a gray suit, legs crossed, reading the morning paper. After a moment the man said, "Herr Kruger, good morning."

Kurt was shocked and grew excited, but tried not to show it. "I am here for Frantz Schmidt," the man said calmly from behind his newspaper.

Kurt started to calm down. It was a contact. Of all places. The Moroccan, his brown face scared and aged, permitted himself the resemblance of a smile. "How was your trip?"

"I've had better."

"After breakfast meet me outside the hotel. I'll have your train ticket." He got up and disappeared.

His appetite was lacking and he settled for coffee and a pastry, which he ate quickly, all the while sitting at the table and trying to act calm. A waiter strolled by avoiding eye contact with the German major. "More coffee, sir?"

"Yes, bitte." As he poured Kurt asked, "How far to the train station?"

"Five blocks, sir, due west from here."

Kurt checked his watch. He had a whole day. He needed to be in Bavaria early to contact Schmidt and get the coordinates as to where to go next. He drank his second cup and left. Outside the Moroccan discretely passed him a newspaper. "Inside," he said, "is your ticket. Schmidt will be at the train station waiting for you. Do be careful, the Krauts are everywhere."

Kurt cradled the paper between his elbow and ribs as he began to walk down the street. The station was quite crowded. As Kurt arrived he held his breath. A dozen Nazi officers boarded in front. He pushed himself behind some locals and made his way to a window seat in the corner of the cabin train. Two German civilians sat down next to him, civil engineers who were returning to Bavaria. Both in their late twenties, one man was wearing steel-rimmed spectacles and bow tie, in a dark suit. The other was casually dressed.

After a few moments when everyone found their seat, the train started to move slowly. Kurt unfolded the paper and began to read. He slipped his ticket into his jacket. One of the Germans asked him, "So, Major, you must be very happy with the war, ja?" Kurt nodded. "Our military is invincible," the man said. "Only England now stands in our way."

"But not for long," the other said, and they both laughed.

Kurt smiled. "Where do you gentlemen work?"

"We're at the Alpine Arms Factory. We help build what your soldiers use to conquer Europe." The bespectacled man spoke proudly, and Kurt noticed a German eagle on his right lapel. "And where is your destination, Major?"

"Bavaria. I trust it won't be too long a ride."

"This train makes a stop at every station but we should be in Bavaria this afternoon." The train was picking up speed and the conductor came by asking for tickets.

An hour later Kurt was finishing up his paper when he noticed three Gestapo officers in the aisle ahead of him, glancing at faces as they moved slowly through the car. They were looking for someone. He thumped his foot loudly on the floor. The German next to him sat up, surprised. "What happened?"

"It's my leg. Cramps, you see an injury. I can't sit for too long in one position." Kurt stood up. "Perhaps if I walk around a bit. Keep an eye on my seat for me, please. I shall be back momentarily."

He made a quick exit out of the car and stood on the platform, leaning against the rail. He took a deep breath. The tracks blurred below him as the train steamed ahead, he looked behind him; the Gestapo were closing the line. He stretched across and managed to open the other cabin door. He walked through the corridor and stepped into an unoccupied room, locking the door behind him. He waited several minutes. There was a frenzied attempt to open the door. He could hear in German the Gestapo commanding the conductor to open up all the rooms. Further ahead a door slammed. The Gestapo yelled for a man to stop. He could hear a struggle followed by a silence. They had found their man.

Kurt felt a deep sense of relief. He looked out the window. The countryside was a mixture of fields and farms. He kept his briefcase by his side and his gun in his jacket. Cautiously he stepped out and ran into a beautiful woman. She was a youthful forty, a brunette, dressed in a lovely fur coat and smiling as she nearly ran straight into him.

"Excuse me, sir, I'm so terribly sorry."

He noticed her intense, green eyes. "Excuse me, madame."

"Which way would I go to get to the dining car?"

"I'm trying to find that myself."

"Well, then, lead the way and I shall follow."

They reached the end of the car and entered the next. The conductor was busy collecting tickets. "Would you please tell us which way to the dining car?" Kurt said.

"Yes, sir, two more cabins down."

As they went an SS man sitting in an aisle seat, his head drawn forward, glanced up and stared directly into Kurt's eyes with a surprised look. Then he nodded off again. They came up to the right car and Kurt headed for the bar. He needed to get a drink to steady his nerves. The woman followed suit. "Well, Herr Major, will you buy a girl a drink?"

"And what would the lady be drinking today?"

"Peppermint schnapps."

Kurt looked at the bartender and said, "Make that two." He glanced around the half filled dining car. It was hours until lunch. "We haven't been properly introduced," she said. "I'm Countess Veronica Klinghoper."

Kurt smiled politely. "A pleasure, madame, to be sure. My name is Major Kruger. What brings you on this trip today?"

She fluttered her long eyelashes several times. "Family business." The bartender handed her a drink and one to Kurt.

His eyes lit up. "Countess? My, to think I bumped into a countess."

She smiled and sipped her schnapps. "What a delightful day this is starting to become." She went on about herself in great detail, how her relatives in Austria had been to the courts of Wilhelm the Great and later Bismarck, and how her brother was now in the Luftwaffe and had served with distinction in the invasion of Poland and France.

He pretended to be fascinated and all the while tried to stay a safe distance. She was overtly flirtatious and enjoyed to extend her hand and touch him while she talked.

The train was coming to another stop. He held his schnapps and pretended to listen, but in his mind he was thinking ahead to that evening at the top of Bavaria. He had come all this way to do a mission, the greatest in his career. He was outwardly calm in the way he spoke to her. He had the charm about him all right, as did Kruger. He was convincing. He would survive, he told himself, he would survive anything. It seemed to him in a peculiar way that all the other missions had been a preparation for this one.

He sipped the schnapps and set it aside. She continued to chatter. He kept thinking about meeting Jacqueline and falling in love so immediately and fully.

"Don't you agree?" the countess asked.

"Pardon me?"

"Haven't you heard a word I said?"

"But of course, madame, it's the train. It keeps rattling on." The train was in fact starting to brake.

She smiled again and asked nicely, "Don't you think the Alps are beautiful this time of year?"

"Alps, oh yes, but of course." He looked around and realized they were in Germany. The Munich station in Bavaria would be the next stop.

She excused herself by saying, "I must powder my nose." He polished off his drink, at which point a tall man in a uniform approached, an SS major who was obviously ecstatic. Energetically he extended his hand and exclaimed, "Heinrich, you devil, I thought you were still at the hospital. What are you doing out so soon? And who is that gorgeous woman you were with?"

Despite all his preparations at SOE station he had not the slightest inkling of who was standing before him. Yet surely this man knew Kruger. "The woman?" he said. "Oh, she is just someone I met. Tell me about you."

"What's to tell? I've just got back from Berlin visiting my girlfriend, who is just as fat as ever. Too many bonbons. She worries about me so, she eats all the time now. I think I should get someone new, you know, someone thinner."

At that point several SS officers walked in, sat down at a table and ordered drinks. Things were getting a bit awkward, he thought. "Did you bring them?" the major asked.

"Bring what?"

"The pictures of your girlfriend from Bavaria. You promised me you would show me her when you got out."

Kurt hatched an idea. The SS major was getting loud. He took the countess's drink and proclaimed, "A toast to my friend, Herr—"

Kurt interrupted. "Let me show you the photos. She's a stunner, all right, but my pictures are in my compartment. Will you come with me?"

The German finished the countess's drink and said, "Lead the way." As they exited and entered the next cabin car, German soldiers were heading for the dining room. Kurt stopped momentarily as they saluted him, then continued. He pushed open a door and noticed the end of the cabin just ahead. "Ah, I'm a fool," he said. "My pictures were in my wallet all the time. Come, to the window here. I'll show you."

The SS major leaned up against the wall, grinning. "How big are her cups?"

Kurt noticed a tunnel straight ahead. The train was slowing a bit. "Oh, they're big enough my friend, let me show you." He pulled out his gun and shot him dead. The silencer made nothing more than a coughing sound as the gun discharged. He waited until they entered the tunnel, opened the door, and pushed the body outside over the railing. The train's engine echoed loudly in the tunnel. Kurt took a deep breath, straightened up and headed to his room.

Chapter Twelve

The splendor of Bavaria was truly impressive. From the baroque cities along the Danube to the turreted castles perched high in the Alps, to the charming villages of the Bavarian forests, the region was the backdrop to Wagnerian operas and Teutonic myth.

The train stopped on time at the Munich station. Kurt got out as a large group of Nazis marched passed him. Over in a clearing he saw a figure wearing an old hat and gray trench coat. He took a step forward and the figure turned and started to walk away. He ran up to the man. "Frantz Schmidt," he said with expectation in his voice.

"Nein," the man said and hurried off.

The train began to move again, the boarding platform cleared and he was left alone except for a solitary figure by the ticket window. He was dressed in a distinguished suit and tie. He folded his paper and tossed it into a trash can, and with brisk steps approached Kurt. "Good afternoon, Major Kruger."

Kurt was silent, his face tightened with nerves. "Welcome to Bavaria," the man said. "My name is Schmidt."

Kurt extended his hand. As they shook he said, "Where to?"

"Come with me Major Kruger."

They exited the platform and headed toward a parked car. A new Mercedes Benz was waiting for them on the cobbled street. They drove up a roadway for several miles, first following the railway track in a parallel. Later Schmidt abruptly turned off into a wilderness dotted with jagged ridges. After many miles they reached a clearing. Schmidt switched off the engine. "We walk from here," he said.

Kurt followed him to a small cabin hidden by a cluster of trees. Once inside, Schmidt said, "We will wait until early evening. I will drive you to a town near Berchtesgarden, and there a car will pick you up and take you to the peak of Kehlsteinhaus Eagle's Nest." Schmidt had the face of a drill sergeant, stern and spiteful. He made his way to a table and sat down, took out his revolver from inside his suit and placed it on the table before him.

"Relax," he said poignantly.

Kurt found a chair to sit in and had some breathing space. Closing his eyes a moment, he found that his neck and shoulder muscles were tight from the train ride. He scrambled to his feet when he heard the sounds of engines. German military vehicles and trucks were approaching along the winding road. "What's that?"

Schmidt shook his head. "Don't worry. The Germans use this road all the time. That's why I have my retreat here, a perfect location and a perfect cover. On occasion, some of the soldiers come in for coffee and tell me some bits of information." He walked over to his writing desk and pointed toward the typewriter. He turned it around and revealed a radio transmitter in the back. "Everything worth telling SOE I do with this."

Kurt looked on in interest. "I see."

"It's an interesting life. It's worth every minute of it. Just last week I reported German troop movements to British Intelligence. They had no idea that so many soldiers existed in this part of the country." As Schmidt looked out his window with binoculars in hand, he jotted down notes on their size and strength.

Kurt watched with curiosity and reserve. When the man finished he said, quite contentedly, "Well, that's that. They won't be coming back to bother us today."

"Do you stay here alone?"

"Well, most of the time. There is another agent I work with." His voice rose slightly as he sat back into his chair. "But he's been gone several days now to Berlin."

"They told me that you would be able to get minimum access to my destination. Why just minimum, why doesn't the high command make allowances for you as they do for Kruger?"

Schmidt put his binoculars away and chuckled a bit under his breath. "If I looked like Kruger, young and handsome, charming, with all the ladies chasing me at every party, I suppose high command would embrace me just as much. None of them would win a beauty contest, you know. They need someone like Kruger to provide a certain inspiration to the opposite sex. They simply flock to Kruger. That one, he can have his pick of any woman day or night. He always has first crack at them, to soften them up before fat man Göring has his indulgences—you understand, don't you?"

Kurt just laughed off the remark. He lit a cigarette. It was starting to get cold and the winds began to howl under the front door. "Suppose those Nazis make it?" Schmidt said.

Kurt looked up. "What do you mean?"

"You know, beat us, invade England."

"That's not suppose to happen with agents like us out in the field."

"No, really. What if..." He thought about it to himself, taking a drag off his cigarette.

Kurt sighed. "Well I suppose guerilla warfare inside of Britain would be the next step."

"Something extremely frightening about that," Schmidt said. "But if Germany does conquer the British Isles with all of Europe already fallen, there would be little else for them to do. I've heard talk about scientific matters, the practical possibility of an atomic bomb. The German empire could use the immense resources of Europe to build an atomic bomb. Think of it."

Placing a cigarette back in his mouth, Kurt said, "Here now, slow down, England is still free."

The old man sunk deeper in despair. "For now. But if Germany conquers England the way will be clear to develop this weapon, don't you see? Hitler can blackmail anyone who is left to resist."

"Get a grip on yourself, man. All of this is theory."

"Theory?" Schmidt said. "Hah, theory! Let me tell you something about that. Hitler has under his control the greatest of the nuclear physicists, Niels Bohr, in occupied Denmark."

Kurt leaned forward, his expression intense. "The English countryside is sprinkled with old mansions earmarked as schools for spies. There are agencies for political warfare and special operations. Our boys in SOE are training over twenty thousand Dutch, Norwegians, Frenchmen, and Belgians who escaped across the seas to continue in the fight against Nazism. Their instructors have been on covert missions to Russia and China. They have studied the art of guerilla warfare, from the civil war in Spain to the Boer War in South Africa. These regulars work behind a facade of commercial offices between Soho and Westminster. Once their training is completed, they will be some of the best agent saboteurs and leaders of the secret army we've got. Thousands of top secret threads are joined together to prevent the Germans from developing this bomb."

He leaned back and dragged on his cigarette. "Now I suggest you take a day off. You're getting quite paranoid here."

The man eased back in his seat and smiled broadly. "I suppose you are right. This place does tend to get to me at times."

Kurt walked over and placed his hand on Schmidt's shoulder. The end of the month would mark three years Schmidt had served at the station in the thick of Bavaria. Three long and difficult years. It would have ruined a lesser man. Schmidt reached over and turned on the radio to a symphony by Beethoven. "This is better than nothing, I suppose," he said. The cabin had a somber interior, simple furnishings, an oil lamp in the corner for emergencies when the electricity didn't work during thunderstorms.

Kurt stood there for a time as the music filled the room.

Göring arrived in Berchtesgarden with the party only a few hours away. The field marshal saw fit to recruit some local talent apart from the standard fare. He craved new faces and at his private house made his selections. The women who saw him were the cream of Bavaria, seductive, young, idealistic, highly attractive and friendly. Göring's passion for such decadence found few parallels amongst his elite associates.

It was a quarter to six and Schmidt had driven Kurt down to his designated drop-off point. After their heated exchanged that afternoon they still managed to part as friends. Kurt had come to look forward to the social affair with an optimistic boyishness that surprised even himself. He was now Kruger; he felt that wholeheartedly. He walked and talked and even thought like the man. This was to be his greatest assignment and he was up to the challenge.

Just across the street lay waiting a black Mercedes limousine. He made a straight line to it. As he approached, the driver, a young German corporal, stepped out. He saluted and awaited his instructions.

"Where is everybody?" Kurt said in his best Kruger voice.

"The field marshal is on his way down from his estate, sir. Field Marshal Keitel and Herr Ribbentrop are inside the limousine, Major."

At that point the rear window rolled down and Ribbentrop greeted Kurt with a wave of his hand. "Guten tag, Herr, Major, and how are we today?" Here was one of the most despicable men of the Third Reich sitting not more than several feet away from him, and Kurt had to muster all of his will power just to remain composed.

"Very good," he said.

Keitel emerged from the shadows of the interior. "The operation went well, ja? I see very little change in you." After a pause he added, "Except..." Kurt grew nervous. He waited. "Perhaps the doctors made you a bit prettier."

Ribbentrop and Keitel both laughed as Kurt stood there smiling pretentiously through it all. His moment of truth had come and he had passed. Now it was a matter of putting up with the pompous bastards until he could get to the safe.

"Get in quickly now," said Ribbentrop. "Göring told us to meet him on top." The interior of the limousine was filled with all the trappings of a privileged life: liquor cabinet with only the best liqueurs, leather upholstery, plush carpeting.

Kurt sat down and the chauffeur closed the door behind him. "What will it be, Heinrich?" said Keitel, moving toward the liquor cabinet. "We have French cognac, or perhaps some of this fine cherry brandy?"

Keitel poured him a cognac and one for himself. "Salut. To the new major, with my compliments."

"Here, here!" said Ribbentrop.

The limousine drove off. It was half an hour later when they reached their destination. Outside, smartly dressed SS guards stood at attention in their black uniforms and white gloves, rifles over their shoulders, eyes fixed far into space. The air was thinner and it took a moment to adjust. As everyone got out Kurt managed to gulp in some deep breaths to sustain himself. The limousine had stopped in a broad parking space carved out of the mountain in front of a tunnel, which led directly to an elevator. The ride up lasted all of forty-five seconds. When the elevator door opened into the Eagle's Nest itself, the reception was overwhelming. Party favors rained down from all corners of the room and champagne bottles popped and cheers and applause filled the interior.

Keitel and Ribbentrop stepped in lively. A waltz by Strauss was being played by a small orchestra in the corner and the Nazi elite had made themselves right at home. Officers of the SS served them drinks. Kurt entered last. He put up his best fake smile and gritted his teeth as a tray with champagne floated past him. He took a glass and worked his way over to the middle of the room. There he spotted a couch and sat himself down, placing his briefcase in the corner.

A kind of euphoria enveloped the room as the elevator opened and Göring himself stepped in with a bevy of beauties at his side. Blondes, brunettes and redheads filled the reception room, giggling and flirting as they went. Göring stopped, his eyes flickered and a big smile spread across his face. "Heinrich, old man, come here! Kommen sie."

Kurt sprang up and walked across the room. Göring embraced him. "Thank God you're all right. The reports I got about you had me worried. You look quite good."

As he stepped back Kurt took a deep breath and felt his heart racing. Convincing Göring was the white glove test. If he could do that, the rest would be easy.

The field marshal bellowed, "Dear woman, please come here." A statuesque blonde with considerable cleavage approached, smiling amiably at her host. Göring took her by the hand and kissed her. She beamed. Göring clapped his hand on Kurt's shoulder. "Old man, don't just stand there, introduce yourself."

He hesitated clearing his throat and bent down, clicking his heels together. "Good evening, my name is Major Kruger, a pleasure."

"The pleasure is all mine," she said in a very soft voice.

Göring said insistently, "Run along now, both of you, I'm sure you have much to talk about."

Kurt led her back to the couch and along the way handed her a drink. As they sat down, she laughed. "Oh my, this is simply wonderful up here. The countryside is magnificent, don't you agree?"

"Yes, to be sure, it is quite charming."

At that moment more women exited the elevator. The men converged on them like love struck college students. "What is your name?" Kurt said.

"Claudia," she replied proudly.

"And what do you do when you don't go to parties?" he asked.

She appeared quite shy all of a sudden, as if ashamed to tell him. "I'm a student," she said in a somewhat distant voice.

"I see, and how old are you?"

"I turned twenty-four last month."

"Well, happy belated birthday to you then."

"I thank you so much." He looked guardedly around him. Göring commanded the center of the room with women at each side. Champagne was flowing, and caviar was consumed, and the cheeriness and laughter were heightened by the comedic talents of several of the officers who consistently enlightened the women with sordid stories from their past. As they eagerly indulged their imaginations in the details, the generals gathered around Göring and raised their champagne glasses to a salute.

Göring stood up and robustly proclaimed for all to hear, "To our Führer, and to victory over England!" Cheers and applauds thundered throughout.

Kurt stood up, clapped in earnest with the others. He noticed a black briefcase by Göring's feet. This might contain the secret plans for invasion. Then again it might not. He would have to wait patiently as the party progressed before he had a chance to find out. The orchestra played another waltz and people started dancing in the middle of the floor. The party started to flow over into other rooms now, as formalities ended. Duran noticed Göring handing his briefcase to an SS officer, who in turn took it away abruptly into another room.

"Why aren't you dancing?" someone asked from behind. Kurt turned around, it was Ribbentrop with champagne glass in hand. "Is she not your type?"

Kurt smiled tactfully. "Ah, but she is." With that he took her by the hand and they made their way across to the dance floor. They swerved around into a second room that was larger than the first but less crowded. Inside it had wood paneling and burgundy carpeting on the floor. There was also a large oil painting of Hitler hanging over the north wall in a lavish, gold frame, antique chairs and couches off to the side, and a magnificent French mirror on the opposite wall, highly intricate in its design.

Claudia was flustered. Kurt was a good dancer and the lady was quite impressed. "Marvelous to see those moves of yours," she said coyly, as she eyed herself with him in the mirror.

"I thank you, my lady, a dancer is only as good as his partner."

"Yes, but you lead and I follow." With that, she pressed her ample bosom up close against his chest. Her eyes flickered with a passion. She clearly knew Kruger's reputation and was thrilled by the chance to be in his arms.

Keitel strolled by with a brunette who giggled uncontrollably. More officers started to filter into the room, along with their dates for the evening. Kurt looked over and Göring, who hadn't even touched his champagne glass, was engaged in an animated dialogue with several of his officers.

Kurt danced her under a crystal chandelier that sparkled in the lamplight like a thousand diamonds. He held her waist firmly and caressed her neck. "Oh, Kurt," she sighed. He did it again. She smiled, closing her eyes momentarily, head tilted in toward his, her hands around his shoulders. She said softly, "I think I'm going to enjoy tonight very much." She leaned into him and gave him a kiss. They circled around and he nodded at Keitel as they passed.

"Not his best," she said.

"And to what do you refer?"

"The music darling, the Strauss waltz, not his best."

He smiled. "Well, then why listen to it. Let's go out for some fresh air." He led her past the other guests through the open French windows and out onto the balcony. It was cold out and she cuddled close to him for warmth. He looked around the balcony. There was no guards in sight. He checked his watch casually.

She kissed him again and moaned. Then she laughed wickedly. "I rather enjoy the cold. It gives me good reason to get closer to you, Herr Major." Then she said dramatically into his ear, "You have one hour to get away."

He pushed her back, staring into her face. "What are you talking about?"

She moved close to him again and in a serious voice said, "My name is Claudia Trudeaux, I'm with the French Underground."

He didn't answer her as he heard guards coming in the distance. He pulled her toward him and wrapped his arms around her in a lover's embrace until the guards went past. When it was clear he stood back. "What the devil are you saying?"

"I work for British Intelligence, SOE. The same people who sent you here arranged for me to be your backup. They weren't sure if I would be called into service tonight. There were three of us, moles. I was handpicked by the field marshal himself."

"But why was I brought here then?"

"Because of your skills and your incredible resemblance to Kruger, of course. They knew you could make it up here, getting me was questionable, I was at the mercy of Göring's tastes of the moment. Tonight he wanted brunettes."

"You told me I have one hour."

"Yes. Later there will be a large party of Waffen SS and things could get out of hand and with all these ladies every room in the place will be a love nest. The guards will be back soon, you must hurry."

He nodded. "I'll mingle with Ribbentrop a bit, then come back and take you to the room with the safe. We'll use the outside terrace to avoid suspicion."

Kurt went inside first. Helping himself to another glass of champagne, he started to strike up a conversation with Ribbentrop, who was finishing up a flirtation with a sultry blonde.

Göring came up to them. "Just the man I wanted to see."

Kurt was quite nervous now. With the field marshal were several Waffen SS lieutenants. Göring said, "I need your opinion on a matter. In view of our upcoming occupation of Britain, the Führer ordered the preparation of a small handbook for our troops, as well as our political and administrative units."

Ribbentrop looked interested. "Ah, Herr Field Marshal what does this small book do?"

"Well, it will describe the most important political, administrative and economic institutions in all of Great Britain, as well as the leading public figures."

"That's all?" Ribbentrop asked.

"No, not at all, it will also contain instructions on the necessary measures that ought to be taken in occupying the premises of the War Office, the Foreign Office, the Home Office, as well as various departments of the Secret Service and Special Branch."

Ribbentrop seemed impressed. He reminded Göring that he had quite a phobia about British espionage. He maintained that every single Englishman who traveled or even lived abroad was in fact given assignments by the British Secret Service. He had a deep hatred of all things English and to this end the handbook, in his opinion, served as an outstanding guide of German organization during Nazi occupation. Göring smiled approvingly as Ribbentrop complimented him on this special project. "Herr Field Marshal, promise me you will give me a copy for my own references."

Göring laughed. "Why, you know England better than Churchill!" The SS around him all joined in his laughter as did Kurt. "None the less, if you wish, I will see to it that you are provided with a copy." With that, Göring and his entourage went back to the reception room.

Ribbentrop confided to Kurt, "This is between us, but I have already seen a copy of that book, and as far as I'm concerned the Army will be far better off without it." He excused himself for some more personal indulgence with his lady friend.

Kurt casually walked to the corner to retrieve his briefcase. From there he headed for the restroom. Inside, he removed the nylon climbing rope and opened the window. He checked to see that there were no guards present as he slipped the rope onto the terrace, hiding it behind the utilities box. He closed the window, turned off the lights and stepped back into the corridor. He left the briefcase in the hall closet. He made his way to Claudia, who had been mingling with a group of officers.

Kurt checked his watch. A full forty minutes before more members of the Waffen SS were due to arrive. The orchestra came back from its break and started another melody, which Claudia proclaimed to be just as distasteful as anything else they had played tonight and in full view of the other guests asked to be taken outside.

He led her to the balcony and began to lean over the railing, hands clasped. The stars were out and the moon shone bright. "How did it go in there?" she asked.

"The Germans have everything covered for invasion all right. Now let's see what we can do to change all that."

The guards made their rounds again. Kurt began to kiss her, his back to them. After they left he told her, "The room with the map is around the corner of the compound. I'll get in through the window, you come in after me and cover the rear." He stepped gingerly into the shadows.

SS Lieutenant Wilhem von Krositch had been hiding along the inside of the reception room with two very charming hostesses. Von Krositch was a man of forty, had the eyes of a hawk and the instincts of a fox. His decorations spoke for themselves, gleaming on his chest. He had finished his glass of champagne. A woman asked him to dance and he stood up and said, "Very well, but just once around." The atmosphere became much more lively and everyone seemed to be busying themselves in all sorts of dialogues.

Göring himself would be leaving the party soon after the Waffen SS was to arrive, as he was due back in Berlin the following morning. He was in a discussion with both Keitel and Ribbentrop as to the finer aspects of German music. The orchestra performed another Strauss waltz.

They reached the windows. Kurt took his rope and placed it on the ground. "Do you have a hairpin?"

She looked rather surprised. "Yes, but why?"

She handed it to him. He bent it. They stood back; there was a click as he worked and the glass door swung open. It was dark inside. It took a minute for the eyes to adjust fully to the darkness. "Stay by the window," he said. "Let me know when the guards come back."

She stood watch as he headed to the Holbein that was hanging on the opposite wall. The picture hung in an ornate gold frame. Behind it there was the safe. He rubbed his cold hands together a few times and glanced once at Claudia. When he felt he was ready he eased himself closer to the dial and began turning it. After a few seconds the door swung open.

The safe was filled with folders and papers of all sorts. He stuck his hand in deeper and pulled out the leather briefcase. It had the field marshal's initials engraved on top. He headed toward the corner and placed it squarely on top a desk. "Quickly," Claudia said. "Someone is coming."

Kurt was reaching for the desk lamp, fingers on the switch. He froze. Claudia closed the glass door and stood by in silence. Two guards walked pass, their silhouettes flickering across the blue-white moonlight that shined through the window curtains.

A moment later she cracked open the door and observed that the coast had become clear. He spread out the papers on the desktop. His face strained as he reviewed the maps for the occupation of his homeland. The first map showed clearly the plan for an all-out invasion starting from points along the French coast with targets for the southeast seaports that were to be captured in the first assault. They had close to 90,000 men. The invaders would ship in a further 170,000 troops to swarm over the home counties and set up a Nazi capital government in London.

He took out his silver cigarette case and started taking pictures. There were more maps than he had film but he got the essentials before Claudia warned him that the guards were returning once again. Switching off the lights, he raced to the window as she closed it up, and stood by the curtains. He noticed the guards outside had stopped and had taken longer in their break time. Claudia started to panic. He gestured her to stay still. He took out his revolver and cocked it. He parted the side of the curtain a tad and saw that one of the guards had taken out a cigarette and was going to have a smoke.

Kurt could do nothing but wait. The Germans did not budge. They started talking and leaning by the railing of the balcony. He heard footsteps coming down the corridor. He pulled Claudia over by her arm and told her to be still. He moved to place the maps back in the briefcase and shove it into the safe, making sure it was locked and pushing the painting back into its proper position.

The doorknob turned slowly and a key was inserted in the lock. It was SS Lieutenant von Krositch. "Why am I not surprised to see you here," he said as he stared at Claudia.

"Don't move," Claudia said.

"Or what?" he replied.

"Or you will be shot," Kurt said, stepping out from behind him.

Von Krositch raised his hands as Duran took his revolver from him and handed it to Claudia. He told the lieutenant to be quiet. He briefly walked over to the curtains and saw that the guards were gone. The lieutenant sat down in a carved, ebony armchair.

Claudia closed the door and locked it. "What do we do now?"

Kurt switched on a lamp and the lieutenant gestured grandly. "How do you like the retreat?"

"It must be nice for scum like you," Kurt said.

The lieutenant had a contented smile on his face. "As you know, we have quite a security system. More Waffen SS are due any minute. I suggest you put down the gun, Herr Duran."

Kurt was stunned. "What did you call me?"

The lieutenant frowned. "Oh, stop with the charades. There is enough of that being played out in the party out there. I know all about you, Kurt Duran, it's my business to know." His leg was crossed and his left boot swung back and forth casually. "You are a bigger fool than I thought if you assumed you could walk into Eagle's Nest and then walk out with our invasion plans."

Kurt was duly mystified. "How the hell—"

The lieutenant smiled contently as he folded his arms across his chest. "I suppose it makes no difference now."

"What?" Kurt said. Claudia came to his side, fear etched in her face.

"You see, Mr. Duran, we in the Gestapo take a certain pride in our espionage techniques. Hitler's Third Reich depends on us to be the eyes and ears of Germany."

"Cut the bull, Lieutenant." Von Krositch stood.

"We have an agent in SOE, and you are well acquainted with him."

"SOE? Who?" Duran said angrily.

"Your personal trainer, Kiel Holmby." The lieutenant sat back down and laughed in delight.

Duran shook his head. "That's impossible."

Von Krositch for a moment said nothing, his eyes fixed on Kurt's gun. "He's been a mole in the SOE for over a decade. He is German born, not far from here in fact, a master of language and deception. One of our best."

Duran aimed his gun straight for the German. He was enraged. "I wouldn't do that if I were you," von Krositch said.

"And why not?"

The lieutenant sank into the armchair.

"Because my guard will shoot you."

Duran turned around to see that two SS men stood behind him, immediately in front of the open French doors that Claudia, in her haste, had forgotten to lock. They held machine pistols at the ready. "These men will not hesitate to shoot."

Duran somberly lowered his firearm and one of the guards took it from him.

"You made the wise choice. Now let's discuss your situation, shall we?" The lieutenant got up, strolled leisurely to the door and opened it. The Waffen SS had come for Göring. He listened to the commotion out in the corridor and closed the door back up. Claudia just stood there staring at him. The Lieutenant smiled at her. "My dear girl, something about you. We suspected you all along but needed you to bring in your contacts, who have been rounded up." He checked his watch. "Exactly twenty minutes ago they were all shot."

"You devils," she cried out.

He slapped her firmly across the face. Her lips started bleeding as von Krositch took the gun with silencer from one of the guards. He examined it. "Not bad, even for English craftsmanship." As Claudia wiped some tears from her face, he pulled the trigger. The muffled gun let out a small coughing sound and she fell forward on the carpet with a bullet hole in her back. Kurt's body tensed up, his fists clenched, the silencer pressed up against his back. "Don't make the same mistake," said von Krositch, "I don't like to be mocked. Where is it?"

"Where is what?"

"The camera, you fool."

Feeling the situation to be hopeless, Kurt pulled it out of his coat pocket.

"Charming," the lieutenant said, "looking it over. How ingenuous. A camera in a cigarette case. This is what you are going to do with it." He stepped over to the desk and placed it on the corner. "There's only you now, and you did quite a commendable job breaking in. It would be a shame to let all of your hard work go to waste. The maps you photographed were fakes. Since we knew you were coming, we prepared forgeries. Misinformation for your high command."

Duran stared at the camera resting on the desk. "You will deliver the film, as planned, to the French Underground."

"And what if I refuse?"

The lieutenant's mouth formed into a smile. "Does the name Jacqueline Pabon mean anything to you?"

Duran stared. His eyes opened wider, yet were distant and unfocused. He felt numb.

"She is a brilliant operative for the SOE, to be sure. The Gestapo never suspected her, but she made the mistake of falling in love with you."

Duran straightened and glared at the lieutenant. "She flew to Europe and hooked up with her ties in the French Underground," von Krositch said. "She wanted to help you in your escape."

At that point Duran's heart felt as if it had been ripped out. The lieutenant grinned triumphantly. "Our men picked her up. If you do not do as we say we shall kill her. Is that understood?"

Chapter Thirteen

When Kurt came to, the back of his head felt as if it had been trampled on by a stampede of horses. He was stretched out in the darkness on the cold, hard cell floor, still dressed in his Nazi uniform. The place had a foul stench to it and the only available light source was a small opening at the top of the locked door guarding his cell. He gingerly felt the back of his head and his fingers became moist. He had been bleeding.

The last thing he could remember was meeting a member of the French Underground at the designated drop-off point. He could clearly see in his mind the exchange of camera and film. Then he returned to the mysterious black car and that was when things went dark. He remembered he talked with von Krositch, and that he had Jacqueline captive. He didn't know where he was. The cell was fifteen square feet with an old cot in the corner, its stuffing half spilling on the floor, the mattress suspended by rusted springs. There was a toilet on one side.

He heard the sound of footsteps approaching; a moment later they stopped. Lieutenant von Krositch walked in front of the opening to the cell, one side of his face framed in the light. He glared down at his captive. He started to laugh.

"Well, just so you know, my superiors are very pleased with the results. You did a fine performance. Now the English will be bluffed."

"And what about Jacqueline?" Kurt said anxiously as he arose from the floor.

"Her? She will be shot at dawn." He paused. "You will be there to keep her company. You are entitled to a last meal, which will be arriving shortly."

"I'm not hungry."

"A pity, it's the chef's specialty tonight. We'll leave it with you in case you change your mind." He turned and walked away.

Kurt, still rather dazed, sat down and leaned up against the door, feeling despondent. He closed his eyes and heard voices speaking in German. Kurt got up quickly and immediately started climbing above the door and then looked down in anticipation. A key was placed in the lock and the door swung open as two burly guards stepped in. He looked at the top of the guards' heads as they entered the cell. One held the dinner tray and the other carried a Schmeisser machine pistol at the ready. The guards looked confused, for he wasn't to be found. Then, they both crashed to the concrete floor, food slammed into the walls, one man was knocked unconscious outright as Kurt dived down from the ledge above the door where he had held himself suspended on the frame. The other guard staggered to his feet. Kurt drove his fist into the German's face, knocking him out on impact, his body slumping to the floor.

He ran to the door and checked the exits. No one else was in sight. He closed the door almost all the way and removed his jacket. He put on the shirt the guard wore and took his helmet and Schmeisser. On the guard's belt were keys. He took them and hurriedly ran along the corridor. There was a cold breeze in it as he stepped lively to each cell door and whispered her name. "Jacqueline? Where are you? Jacqueline?" He heard a faint sound as if someone awoke. He called out again.

"Kurt! Thank God you're all right. Please let me out."

He fumbled with the key chain, trying various keys.

"Hurry," she said.

After several attempts the door finally opened and she raced out, her arms outstretched toward him, her face weary.

They kissed a moment, then he pulled her away. "We must leave now. Do you know which way they brought you in?"

"The staircase, my darling. This way." She pointed to her left.

He took her by the hand and they ran. As they made it to the stairs he asked, "Where are we?"

"The outskirts of Berchtesgärden," she said. "Some kind of Gestapo hell hole for political prisoners."

He held her by her hand as they made it up one flight and started another. "It's two more flights," she said. "There will be guards."

They could hear footsteps charging behind them now as they made their way. The two guards had come around and had murder in their hearts as they gave chase. Kurt swung around the banister and whipped his booted foot into the guard's face, sending both men tumbling backward down the steps. Kurt looked on contently.

She was about to say something, but he put his finger to her lips. He opened the door carefully, slowly. At one end it seemed clear, at the other was a desk sergeant. They had to exit in his direction.

"Stay here," he said. He started to walk casually, straight for the man.

"Guten abend," the man said to him in a friendly voice. Kurt cocked his arm and swung the Schmeisser, knocking the man out of his chair and out cold.

Jacqueline peered out and ran toward Kurt. There was an exit and another door, which was open, and music spilled out from it. Someone was playing the piano and singing badly. Kurt cautiously entered the room, which was a large recreation room for the guards. There was the piano player behind several portable chalkboards that had blocked Kurt's line of sight and a variety of boxes stacked on the floor.

"Move quickly!" he told her, as they made it down the hall.

Hastily they headed toward an exit. "Here," she said confidently, "they brought me in through here."

Kurt walked up to one of the windows and pulled the blinds. Outside were dozens of German soldiers moving in all directions. Kurt looked crushed. A ring of security was being laid out around the entire compound now.

108

Jacqueline came up behind him. "We drove in there." She pointed to a gated entrance in the foreground. There was an unmanned jeep parked in front of the main door.

"I have an idea," he said. He disappeared momentarily. She kept a watchful eye out. In an instant he came back with a gray-black blanket. They made it outside and Kurt had quickly placed Jacqueline in the backseat covered from head to toe. The weather was wretchedly cold. Guards walked by as Duran was getting into the jeep. One of the guards stopped and saluted; Kurt hesitated a moment finally returning the salute. He noticed the sergeant's rank on his shirt.

"What's taking you so long?" she whispered from under the blanket in the backseat.

"Keep quiet, we're off."

He drove down toward the sentry. Just behind the gate was a dirt road and hills dotted with trees. As he drove up the sentry stepped out into the light. "And where are you off to?" he asked in a thick voice.

"I must deliver some papers to Field Marshal Göring."

"Un moment, bitte." The sentry turned to call in for clearance.

Kurt whispered back to Jacqueline. "Hold on." He took out his gun and shot the guard. He floored the gas and the jeep plowed through the wooden gate, which splintered in its wake. Another sentry bolted out from the rear, firing his machine gun from the hip and missed.

"They'll be on us soon," he said.

She lifted the blanket off her head as she sat up behind him. "There's a turn up ahead, take a left."

"Where does it go?"

"The old roadway. You were supposed to take it to fly out of Germany in the first place."

He smiled serenely. "How far?" Her eyes panned the road ahead.

"Five minutes maybe, at the most." He was doing a top speed of sixty five miles per hour now. The headlights behind him were advancing in the distance.

"Get down," he said.

"But why? I've been crouching in that cell all night."

"Just do as I say." A moment later gunshots went off as an SS vehicle opened up.

Kurt turned and now things became familiar. The rest of the way he knew. As he raced along the roadway his headlights glaring, he checked his watch. "My God, it's almost midnight," he said. "The plane was due to pick me up hours ago."

The airstrip was another half mile out. The road changed into a narrow path with a treacherous, sheer drop on its left side. It was not an actual road at all; it was used by the locals in donkey carts and on horseback. Since the Germans knew full well of the British plan they had soldiers waiting for them not far from the takeoff field.

Jacqueline looked behind and said, "They're gone."

"For now," he said.

Soon the road stopped climbing and leveled off. In the clearing ahead the road turned abruptly to the right and Kurt could not believe his eyes. Under the moonlight sat a JU88S, a German night fighter. He spotted several men in dark clothing not far from the plane. He pulled up beside them and an elderly gentleman stepped forward. "Welcome, Mr. Duran. My name is Victor."

The man was at least sixty, world-weary and stocky. "We've been expecting you."

"I'm terribly sorry for being late. The SS has been giving us trouble."

"We'll deal with that from here on." Victor raised his hand as several armed assistants ran to the narrow path.

Kurt got out and helped Jacqueline out of the car. "Can you get word to Ian Richards in SOE for me?"

"I shall try," he said.

"Tell him the film he will be receiving is a fake."

The man nodded. "Very well, consider it done." The sounds of automatic gunfire filled the clearing. Members of the Resistance pounced upon the SS car.

"We must hurry now," the old man said, taking Jacqueline's arm and leading her and Duran to the night fighter. "Just press the red button when you get into radar range of England. It will signal the RAF not to shoot you down."

On the front seats of the plane were two parachutes. As they strapped them on Kurt thanked the man and wished him well. In haste, Kurt and Jacqueline climbed aboard as the old man receded into the brush. Kurt hit several switches and the engine kicked in. The propeller blades began to turn over. Bullets ripped into the side of the plane and it started to catch fire in several places.

Kurt yelled out for Jacqueline to jump. She did, and he followed suit, and together they ran to the brush. The ensuing explosion lifted them into the air. They landed head first in the bushes. The old man ran up nervously and looked them over. As the Resistance continued to hold back the SS, the old man saw that they were all right, just badly shaken, and took them along the weatherbeaten path several feet wide down the mountain. In the distance were the lights of a small village.

He pointed them in the direction of some houses at the outskirts of the village. "Friends of mine in the Resistance live there. Stop for nothing." Cordially, the Frenchman took Jacqueline by the hand and kissed it.

Kurt took her arm and scrambled down the treacherous mountainside, not looking back.

As they negotiated their descent Jacqueline stepped on a stone that slipped from under her, causing her to lose her balance. She started to fall off the cliff.

Kurt held on to her and told her to stay calm as he began to hoist her up. He could see the darkness below her. He was losing his grip, his arm strained. She struggled to get up to the ledge, but she couldn't reach it with her other hand. He swung her carefully from side to side until she had both hands on top.

"Just don't let go," she said breathlessly.

"The thought hadn't crossed my mind," he replied. On the count of three he pulled her over. She lay panting.

"That's a long drop down." She sighed, and her voice trembled. "The gunfire seems closer." They made their way as fast as they could. The streets of the little village were quiet, only the robust sounds of laughter and celebration could be heard echoing out from the beer halls and restaurants. On the corner stood a street lamp and below it a sign in German inviting one and all for drinks.

A bouncer had tossed out an overly aggressive party-goer. As he stood straightening his jacket Kurt walked up and asked, "How late are you open?"

"Until two, sir," the bouncer replied.

"Is there a phone in this place?"

"Yes. Inside and to your right."

Kurt had a contact in Holland, one he needed desperately to reach. With Jacqueline at his side he dialed the number. The phone rang quite a long time and just as he was about to hang up a man answered. "Good evening?" his voice sounded groggy, as if he had just awoken. "Von Krongt here." There was a flash of relief on Kurt's face.

"Charles, Kurt Duran here, good evening."

"Kurt, my God, it has been ages. Where are you? Is everything all right?"

Kurt paused a moment as he saw a man in a SS uniform walk into the bar. He yanked Jacqueline in close to him, his arm around her, and hid from view. "I need your help," he said. "Will you be there tomorrow?"

"Yes, of course."

"Very good then, Peter, I shall see you then." He hung up. A patron walked passed and Kurt grabbed his arm. "Pardon me, is there a back way out of here? My girlfriend had a little too much to drink."

"Certainly, follow me." The stench of alcohol that grew ever stronger as Kurt found the rear exit. Beer bottles by the dozen lay discarded in bins and barrels. The fumes were intoxicating. Once outside Kurt ran down the alley with Jacqueline at his side. Across the cobbled street Kurt noticed an old model Mercedes Benz.

He nodded toward the car. "I need to take us to Holland. That is our only way out." They ran for the car. He picked the door lock and Jacqueline got in first. He closed it up behind her and raced to the other side.

The streets were all deserted and there was not a sign of the SS. He pulled out two wires, from beneath the dashboard and connected them. The engine started up, and they drove off.

111

"Get down," he whispered. There was a Gestapo car on the corner and men in black sat motionless inside. Several blocks later he checked the rearview mirror. "It's all right now."

"Why Holland?" she asked.

"A friend lives there, one I can trust. He can help us get to England."

She sat in silence. The events of the last few days had taken their toll. "How could it be—the invasion plans?"

"They had advance knowledge of my visit," he said grimly.

"How was that possible?"

"Kiel Holmby. He works for the Gestapo."

"Incredible."

"He's been a mole in SOE for over a decade. No telling how many good agents he betrayed. One thing's certain, he won't get away with it, not anymore. I'll see to that." There was a fierce determination etched into his face. After a moment he said thoughtfully, "How did they treat you while you were in the cell?"

She sat passively a moment, taking in a deep breath. "It was close," she said. "It seems I was the only women in the place. I'm just grateful you came along when you did. The only other girl I know in my situation to walk away was Claudia Trudeaux."

"What was her name?"

"Claudia Trudeaux."

"You knew her?"

She nodded. "We did several missions together over the course of a few months. I owed her my life on more than one occasion. I would have been nabbed if it weren't for her alerting me in time."

He sighed.

"What's the matter? What happened?"

"Claudia is dead. So are her contacts here in Bavaria."

She closed her eyes. "My God, how?"

"SOE decided to slip in a backup for me just in case and it turned out to be her. One of the German officers killed her while we were being interrogated. It happened so quickly. The lieutenant wanted to settle a score, so he did."

"Cruelties of war, I suppose. At least she's at her rest now."

Lieutenant von Krositch's car pulled up to an old house. He took off his leather gloves and told his driver to wait as he stepped outside. Steam escaped from his lips and nostrils in the icy cold night air. Inside were SS men vigorously mapping out coordinates in the brightly lit interior. When the lieutenant entered they all stopped. The sergeant in charge saluted. "Heil Hitler. Good to see you, Lieutenant."

Von Krositch stepped into the map room. "All the roads are covered, sir, as are the railroad stations," the sergeant said. "The British spy will not leave

Bavaria alive. We have a company of a hundred men dispatched in all points of the city to see to that."

"Very good, Sergeant. You're response time is commendable." He lit up a cigar and looked up at the clock on the wall. It had been exactly two hours since their escape.

As Kurt came to a turn machine gun fire ripped into the car. Jacqueline ducked down as Kurt tried frantically not to swerve. The shooting seemed to be coming from all directions. He stepped on the gas and headed straight for a roadblock where two Gestapo cars were poised nose to nose at the end of the street. Soldiers were blasting away, but Kurt kept coming, plowing right through the middle. The soldiers dove for cover.

"Are you all right?" Kurt said.

"I think so," she said hesitantly.

"What do we do about the Gestapo?"

"Just hold on."

The agents sprang back to their feet and continued firing on the fast retreating vehicle.

The ancient cobbled streets were narrow in this part of the city, hard to negotiate when driving at top speed. Pedestrians would use them as sidewalks during the day and at night transients would crisscross periodically under the lamplights.

Kurt slowed down and the Gestapo was closer than ever. He could hear them behind them, and suddenly a bullet penetrated the windshield to his left. He tried to accelerate through an alley way. Row upon row of apartments lined the street. He felt his back soaked with sweat as he gripped the steering wheel firmly, constantly checking the rearview mirror.

Jacqueline looked behind them as well and frantically exclaimed, "They're gaining on us!"

Kurt didn't bother to reply; he had thought of something. Below his seat protruded an empty bottle of schnapps. He rolled down his window, and tossed it. She seemed puzzled. A moment later the Gestapo car turned the bend and as Kurt sped away the German's car was rocked by an explosion. Their front tires had erupted running over the broken glass. The driver had lost control and slammed into a street lamp.

It was close. Kurt braked to a halt; the roadway split in two. Jacqueline saw his hesitation and told him, "Go left. The right side only leads back into the city."

The wheels skidded as he accelerated. He held the wheel forcefully, spun out of the slide, and headed up the street. He was driving for the top of a hill. She knew the area quite well, but neither could guess where the Gestapo would turn up next.

When they reached the top he parked the Mercedes and turned off the engine. He could see cars plainly now, coming and going, and they had time to plan an escape. "Where exactly are we now?"

"Five minutes from the train station," she said, "but it will be watched."

"I know." His hand slid down the steering wheel, his fingers tapping it as they went.

"There's also the forest, and the river."

"River?" his eyes lit up. "How far?"

"A kilometer, maybe two."

"And how far does it go?"

"That I don't know, but it stretches through all of Bavaria and beyond."

They could see an oncoming Gestapo car driving in the street below. The vehicle was moving slowly, searching.

All of a sudden she smiled and laughed uncontrollably. "What's so funny?" he said.

"Well, who would have thought the two of us would wind up here like this, being chased all over Bavaria by the Nazis over some idiotic maps that turned out to be fakes."

He smiled and stroked her cheek. They moved closer, his lips near hers. "God, I love you," he said. She kissed him, aglow in the light, running her hand through his slick, black hair. For the next moment they embraced, remembering the night of passion that they shared at the SOE training center.

"Why do men have to fight and kill," she said. "Why can't they spend their time making love instead, like we are."

"Maybe it's because they don't have you, my dear."

The sound of an automobile brought them back to reality. Just behind them, at the base of the hill, were the Gestapo. Kurt turned on the engine but it wouldn't turn over. He tried again and again, and still nothing.

"Get out," he said.

The Germans drove up the street, checking each alley and parked car as they went. Kurt led her along the steps of a house and told her to wait by the entrance. It was nice and dark and she would be out of sight. He crept up to the Mercedes and turned the steering wheel, releasing the hand brake. The vehicle started to roll and picked up speed as it headed directly for the Gestapo car below, which swerved to avoid it, but too late. In the collision the Gestapo car overturned, and the Mercedes came to rest across the road, blocking it.

"We don't have much time," he said. "Show me where the river is."

They ran down the steps. He clutched the Schmeisser in one hand and told her his plan as they went. "We should make it to Holland tomorrow by nightfall, that's if we can slip away unnoticed down the river and somehow find a car once we are out of Bavaria. I just hope the weather holds out." The sloping mountain peaks in the distance were silhouetted against the clear night sky. There were no signs of the Gestapo now and they started walking. They still had quite a distance to go. "So you lied about having a sister," he said.

"I did not. I lied about her being in London."

"You honestly believed you could help me?"

"Yes, of course. That was my intent. I don't trust SOE any better than I do the Gestapo, not when it comes to these matters. I worked with a man last year in France. British Intelligence promised him political asylum in exchange for industrial secrets. As soon as he provided them, they washed their hands of the whole thing. He was picked up by the Gestapo and shot."

"So why did you go to work for them?"

"The lesser of two evils. As long as we fight the Nazis I serve British Intelligence."

A little further they came to a street crossing. Several cars rolled by in different directions. "Act natural," he said. "And don't look so nervous."

As they crossed, a car's headlights shined on them brightly. He held his machine pistol tightly at his side, away from view. As they walked the last block they came to the outskirts of the city. She marveled at the thickness of the woods ahead. She noticed the clock tower further up and pointed the way. "We go over there now."

The wind had picked up, howling through the trees. "I need to rest," she said. "My legs are tired." They came up to a tree stump by some bushes. As he led her, he looked the ground over carefully. The terrain had a particular shine that flickered in places. Small stones of all colors lay scattered on the damp ground below.

He scooped up a handful. "I use to collect these kinds of stones back home when I was a child."

"I've always picked the red ones myself. They were the most charming and had white veins running through them, which gave them the look of marble." As she sat down he kept an apprehensive watch on the surroundings. "Now that feels good," she exclaimed as she stretched her legs out.

"How much further?" he said.

"Not too far. The river should be a few minutes from here, that's all." He came up behind her and caressed her. She held his arm across her bosom. "All those people," she sighed.

"What, dear?" He listened intently.

"The sacrifice of the war," she said. "Claudia and the others, and to still fall short."

He shook his head. "No, not so. We still can turn this around. I need to contact Ian and make sure London doesn't fall for the hoax. If the Germans think we're dead, they would never suspect."

"Dead?" she asked.

"It doesn't really guarantee anything, but it might work to the British advantage if the Nazi high command thought SOE was duped to expecting a fake mission."

"And how do we accomplish that?"

Just then oncoming headlights appeared. He hustled her off and hid her behind a tree. They observed a Gestapo unit with SS troops marching into the woods not more than fifty yards away. The Germans in the car disembarked.

"What do we do?" she whispered.

"Take me to the river now."

The SS pushed onward through the woods, guns drawn at the ready, their search lights slicing through the dark. Kurt and Jacqueline ran feverishly through the trees. Soon they could both hear the sound of the river churning below.

They stopped, and ahead of them was an old stone bridge, but at the end it was blocked by a fallen tree. He stepped closer and saw the onrush of water as it passed below him. He searched frantically for a way out. There on the side near Jacqueline he spotted a half-covered trail and that zigzagged down the incline to the base of the river.

She ran to him, struggling to contain her fears. "They're getting closer."

He held her by the shoulders. "You must go down by the riverbank and wait for me. Under no circumstances must they hear you. Understand?"

"I don't want to leave you."

"Don't worry, just do as I say. No matter what happens, stay quiet. All right?"

She nodded.

"Go."

She made her way to the edge, scrambling down out of sight along the narrow ravine. She held the Schmeisser firmly in hand and looked up lovingly as he disappeared from view.

It became quiet. Then Kurt heard voices approaching close by.

He positioned himself in the middle of the bridge and waited. A few moments later he heard the breaking of branches. He turned, and a member of the Gestapo stood with Luger drawn in his black hat and uniform, his long field coat unbuttoned, a half dozen SS troops at either side of him.

"Well, well. Herr Duran I presume." His face exhibited a stern and loathsome stare. "That was quiet a walk. You must be tired."

"Nothing like some fresh air late at night, it works wonders," Kurt smiled sarcastically.

"In a manner of speaking," the German replied. "So then, Herr Duran, how is your lady friend?"

Kurt was silent, his eyes deepened, he frowned, shaking his head. "She's dead. Your men killed her."

"Is that so? Well, how is that we did not find her body?"

"There was a car wreck," he said. "We collided with one of your vehicles. I managed to jump out in time. She couldn't unfasten her seat belt."

The German looked at him crossly. "A pity," he said. "On the other hand, a quick death. I prefer a slower, more dramatic conclusion for you. Something with bravado. Lieutenant von Krositch ordered me to have you killed at any cost." There was a drawn-out silence as the German looked Kurt over. "So what does the condemned man want? A cigarette perhaps?"

"Why not," Duran replied. "Just out of curiosity, when will England be invaded."

He took out a cigarette and matches, lit the cigarette, and handed it to Duran. "Sooner than you would expect."

Duran spotted a noose hanging over a branch. Two Germans secured the rope at the base of the tree.

"What do you think, Herr Duran? Won't this be a fitting end to a dirty old spy, dangling from the willows like a white flag. I think it rather fitting."

Duran looked dejected, lowered his cigarette and said, "I must disagree."

The Gestapo agent glanced at the noose and back. "How so?"

Duran tossed the burning cigarette on to the bridge and stepped forward on it, arms at his side. As the SS men approached Duran spun around, his hands extended out and he leaped over the stone bridge, plunging head first into the water.

From below Jacqueline watched as his body fell, dove into the rushing river and vanished. She was stunned, but dared not cry out.

The Gestapo ran up to the side of the bridge and stared down. He shook his head.

The SS cleared out. Jacqueline lowered her gun and sat on the riverbank directly below the bridge. She started to cry, covering her face with her hands as she sobbed. After a moment she looked up, tears streaming down her face, when she saw bubbles churning in front of her in the water. He surfaced, taking in huge gulps of air as he swam up to her and spread out on the rocks.

She gasped and smiled. "You're alive!"

"Barely," he replied.

"But how?"

"I held onto the rocks along the riverbed."

"You bastard. I almost died watching you fall."

"Now that would have been foolish," he replied. He stood. "Let's get a move on."

Chapter Fourteen

It had been over an hour since they had pirated the fishing boat they spotted docked near a cabin at the river bend. With a simple motor in the rear, the wooden boat kept reasonably good time. The river itself grew more unpredictable the further they went, until finally they hit the rapids.

"Bad sign," Kurt muttered.

"What's wrong?" Jacqueline asked, her eyes frantically searching the space around them.

"When you get rapids, waterfalls sometimes follow." He made an all-out effort to cross the river onto the bank on the other end. When they reached it he cut the engine. "Quiet," he said. There were sounds; he could hear automobiles in the distance.

He helped her out of the boat, and they hastily made their way below the cover of tree branches that populated the hillside. They didn't stop until they reached the spine of the rocks that ran along the crest of the hill. There he pushed her down and dove on top of her. "Don't move," he said.

Seconds later, a German truck filled with storm troopers came by, followed by a motorcade. Once they had passed, they both stood. "I hope that was necessary," she said. "My clothes are ruined now."

They had reached a small town fifty miles north of Riems in France. Holland was just a few hours away. There was a hotel across the street and a nightclub next to it.

They strolled to the club and Duran whispered, "The last thing we need is attention. We'll simply go in, order a couple of drinks, then leave. Someone will have a car parked around and I'll do it a bit of mingling and we'll be on our way."

Couples kissed and cuddled throughout the place. The war seemed irrelevant to them there. Taking an inconspicuous table in the corner, Duran ordered two glasses of red wine. In a breathtaking display of vigor one couple danced to an enthralled audience at the side of the club. The other side was reserved for dining, food and drink. There was no sign of any Germans, no SS or Gestapo for that matter.

Kurt's presence on the other hand, in the full Nazi uniform, a wet, dirty uniform at that, brought no more than a passing glance from uninterested onlookers. Everyone was too busy with love, wine, dancing and song. The merrymaking was contagious as Kurt saw Jacqueline smile enthusiastically and ease into her chair with a sudden relish, observing the festivities.

As the young lady brought the drinks Jacqueline glanced down, her voice becoming introspective. "Those men we left are very dangerous, they won't give up unless they're sure we're dead."

Kurt was taken aback. "Relax," he said, "we're free. Just one more step and we're in London. I think I covered things with those butchers. There could be no doubt in anyone's mind."

"I hope you're right." She tasted the wine. "It's a bit too sweet, don't you think?"

"The wine is all right, but you've got to lighten up. It's been a long night, and it's going to get longer. I'd best find us a ride."

The following day at midmorning, on Thursday, August 15, Oberst Paul Deichmann, the chief of staff, looked out from the second story window of a farmhouse at Bonninques, near Calais, which was Second Flying Corps headquarters. He saw blue skies and golden sunshine. The wind was zephyr-calm. Its direction was west-northwest at little more than two miles an hour, and clouds were negligible, a scattered front around three thousand feet. It was ideal weather for Eagle Day.

Sorties were in fact part of a complex blueprint applicable for any time the weather held fair. This was the case in airfields all down the coast. Deichmann knew that more than eight hundred bombers and one thousand fighters of the Second Flying Corps were scheduled to lead the attack and were already fueled up and alert for takeoff once the signal was given.

Reaching for his phone Deichmann gave firm orders. One dozen Stukas under Hauptmann von Brauchitsch, airborne from Tramecourt, were to form the spearhead of the attack, bound for Hawkinge. Then two dozen more under Hauptmann Keil, loaded with 500-kilo and 250-kilo bombs destined for Lympne. Twenty-five Dorniers of Obest Chamier-Glisczinski's Third Bomber Group were to attack Eastchurch and another wing of the same group were bound for Rochester Airfield. Here they would use both delayed action and incendiaries. Rubensdörffer's Test Group 210 would slug away against Marhesham Heath on the Suffolk coast. With his orders acknowledged, Deichmann hung up.

He had his aide drive him to the Holy Mountain, a nickname for Kesselering's bomb group underground headquarters at Cap Blanc Nez. Kesselering had in fact installed himself there long before the battle was to commence, along with fourteen officers who manned a battery of telephones. Resolved on checking the success or failure of each and every plane that took off, Kesselering was an astute perfectionist and was driving himself as well as his entire staff beyond the level of endurance. Everything was confined to this dugout and when Deichmann arrived the interior was gloomy, lit only by a flickering oil lamp, so that Deichmann had to strain just to see Major Hans-Jürgen Rieckhoff, Kesselering's operations officer.

"Herr Oberst," Rieckhoff said, "welcome. I trust you had a pleasant trip."

"Very. It was the first time I had a chance to relax in weeks." Together the two men made their way up the rough-hewn steps to Kesslering's private lookout post, which was a sandbagged, chest-high parapet that jutted from the Channel cliffs. They stood in silence, hands pressed over their ears, as planes roared overhead—wave upon wave of black, hump-winged Stukas and silver shark-nosed 109's.

Twenty-seven miles away at Dunlop Farm in Hawkinge, John Wingate was in the field with his tractor. George Koolidge was repairing a broken fence when out of the sky came a strange, high-pitched whining followed by the snarl of engines. Without further warning the Stukas of Hauptmann von Brauchitsch's 4th Wing Lehreqeschwader 1 fell down from the skies like screaming phantoms. The picturesque, sunbathed farm became a nightmare of devilish fury. From the high-pitched screams of the diving Stukas to the metallic panging of the airfield's Bofor guns, as well as the pandemonium of exploding hangars as bombers made their marks.

The farmers felt totally exposed standing in the center of a ten acre field. They abandoned their tools and ran like madmen to the distant shelter of an elm grove. They had just witnessed the first vicious bomb attack of Eagle Day proper. Between then and eight p.m. that evening over two thousand German planes of all types would be unleashed in a massive driving effort to bring the RAF in the air to meet them, and smash fighter command totally.

They arrived in Amsterdam by the grace of God and good luck in a vintage roadster. Kurt had persuaded a disillusioned and drunken aristocrat to loan him his form of transportation the night before. Jacqueline slept like a child in the passenger seat while they headed for the house of his friend, Charles von Krongt. She started to come around as they passed a street vendor who cursed vehemently at a woman who was pinching his produce.

"Did you sleep well," he asked.

"Oh my, I think my neck is broken." She sat up and twisted her head from side to side.

"At least we didn't have to walk." As he spoke he spotted the street von Krongt lived on and made a sharp left. Half a block up and they were inside.

"Well, well, it's been so long. What are you doing in that getup?" von Krongt hugged Kurt with both arms. He stood back in awe. "And who is this charming creature?"

"My fiancée," he said.

"Congratulations, my boy. Please sit down and let me get you something to drink."

As he prepared some Dutch coffee Kurt said softly to Jacqueline, "He is a very good man. He'll get us out of the country, if anyone can be sure." She held his arm securely as they reclined on the sofa.

Charles placed the coffee on a small marble table in front of them. "Drink up. You sounded as if you lost your head last night. So tell me, how can I be of service?"

"I trust you with my life, Charles, you know that, that's why we're here. I haven't much time to explain except to say that the Gestapo is on to us. I've been on a special mission that has gone astray. Thus my attire." He took in a deep breath. "We'll be dead soon if you don't get us out of the country and back to England."

"My God, you are in trouble, aren't you?" He brushed the fine whiskers of his gray beard, his droopy eyes looked affectionately at the two of them sitting there. "It's within my power to try. I have a little bit of time to make some phone calls. Would tonight be soon enough for you?"

"Perfect."

"Why don't you both make yourselves at home. I'll be back in a bit."

As he exited the room Jacqueline looked around the place in awe. "What did you say he did for a living?"

"He's an antique dealer, the best in Amsterdam."

She smiled delightfully. "I can see why. Is that a real Louis XVI vase?"

"I would imagine so, he doesn't deal with imitations."

The whole room was in fact a sprawling showcase studded with exquisite antique furniture, rugs, oil paintings, candelabras, sofas, and more. There was a jewelry case in the corner and silverware displayed in red boxes along the tabletops. Before the pandemonium of occupation he'd had a thriving business.

"Now," von Krongt said as he reentered the room, "only high-stepping Nazis show up here. It's a miracle they hadn't looted me out of business."

"They actually pay you? Are you not in danger staying here?" she said.

"My dear, I have specialty items only I know where to get. They understand this. So instead of robbing me once, they come back every so often as I get new things in, and they just help themselves. As long as my family and I are still alive that's all that matters."

"Speaking of specialty items, I need to use your radio right away," Kurt said.

"I'm sorry to say I cannot oblige you. The radio was knocked out during a Stukas air strike to crush local resistance. My boys are bringing in new parts tonight. You're welcome to try after they fix it. In the meantime I suggest you both have something to eat. The skin on your bones looks tighter than a drum."

It was almost noon and his wife was preparing lunch in the kitchen. "Grab two more plates, we're having company," he called out from across the room. As he turned around he noticed his wife had already come in and took notice.

"I see, and who might you be?"

Her husband held up a hand. "Oh now, Agatha, they're my friends. You remember Kurt Duran, I told you about him, and he's brought his fiancée."

"How charming, a pleasure to meet you both." His wife was a woman of sixty, white hair neatly combed behind her head, held into place by hairpins, simple country attire with a white apron over her dress. Her hands were those of a worker, coarse and stubby, and her face revealed many years of toil. She outstretched her arms and smiled. "Welcome to our home."

Jacqueline came up and hugged her gently. "Thank you so much, Mrs. von Krongt."

Kurt stepped up. "You're too kind."

"You know," she said, "I try, but then you see I have six children and eighteen grandchildren and they all love their grandmother, so I get lots of practice." As he held her he saw her eyes well up. "I'm sorry, but you remind me so much of one of my boys. He was also young and handsome..." She hadn't the strength to continue. She excused herself.

"Is she all right?" Kurt said.

Von Krongt nodded. "Ah, Mama will be fine. She just worries about the boys, you know."

Kurt stepped forward. "I need to get to a radio to contact London. It's of vital importance."

The old man shrugged. "I would like to oblige, but as I say the radio I have upstairs is knocked out. My boys are due in tonight, I assure you, with new parts. You're free to try at that time."

Kurt nodded in compliance yet was visibly distraught. He had to call Ian, and fast. "Would you excuse me a bit, I need to step outside." As he opened the door the Gestapo drove past. The car stopped a moment as if searching. Kurt moved to close the door.

"Best you stay inside until tonight," the old man warned.

At three p.m. London Standard Time, Churchill had boarded his private airplane to be flown to Edinburgh for a secret conference. President Roosevelt had sent three senior staff officers as personal representatives of the United States. The U.S. was still officially neutral but began to view the erupting conflict with increased concern as the air war continued to engulf the British Isles. Roosevelt knew that if England fell, nothing would stand in Hitler's way.

The day before Churchill had given a speech in the House of Commons with typical tenacity; his oratory was well received. His praise of the airmen who rose to meet the challenge of the Nazi juggernaut was poignant and precise. "In the four days of intense air attacks between the 10th and 14th of August, Hitler failed to achieve his one condition for invasion," he said passionately, "which was to break England's air power."

On August 15th Churchill was astutely entertaining various possibilities that his guests, who were all staying with him at an undisclosed location outside of Edinburgh, could review. In the guise of being there on a relatively low-grade mission to discuss the standardization of arms, those three officers, Admiral

Ghormley, Brigadier General Strong and General Emmons, were in fact engaged in the first staff conversations between the United States and Britain. Churchill was adamant about the U.S. sharing intelligence, as well as realizing that the common good of both nations were interwoven in military matters.

As the Battle of Britain was being waged in the skies over England, Churchill received reports. On August 15th after careful scrutiny of the German air force messages decoded by the Enigma machine, the combined forces of the Intelligence Community gave as their view to the prime minister that no final decision for the planned invasion of England would be taken by the German high command. They based their opinion solely on the results of the existing struggle for air superiority.

Crowded into the small room at the end of the hallway, Churchill was studiously puffing on his cigar when during the course of the conversation Admiral Ghormley said, "We would like to negotiate a possible release to Britain of a total of fifty American destroyers." As he read his papers he strained his eyes over the type. The admiral put on his reading glasses and continued.

When he had finished reading, Churchill smacked his cigar, pushed his own reading glasses up to the bridge of his nose. The other men in the room looked on patiently as Churchill sat back in the upholstered armchair, his feet stuck out beneath his rotund self. He lamented over his country's predicament, its future.

"Gentlemen, it's good of you to come." He eased into his chair a bit more. "Let me share with you my concerns," his manner of speech was cordial, his voice low-key. He eyed the men before him. "Several nights ago a German air raid was launched against British aerodromes throughout southern England, and fortunately for us the first time, all but one of the German formations were forced back by our fighters. The next day, some of our boys who were reading the German air force messages concluded, with a certain degree of confidence, that upon the success of this operation would depend the future decision as to the actual invasion itself. Not only the feasibility but whether in fact it would take place at all."

The admiral cleared his throat. "Sir, would you concede then that the RAF had broken the Luftwaffe?"

Churchill paused a moment, removed his cigar and replaced it on the rim of his ashtray. He started to take some papers out from his briefcase. "These reports, gentlemen, are not from British Intelligence. They are from a man I highly admire. He commutes to London by military aircraft for my regular meetings with him. He has a close circle of agents in his secret operations and his name is Intrepid." He removed the papers and placed them on his lap. "Just three days ago a German bomber struck at a British armament factory. Due to some confusion caused by a low ceiling of clouds the bomber inadvertently flew off course and dropped its bombs on the city. What happened next was most astonishing," he said as he continued to read the report.

"The concentration of anti-aircraft fire was immense and yet strangely ineffective. Not a single plane was brought down. Not one was even picked up by the searchlights. This, gentlemen, you'll never hear in the official British Intelligence reports, nor what I'm about to add to it. Intrepid's spies have made a particular discovery." As Churchill spoke referring to some peculiar events taking place in his native England that same day Kurt still waited along with Jacqueline for Charles' sons to come through with the spare radio parts. It was quite debilitating all in all and their patience was in fact wearing quite thin. Churchill had gone on in length to describe the events of the day. It seemed that England was assaulted. A total of fifty-eight empty parachutes were found in various parts of the country, principally the Midlands and also the Scottish lowlands. "But that's not all."

There was a hush in the room as he continued. "There were also uncovered maps, wireless transmitters, along with a list of addresses of various prominent people. The admiral gasped, but Churchill ignored him. "I've offered a reward for the capture of these parachuters. Much to my displeasure I must concede that British Intelligence has been duped by German propaganda. The alleged Enigma messages were deciphered too easily and I think I should tell you gentlemen, England is in a very grave situation indeed."

It was five o'clock in the afternoon when Ian Richards' Bentley drove up to SOE headquarters in London. His men had been processing the data obtained by Kurt Duran at Eagle's Nest. Hugh Hardwick sat next to him, studying the teletype sent from southern England. "Well I'd say they've softened us up pretty good." His eyes were wide and distant as he placed the report down. The car remained parked out front.

The teletype detailed the destructive power of the incoming Luftwaffe and the devastation they had left in their wake. It was not pleasant news. Next to Ian on the car seat lay a gas mask. There were two more in front. Reports of all types filtered in as to what London could expect next. The men hastily exited the vehicle and made their way up the front steps.

Once in the office of Strategic Affairs, Ian demanded to see the results of Operation Eagle's Nest. The lights were turned off as the men in the room observed on a projection screen numerous snapshots. They depicted various maps of England and close-ups of the coastal line, with dark arrows pointing to designated targets.

"My God," Ian said. "They're coming at us from both sides."

The room was abuzz with nervous tension. The maps revealed a massive contingency force from the continent of Europe to strike at England at the farthest reaches of the Isle, both north and south, splitting her right in two. Ian shook his head. "Defensively speaking, very bad indeed."

Churchill drew in his cigar and exhaled a mountain of smoke. After a solemn moment he went into a cascade of dialogue with his American guests. "Gentlemen, I have another issue of vital importance to discuss." He in fact was trying to cement a long held goal. The deal for the destroyers marked just another step forward. He was now negotiating a merger of intelligence work. He had heard of an ingenious undercover agent by the name of Rolin Jacobs who worked for President Roosevelt. Stephenson had created a police force to safeguard cargoes of supplies and arms that were under constant U-boat attack. Convoys had been betrayed by German agents in U.S. ports. But Churchill wanted more help from U.S. radar detection stations to hunt enemy submarines.

The admiral explained that fifty destroyers presented a difficult problem. And Churchill was unwilling to acknowledge the constitutional difficulties involved in handing them over, and kept up an unrelenting pressure. "In the event of a Nazi conquest I cannot tell what policy might be developed by a pro-German administration, such as would be undoubtedly set up." He said this to underscore what would happen if the British Navy were in fact captured. "The British fleet," he said, "would be the sole remaining bargaining counter with the Germans." He wanted to strengthen his cause by arguing that the fifty American destroyers would in fact enable the British Navy to prevent any such capitalization from occurring.

"Three British destroyers were badly damaged recently," the prime minister looked them over with calm reserve. "The situation, gentlemen, is growing desperate. German invasion troops have assembled in the newly captured ports. They subsequently have amassed every kind of ship and small craft available. Thus I put to you my plea. The urgent need for destroyers to combat invasion is paramount."

"And what type of payment is England ready to make?" said Brigadier Strong."

Churchill scowled, "Britain's resources of gold and dollars are nearly exhausted. One third of British Army's budget went to purchase a single type of special American shell. All I could offer is your fleet's use of our bases in the Caribbean and Western Atlantic."

He sank deeper in his chair. "In the previous two weeks," he said grimly, "England has lost over one hundred and forty thousand tons of ships. That, along with twenty percent of the total British fighter aircraft strength, which has been destroyed in battle."

"So," the admiral said slowly, "these old four-funnel destroyers, ill-equipped as they are for modern fleet action, would help cut down the losses?"

Churchill sprang to life. "Yes. They would. And they could be used to escort cargoes of new aircraft now being dispatched through Canada."

In his closing arguments, Churchill concluded that the RAF, even though offering a noble defense, was not capable of making best use of its most secret weapon which of course was radar. "Part of our coastal battery stations have been out of commission during the course of the first day of the new German attack." His voice dropped.

"Our intelligence recovery of German attack orders was neither swift nor complete enough for our fighter pilots to be sure how to handle the new threat."

All three men listened intently. Admiral Ghromley said, "Mr. Prime Minister, President Roosevelt has expressed his deepest concern for the British Commonwealth. We will stress to him the importance of the destroyers. He also has suggested that you may be interested in establishing a base of operations in the United States for your secret intelligence agencies and uncover operations."

Churchill nearly leaped out of his chair at the mere mention. "That's a marvelous idea, Admiral," he said. "One I would whole heartily like to pursue. Even in the event of a German occupation of the British Isles, England would contribute to the wars fought on by the existing secret armies. A central agency to bring together the manifold strands—let's say New York, gentlemen, for the sake of argument. On neutral soil so no threats of aggravation by the enemy or bombing."

Churchill beamed in delight. "Why, yes, experts could realistically tackle any host of problems in relative calm and their findings be dispatched to London. Yes, gentlemen I think this would be a most enjoyable alliance."

Chapter Fifteen

Kurt Duran stood by the curtain-strung window with a look of impatience on his face. It was seven fifteen in the evening and there was no sign of the old man. Jacqueline was anything but calm as she finished off a second cup of coffee. "When are they coming?" she asked.

"Any time now." He checked his watch.

Her voice sharpened. "And when do we leave?"

"Your guess is as good as mine."

Out of nowhere came a company of German soldiers briskly marching down the street. Von Krongt's wife came out from the kitchen. "Those swine on parade again," she said in disgust.

"And where do they go?" Kurt asked.

"The docks."

"Really. Why so many?"

"Mrs. von Krongt mentioned something about ships coming in tonight. "I suppose it has something to do with that."

Kurt's face was quickly suffused with passion. "And how long has this been taking place?" he asked.

"Can't say for sure but a week at least." She picked up Jacqueline's empty coffee cup and offered more.

"No thank you, I've had my share. Perhaps Kurt would like some."

But he was transfixed, staring at the columns of Nazis marching past. Mrs. von Krongt walked up to him and said, "Please, don't worry, Papa will be back soon. Then you can go to England."

He turned and thanked her graciously. As Mrs. von Krongt left the room Jacqueline got to her feet wild-eyed.

"Those soldiers out there, it's not good."

"Not much I can do about it."

Without notice Charles pulled up and came in through the front door. "Hello again." He smiled enthusiastically as a tall man with simple features stepped in behind him. "We will be leaving soon. Close the door." He placed his coat at the end of the couch. He held firmly a small bag. "This, my boy, is for the radio. My son Albert will fix it momentarily, and you can call London."

The tall man took the bag and left the room. The old man sat down in his wing chair, letting out a deep sigh of relief. "Well, when do we leave?" Kurt said.

"That is a question for the captain. You will be driven to an inlet half a mile outside the city. But it will have to be between ten o'clock and eleven, and no later. SS patrol the area after midnight, it's not safe out there.

"This is very kind of you. We greatly appreciate it. If there is anything I can do for you..."

The old man looked up pleasantly. "As a matter of fact there is. Pour me some brandy and help yourself."

Jacqueline was incensed. "Don't you men have anything better to do?"

Kurt distributed the drinks.

"We'll be leaving soon," he said. "Calm down."

"I'm sorry," she said. Her complexion was pale.

"Your apology is accepted," Kurt replied. "Now take a swig of this."

She cupped the glass in both hands and began to sip.

Halfway through he stopped her. "Not too much."

She giggled. "You're right. Here, have some. I don't know what's wrong with me, I haven't been myself lately."

Charles smiled. "I don't blame you." Jacqueline struggled to keep a handle on her emotions. All those sordid hours in a dark cell with those brutish men and what they did were all catching up with her. When it finally came to her what she had gone through, the humiliation, the abuse, both physical and psychological, the sheer cruelty of it, she couldn't believe it. She felt like exploding a million different ways all at once. She knew quite well that would be useless now, and not here, not in front of the man who was responsible for her rescue. She wanted revenge. Still, a feeling of total helplessness enveloped her.

"You can't pretend to be indifferent about what you went through," Kurt said in a soft, loving voice. Putting his glass down he reached out and held her hand.

Jacqueline observed his kind face. "I'm not trying to," she said. "My only wish is that the culprits in this war be punished."

"They will be, my dear, they will." He couldn't be more reassuring, more noble and determined. He meant what he said and she knew it.

He poured himself a half glass of Scotch. He took it firmly in hand, tilted his head back and let it splash down his throat. He turned and glared broodingly out through the window. More Germans could be seen passing in the street.

The old man got his attention by asking, "And when you get back, what will you do?"

They both turned around. "Keep fighting," Kurt said.

Jacqueline smiled at his reply.

The old man nodded. "It will be a while longer before you can use the radio. Would either of you care for anything?"

"No, nothing, thank you," Jacqueline said politely. "I'm not particularly hungry. She turned to Kurt. "I could do with some fresh air."

"Have you a back door?"

"Certainly," said Charles. "It leads to a small garden between the buildings. You will be perfectly safe there." He escorted them to the door and Kurt pulled out a cigarette and took a glimpse outside. It was a quaint little garden with concrete benches and a grassy area in the middle with flower beds growing around the walkway. The old man closed the door behind them.

She sighed. "My God, I think I'm going mad."

"No, not now, just tired," he said. "You've got to detach yourself from the day's events. You've got to put it out of your mind, as difficult as it might be." He handed her a cigarette, reaching over and lighting it for her.

She exhaled a silvery cloud of smoke that drifted away in the breeze. She sat on the bench and crossed her legs.

"Hitler is a madman," he said. "He is bound to lose the war, it is all a matter of time."

"And in the meantime good people get killed."

He lowered his smoke. "You know *Mein Kampf*?"

"Who doesn't know?"

"Yes, exactly. In it he wrote of the need to expand eastward."

"So that would be Russia."

"Yes, after England he plans an attack on Russia and that, my dear, will be the end of him."

"And in the meantime?"

"In the meantime I need to get you to England where it's safe. To my house in the country. I've seldom used it over the past few years but it would be the perfect place for us, out by the Shetfield coast, far away from the bombing."

She rolled her eyes. "Oh, Kurt, you don't mean we just stay there?"

He let out a slight laugh. "And you're serious about returning to fight? Look at you. Think about what you are saying. Do you love me?"

"What's that got to do with it?"

"Just answer the damn question."

"Yes, of course I do."

"Then prove it," he said. "Stay at my house in Shetfield until this bloody nightmare ends. I've lost enough loved ones to war, I don't want you becoming another statistic."

She discarded her cigarette, tossing the burning butt onto the gravel pavement. She gazed at him admiringly. "God knows I love you, never think otherwise. When we get back I will do as you ask."

He stood up and approached her, his hands outstretched. She rose to meet him and they embraced. He held her tightly in his arms and they kissed. He felt his lips against hers, the warmth of her body, the softness of her face. She whispered in his ear, "Thank you for everything."

His heart filled with delight.

Upstairs, Charles' son negotiated gingerly working on the radio in the dimly lit room. The transmitter sat on a small wooden table that was chipped in places and cracked in others. The table was covered by a dull green tablecloth in the middle, and on it lay various radio parts and tools. The old man stood next to him overseeing the work. He looked out the attic window and in the distance he could see Kurt passing the walkway as Jacqueline lit up another cigarette. It was a full twenty minutes since they had gone outside. Charles called from the third story window.

"All right, young man, all yours."

The couple stepped back inside and headed toward the staircase. Von Krongt's son stood by and gestured them to the open door, leading a way up a narrow staircase. It was dark inside and Jacqueline asked Kurt to hold her hand as they went. She grunted as her face caught in a spider's web. "Careful dear," Kurt said, "we're almost there."

Upon entering the attic, they felt as if they had been magically transported in time to an era two centuries ago. Everything was 17th century—clocks, hand-painted porcelain, fine upholstered chairs, small marble tables, and a number of bookcases filled to capacity with rare volumes. The air was bad and Jacqueline started to feel poorly. She found a stool by the open window and breathed in some night air.

"All right, let's get started." Kurt looked over the dials and switches and Charles gave him a quick run-through. He finally started to transmit. He removed the headset as the booming static painfully intruded on his eardrums. "Good God! Are your wires crossed?"

Charles sighed. "It should have worked fine," he said. He took the headset and listened in as the crackling noise resonated through the lines. He flipped a couple of dials but it still crackled. "Here, let's move in closer to the window."

Jacqueline got out of their way as they gently placed it by the window sill.

Again, there was nothing but static. "Do you realize how important this is?" Kurt said to von Krongt.

"My boy, I give you my word this is the only transmitter in the city you can possibly use tonight."

Kurt checked the back panel. "No wonder." He found the wiring was placed incorrectly. He took a knife off the table and carefully began to reset the wires. The old man looked on nervously as Jacqueline shook her head in disbelief. Charles' son grew red in the face but said nothing. Kurt in turn without looking at him said outloud, "I've almost got it," he said. "There, that should do it." He put the knife aside and positioned himself again to try transmitting. He found he could hear the calm of a clear line. "Bay Station, come in, please."

There was nothing but silence. In a more aggressive tone of voice he said, "Bay Station, do you hear me, come in." Exasperated, he stopped momentarily. He stared at his friend. "What's wrong with this thing?"

"I don't know. It normally takes a moment to get going. Give it another try."

"No," Kurt said.

"No?" Jacqueline said anxiously.

"No," Kurt said. He took off his headset and stood up. "My primary concern now is to get you safely back to England."

She stood and shook her head slowly. "Charles here will take you to the submarine just outside the city," he said. "I'll stay on and keep trying to transmit. I'm bound to get through sooner or later."

"I won't leave without you," she said, her lips trembling.

"Remember what we talked about," he said.

"Prove that to me, that you love me unconditionally, as much as I love you."

"Do as I ask, this once."

"What difference can a few hours make?" she asked.

"If you were to tell SOE in person once we landed in England, would that change everything so dramatically?"

He paused a moment, looked over at von Krongt and back to Jacqueline. He placed the headset on the table. "You are absolutely right. Let's get out of here while we can." She smiled and kissed him.

Kurt told Charles to ready the transportation. Meanwhile, downstairs von Krongt's son was finishing up a phone conversation. The old man came down the steps. "All set. We leave now."

"Yes, father, the car will be here momentarily."

"What about the curfew?" Kurt asked.

"That's for non-Germans. We took care of things."

Jacqueline grew apprehensive and held on to Kurt's arm tightly as a car drove up outside. It was the Gestapo. There was a thunderous knock at the front door. Charles stepped over lively and opened it. "Good evening, come in."

Kurt and Jacqueline were both stunned by the presence of a tall man dressed all in black with a long leather coat—full fascist attire. "You need a ride tonight to that submarine?" he asked.

Kurt smiled. "Indeed we do." The man was a tad past fifty with graying hair and sunken cheekbones. He had the air of an aristocrat and his demeanor was cool and aloof. He was one of theirs, and his name was Winthrop, an old respected family from Amsterdam.

"What if somebody stops us, what then?" Kurt said.

"No need to worry, there is a trap door in the back seat. Both of you will be in the trunk during the trip."

Kurt turned to von Krongt and extended his hand. "For everything you've done."

"My pleasure, my boy. Now say hello to Ian for me when you get back."

Charles stepped over to Jacqueline and kissed her hand. "Good-bye, madame. It has been a delight. I wish you and Kurt all the best."

Winthrop urged them to hurry. "This is a very risky time to be out." He exited first and opened the back door of the vehicle. He checked the streets to make sure the coast was indeed clear.

With the trap door open Kurt got in first, straining to find his way until he slid sideways into the rear of the trunk. "Quickly," he said, and Jacqueline followed. The side door closed, the engine started, and the vehicle drove off.

Loud enough to hear in the back, Winthrop said, "Whatever happens, stay quiet. They won't suspect anything as long as they don't hear anything."

It was cramped and difficult to do anything but breath. Kurt's knees started to give him problems.

"Are you all right?" he whispered.

"I suppose," she replied. She struggled to get her breath as there was barely enough air to sustain them. "Do you think we have a chance?"

"There is always a chance," he said. "Our only hope now is to get to SOE and to make sure no radical changes in defense were made." He started coughing. His throat was as dry as cardboard.

After what seemed like hours of driving, the car stopped and all was quiet outside. "What do you make of that?" she asked.

Kurt, with a light squeeze of her hand, told her to be still. He heard voices outside. He tried to spy out of the slit, but it was too dark to see anything clearly. For several more nerve-racking minutes, there was nothing. No engine sound, no voices, no car doors closing.

In an exasperated voice she said, "The least he could do is let us know what happened?"

The back door was pulled open. Winthrop slipped the escape panel out. "How are you holding up in there?" he asked.

"We're still here, more or less."

"It is time for you folks to get out."

Jacqueline lunged for the opening. "Did we make it?" she asked.

"No, not quite, half way there."

"Why, what's going on?" Kurt asked excitedly.

"SS. The woods are crawling with them. It seems some Resistance fighters are giving the German's problems. They are trying to flush them out. Hold on." He slid the door back to a mere crack.

Jacqueline became wearisome and wanted to get out. They made their way to a large tree some yards away and stayed quiet.

"More SS," she said. "This is all just a bad dream, isn't it?" she leaned into Kurt and grew silent.

The driver sat back behind the steering wheel when a flash of light streaked across his face. "Was ist los?" a voice demanded in the darkness.

"Ein moment," Winthrop said impassionately.

Searching his pocket he produced papers. The SS guard carefully read them over and returned them. "Danke schön."

Winthrop wasted no time in starting up the automobile. Kurt and Jacqueline were carefully concealed behind that tree not more than ten feet away. When the SS cleared out, they both ran back to the car and got into their hiding space.

Chapter Sixteen

Devout adherent of the monarchy though he was, Churchill was incapable of sharing King George VI's pleasure in the fact that England had no official allies, neither to court nor pamper. He hovered over a cup of black coffee in an old armchair in his bedroom reading a memo sent by Sir Stafford Cripps. It went to SOE and was decoded first before finally arriving for review by the prime minister, who knew that tensions between the U.S. and England still existed and that any great alliance was purely speculative.

He had placed too much optimism on his meeting with Roosevelt's representatives. They had not brought about the effects for which he had hoped. Progress was slow in coming, even his grand idea of a base of operations for British Intelligence was still only a dream. He felt a need to reach beyond the West and secure help from the East as well.

That afternoon he had hurriedly sent Cripps as ambassador to Moscow. A left wing politician, Cripps was a man with a strong sense of mission. Cripps met with Stalin as Molotov the Russian foreign minister looked on. Cripps was empowered by Churchill himself to appease the Russians by offering them British recognitions of the Balkans as the Russian sphere of influence, and to acknowledge Russian aspirations in the Dardanelles.

As Churchill read through the papers it was apparent that Stalin saw through Churchill's overt and sudden friendship and preferred to avoid any conflict with the Germans for as long as possible. Churchill knew that the United States was in no position to help either. It was, in fact, militarily weaker than Britain. America was heavily dependent on the French and British navies for her Atlantic defenses. Churchill was also familiar with the German assessment made the same year that America could not be ready for conflict until the following year, 1941 at the earliest. Churchill had reviewed reports from the British Embassy in Washington, D.C., which stated clearly that Congress had passed a bill providing that no material belonging to the United States government could be delivered to foreign forces unless the American chief of staff certified that it was surplus to requirements.

Sipping his coffee slowly, he closed his eyes and felt a terrible strain. Here was a juncture, an episode of the highest drama. Churchill worried about the possibility of American aid coming in for the British fleet and for the future of the French Navy. During the final days before the French armistice the British government had put all its pressure on the French to secure a binding guarantee that the French fleet, which was the forth largest in the world, would not fall into Italian or German hands. But a clause of the armistice agreement prescribed that the whole of the French fleet—except that part left free for safeguarding French colonial interests—should be collected in ports, disarmed and placed under Italian or German control.

There was a knock at his door. "Come in," he said as he lowered his cup, placing it on a nearby night table. He sat there glumly, dressed only in pajamas and robe.

"Prime Minister," his aide said nervously, "forgive me, but there is a call from SOE."

Churchill got up and hurriedly made his way to the phone in the other room. He was informed of Hitler's invasion plans. His eyes widened until they almost popped. He stood there in silence as he listened to the report. He reached for another of his cigars and with due patience he digested all the facts that were reported to him. He thanked the caller and placed the phone down.

Sitting in his mahogany chair he stared at the large globe on his desk.

Finally the coast was in sight. Winthrop pulled up next to an ancient tree for cover. Its thick branches sprawling out. He cut the engines, checked the surroundings, and rushed to the back to let out his cargo. Jacqueline leaned out first again and almost fell as she tried to walk. Her legs were cramped and Kurt came out to aid her.

"Dammit, if I ever do that again," she said under her breath.

"Where's the sub?" he asked.

Winthrop, who at that point was halfway down the roadway and looking into the murky distance, could see an English submarine in the surf, her great hull peaking out of the waves. Winthrop turned hurriedly and came back down. "It's here."

They went over the side and carefully worked their way down the incline until they reached the beach. There was a mist drifting across as they made their way through the sand. The captain of the sub stared through binoculars at the figures approaching. A moment later a launch was sent, heading for the shore, piloted by two armed crewmen.

"I need to catch my breath," she said, as they struggled through the thick, deep sand.

"We're almost there," Kurt checked his watched as he reached around her waist and helped Jacqueline up. They raced toward the oncoming boat. The launch landed.

"Welcome," said one of the crewmen. "Glad you made it all right. We must be off now. The Nazi U-boats will be out later."

"Do you have a radio I could use aboard the sub?" Kurt said. "It's vitally important."

The seaman looked stern. "I'm afraid not. We're operating under strict radio silence. The sea is crawling with Germans. I'm afraid that whatever it is will have to wait until we arrive back in England. Now let's get out of here."

As the crewman helped Jacqueline into the launch, machine pistols opened up from the cliffs. Two SS men fired long bursts and several volleys hit Winthrop in the back. He went down hard, his face buried in the sand. Jacqueline shrieked as more rounds found their way dangerously close to her, as well as Kurt, who dove into the gray mix of sand and seaweed at the water's edge.

"Come on, Kurt, hurry!" she called out frantically as the launch began to pull back into the cold sea. But the fire-power was too intense and he was pinned down between the volleys coming from the cliffs and the launch. The pilot of the launch accelerated toward the sub.

"My God! What are you doing?" she said. "You can't just leave him there. Turn back, quickly!"

"We have our orders, ma'am."

Kurt reached around Winthrop's lifeless body and pulled out his Luger. He rested his arm on the dead man's back, took careful aim and fired four quick bursts. One SS man fell off the cliff instantly, the other disappeared behind the rocks. The fighting had stopped. Kurt turned and looked at the sub, which was diving.

"I don't believe this," he said with exasperation, as he slammed his fist into the sand. "I don't bloody believe it." He took a spare clip from the dead man's belt and started running back up toward the cliffs. His legs felt as if they were weighted in cement as he struggled along the difficult terrain. Panting, he reached the base of the cliffs and frantically began his ascent.

As he neared the top he bent down. The peak was within reach and he was not sure if the second SS man was in fact dead. He stopped a moment to pick up a small stone and tossed it overhead into the brush. There was no sound, no reaction of any kind. He took his chance and stood up. Kurt was surprised; the SS man was dead, a bullet lodged in the side of his head. He raced back to the Gestapo car that was parked under the tree by the side of the road.

The mist started to blanket the countryside now, and as he eased himself behind the wheel he started up the engine. He realized he had only one choice now—to play out his hand all the way. The visibility was a nightmare. He remembered a few key landmarks along the route and hoped to retrace his steps back to von Krongt as quickly as possible.

Forty minutes later he pulled up a block away from Charles' house, parking in an alleyway. The lights were still on at the old man's place and not a soul stirred outside. He took in a deep breath, popped his car door open, the Luger wedged at his side, and he ran along the street staying close to the houses away from the streetlights. He reached von Krongt's door and knocked feverishly.

The old man answered. "My God, Kurt, you're still here? What happened?"

He stepped in, closing the door behind him. "I need to try your transmitter once again, please."

"Of course, you know the way."

Kurt climbed the steps in a daze. The darkened staircase ended at the attic door. Inside, all was as he left it.

He put on the headset and started transmitting to London. All he got was static. He tried again. Finally, there was an open line and he began to transmit.

Ten blocks away, a black Gestapo van was picking up the transmission signals. The van was equipped with a tracking device and there was a C-shaped aerial on top, twisting left to right in an effort to pinpoint the sender's location. "Ein moment," the tracker said. His eyes perked, straining and staring at his radar scope as he narrowed down the location. The captain in charge looked on in intense anticipation.

"Groble Street," the tracker said.

"Move out," the captain ordered the driver of the van.

Kurt kept up the transmission. Having sent the full message once already, he was asking for confirmation. The reply was coming in sketchy at best. It kept breaking up. The line started to develop excessive static and he wasn't able to make out if they had understood his message in full. Then outside the window he spotted the Gestapo van pulling up to von Krongt's. In a panic, he hurriedly put down the headset.

The Germans kicked down the front door. "Where is he?" the captain demanded.

"Who?" the old woman said.

Charles entered the room. "By what right do you invade our house?"

"By the orders of the state." He drew his Luger. "Now then, where is your transmitter?"

Von Krongt was silent.

"Speak, old man."

He said nothing.

The German fired a round that hit Charles in his upper shoulder. "Papa!" she cried. "What have you done to him? Leave us alone." She ran at the German, her fists flying until she was restrained.

The old man held his shoulder as the captain pressed the barrel of the gun against her head. "Now talk."

"All right. It is upstairs in the attic. Now leave her be."

The captain made a gesture as he lowered his gun. Five men stormed up the stairwell.

Upon entering the room they found the transmitter had been smashed and its wires pulled out. The window was half open. One of the men stuck his head out and saw a figure escaping along the rooftops. He fired several shots, but the figure kept running and finally disappeared.

"How could you?" Jacqueline exclaimed as she wiped a tear from her cheek. "How could you leave him there?"

The captain of the sub was stoic. He stared at her blankly. "We have our orders."

"I was right about you people all along," she said bitterly. "It doesn't make any difference what uniform you wear, German or British. Your kind would sell your own soul to the devil for the right price."

"If need be," he said. "Be quiet now, or I'll have you removed to your quarters. We must stay clear of Nazi sonar. Our objective now is to make it safely back to port."

The submarine propelled itself through the murky depths, when suddenly the pilot said to the captain, "A moment, sir, we are being tailed." Their radar had picked up a vessel heading full speed toward them, topside.

The captain studied the screen. "It must be a destroyer," he said. Depth charges exploded above. The sub shook profusely as it withstood the explosions. "Dive!" the captain ordered. Another depth charge went off. The sub was heading for the bottom.

Jacqueline could think of a thousand deaths more noble than dying in the claustrophobic confines of a submarine. There was panic running through the ranks as the crew of the *King George* braced themselves for a crash landing on the bottom of the sea. Another depth charge exploded farther away. They had distanced themselves. There was a huge thrashing motion as the sub jerked and finally settled on the sea floor.

The captain ordered total silence. "Let them think they got us."

"What are you planning to do?" Jacqueline asked.

"On saving our skins."

He ordered his men to get ready to launch Operation Decoy, a code name he used for tactical response. A leak sprang from the ceiling of the sub interior and water spread across the floor.

"Hurry!" the captain demanded as he eyed the leak. "We got only one chance now to make a clean escape," the captain told his crew as Jacqueline listed on. "In a few moments we will have one of our compartments flooded from structural damage. If the German's find us they'll blow us out of the water. If we stay down here much longer, we'll drown."

One of the crewmen ran in. "Captain, everything is loaded and sealed."

"Very good." The captain stepped up to the radar screen. The Germans were directly above them. He raised his right hand onto the torpedo release button, took in a deep breath, and momentarily closed his eyes.

The tube shot out its load and floated upward with an onrush of bubbles. The captain of the German destroyer looked on in the distance as the ocean simmered with an explosion of white foam, then sprang up uniforms, pieces of furniture and papers, all in plain sight, along with a stream of oil that covered the objects in a slick-black film.

The captain said nothing, just looked on. There was a wave of tension below as the crew of the *King George* waited. The captain continued to study his radar screen. Two rooms were already sealed up due to the flooding.

The destroyer made an about face and disappeared off screen. The captain breathed a sigh of relief. "That was a close one," he said.

"Too close," one of the crewmen added.

The captain gave the order. "Let's get moving. Full speed ahead." The sub lifted up and kept a low profile for the rest of the trip. It had sustained some damage but was not totally crippled.

Kurt took out his gun and fired back, hitting the German in the chest. His hand flew up over his heart. He gasped and tumbled off the side of the steep incline, falling along the shingled roof. From the window, another German opened up with his revolver. This time a bullet grazed Kurt's shoulder as he dropped down onto his stomach. His gun slipped out from under him and fell into the railing running the length of the roof. He tried to reach for it, but it was simply too far down. He heard voices in the background as the Germans started to carefully climb onto the roof after him.

He grimaced, sprang back up, and ran to the edge of the roof. There was a sheer drop down and behind him he saw four Germans approaching, firing sporadically. He took a step back and leaped off, arms and legs strained, trying to keep his balance. As he landed he rolled across the flat of the second roof. A bullet slammed into the wall behind him; he got up and ran. His heart was beating rapidly and he broke out into a cold sweat as he reached the edge of an attic. He peered around the corner of the roof and all was silent.

He moved along the edge, placing his hand on the side of the wall as he looked back. It was clear for the moment, so he raced with all his might and leaped across to the third roof. His arm felt as if it had splinted in two, but he ignored the pain and pressed on. He neared the edge of the roof and saw a balcony below. There was no time to try to outrun four determined men.

He slipped out over the edge and held himself aloft. As he started to ease down his left arm gave him tremendous discomfort and he slipped, then fell, and it was all over. In the stillness of the night he laid their motionless. His right leg moved slightly. He took in a deep breath, and another. He opened his eyes to see he had landed squarely on the balcony floor. He managed a slight smile.

He tried to open the window but it would not budge. There were no lights inside and it seemed the place was deserted. Two Gestapo men ran for the edge and he could hear them coming. He pressed his back against the window frame, arms at his side, standing as silently as he could. Overhead he saw one of the Germans jump onto the second rooftop, but he fell short and dangled for his life with one hand. The other man leaped across and tried to help him. Then he spotted Kurt on the balcony.

The distance between them was no more than ten feet. As he was pulling up his partner he raised his Luger and started to take aim. Kurt reached behind the back of his head and flung his throwing knife, hitting the German directly in the base of his throat. He in turn dropped his partner, who let out a horrific cry as he fell. The other German held his throat with both hands before he went over the side as well.

Kurt began to climb over the railing and made his way down to the street below, when the Gestapo car drove out, sticking its nose out from behind the corner directly underneath. He cringed in disbelief as he dangled in midair, his feet strained to reach the stone wall in front of him. He got a foothold and swung himself back up. Resting momentarily in the safety of the darkened landing, breathing heavily, he spied out the activity below. Germans swarmed the houses in their relentless search for him. People were awakened in their beds, and he saw lights coming on all around the neighborhood.

His only escape route now was up and over the next rooftop. The Gestapo chief below barked orders at his men.

"Find the swine, he must not get away."

Kurt shook his head, trying to come back to his senses. Every inch of his body ached. There were two remaining Germans on the roof somewhere, he thought to himself. He decided to climb up the fire escape and see how far they'd got. Silver light was pouring into the alley below him as the Gestapo officer wielding a flashlight began a close inspection of the grounds below.

Kurt made his ascent as quickly as he could, gripping the metal steps awkwardly. Just then he saw one of the Germans. "Damn it," he said under his breath. The metal fire escape creaked a bit, enough for the German to hear. He started to come to the edge of the roof. Kurt lunged up at him, and using both hands he snapped the German's neck. The lifeless body fell helplessly to the side. He climbed over and onto the roof. He took the dead man's gun, making his way toward the attic door. There was nothing but silence to greet him.

A moment later Kurt heard a voice below speaking in German. He was giving orders to the dozen SS men coming up the back staircase. As the German made his final ascent to the front door, it slammed shut in his face. He fell backward, tumbling in the semi-darkness of the staircase, thundering down as he went. Kurt paused a moment and cautiously opened the door. There was no sign of him, except a bloody spot on the inside of the doorway. He could make out more voices downstairs. The Gestapo now had made their entry on the first floor. It would be a few more minutes before they found the body.

Kurt raced along the roof to the edge. The Gestapo was still below searching with their flashlights through the alley and side doors, checking every doorway and hiding place as they went. Staring at them a moment, his face sullen, he noticed the attic lights come on behind him. The Gestapo had entered the rooftop now. He leaped to the next building but almost missed his mark. The roof was angled downward with several small stone chimneys sticking out into the night sky. He held on to one with all his might. He was in its shadow and watched as the figures in black spread out over the opposite roof.

"Over here!" one of the Germans yelled out as he discovered the body of the dead German. "He is here somewhere, find him!" Their guns drawn, they peered over the roof. One of them started to descend the fire escape.

He called out to the Germans below. "Any sign of him?"

"Nein, nothing so far."

Kurt's grip began to weaken. Not now, dear God, he thought to himself. He strained with all his might just to hold on. Then his luck changed. A drunk had fallen over some garbage cans half a block away and made enough noise to bring the Gestapo down on him in a hurry. Those who were on the roof sped down to join the others below. Using all of his powers of concentration Kurt managed to reposition himself along the slanted, shingled roof, his right hand gripping into the stone like a steel clamp. Using his left leg he pushed his body up between the two chimneys.

Taking in deep, hard breaths of the cold air, he looked across the roof to see cables running in every direction. He unfastened his belt and slid it out over one cable running overhead. Holding on with both hands he tested the line. It was quite taut. He followed that line as he carefully walked along the roof, at times stumbling. When finally he reached the edge he gasped. "Good God," he said to himself. The line ran across the breadth of the entire city street, ending over the harbor.

There was a ship docked and he could see activity of some kind as if they were loading her up. He clenched his lips firmly together and pushed off. He became airborne and could see more Gestapo below. They had discovered the drunk had broken curfew. He was gaining momentum and realized he had only one place to land and her name was *Valhalla*. The ship was docked parallel to the harbor. He could see soldiers finishing loading cargo as he sailed overhead. He held his breath and let go. He landed on the course, linen padding used for tying over the cargo for voyage. There was a strange marking on the top, left side of the crate he was on. It had the German eagle holding a swastika. Below that, he saw a design reminiscent of a bomb.

The Germans were no more than fifteen feet away finishing the loading. He could see the captain of the *Valhalla* salute the German sergeant whose men helped with the deliveries.

"Excellent," the sergeant said. "We are set and on schedule."

Kurt strained to hear the captain speak. "We should arrive in Calais in a matter of hours. From their our bombers will make light work of London."

"Heil Hitler."

Kurt grew pale. This operation was on no one's charts. It was an order by the decree of Hitler himself to retaliate against an embarrassing air raid made by several British planes a week before. Inexplicably they had appeared over Berlin and dropped several bombs on the Führer's capital. The damage was insignificant, in fact no fatalities were recorded, but the thought of British bombers over Berlin had enraged the Führer to a retaliatory strike that he hoped would crush Churchill's brazenness.

Chapter Seventeen

The *Valhalla* pitched in the high white caps of the stormy sea as the gale intensified, striking her starboard side. There were several lookouts top deck, everyone else was safely below. The captain took refuge at his post in the wheelhouse, on course for Calais. Looking over his bearings he sipped an occasional cup of hot coffee and checked his watch.

"Would you care for anything from the mess, Captain?" an aide asked.

"A good idea, Karl. Bring me some schnapps and something to eat."

"Jawohl, Herr Kapitän."

Kurt was on the point of freezing, his face wind-bitten. He squinted out over the edge of the crate. With one hand he held onto a rope lashed around the cargo. The other he used to shield his eyes as he surveyed the top deck. He knew the seas and he could guess that they were nearing their point of destination. He hoped he had enough time to marshal a plan.

In the galley below an aide prepared a modest meal for the captain consisting of sausage, sauerkraut, and a bottle of schnapps, all placed neatly on a serving tray. He reached for it when Kurt's hand came out and snatched it away.

"For the wheelhouse, ja?" Kurt disguised as a cabin boy said.

"Yes, quickly, the captain is hungry."

Walking along the corridor, Kurt, dressed in dulled gray, opened the door. "Bitte," he said, as he served his superior.

"Danke. Please come in and place it on the table," the captain said, both hands on the telescope scouting the seas. "We will be in Calais soon then the air force will have its day."

Kurt, his cap pulled over and down in front of his face, listened as the captain continued. "England is no match for the German air force. Tonight the Luftwaffe will set London ablaze." The captain laughed.

"Now, pour me some schnapps, my boy."

"Yes."

"Fifteen thousand pounds of incendiary bombs, plus eight specially designed high explosive bombs weighing five thousand pounds each. Can you image? Between them they could flatten all of Buckingham Palace, Parliament, and the House of Commons in one stroke." He reached for his drink and sighed. "Ah, nothing like good schnapps to warm you through. Have a glass, my boy, it's all right. Can you imagine the brilliant strategy of our Führer? Our night fighters will guide the heavy bombers into London, drawing RAF fire and leaving the big boys free to find their targets. Salut."

Kurt raised his glass to him. "Here, here," as he downed his shot his steely eyes observed the captain's every move.

Kurt Duran got more than an earful now. He knew the mission and the weapons that were to be used. He also understood that for as long as he was aboard ship he was part of a floating bomb. If any English planes or ships were in the area and a firefight erupted, there would be no escaping.

"What's the matter, boy, don't you like liquor?"

"It's very good, sir."

"Then pour me another glass."

Jacqueline's face had turned white, her eyes strained out and her hands clutched her knees so strongly that her legs all but went numb. She glanced around her surroundings. A small night table by a bunk, a tiny lamp barely fit for reading. The room itself was no bigger than a walk-in closet. But what could she expect aboard a British war submarine.

There was someone at the door. "Who is it?" she asked hesitantly.

"The captain, ma'am."

She stood up, stretching a bit, and walked to the door. "Yes, Captain, what is it? Is everything all right? Are we still leaking?"

He smiled broadly, stepping closer to her. "As a matter of fact the leaks have been patched up. I just wanted to stop by and see if you were all right. I mean, I was a bit rough with you earlier this evening, I wish to give you my apology."

"Accepted. When do you think we'll reach England?"

"My guess will be within the hour."

"Well that's the best news I've heard all evening," she said.

The captain leaned against the doorframe and smiled. "We have time, you know."

She saw that sparkle in his eyes, the arrogant advances of an arrogant man. She replied carefully, "Well, Captain, I am flattered, truly I am, but the last few days have been very trying for me. They've taken quite a toll and I'm afraid I'm fit to be tied. In fact, my eyes are growing heavy as I speak. Would you kindly let me know when we reach port? I must lay down a bit."

"Why, I'd be happy to, madame. If there is anything you need..."

"Yes, Captain, I'll be sure and call you."

She closed the door and locked it, feeling quite disgusted. She stretched out on her cot as best she could and rested her head against the pillow. Not wanting to lay in total darkness she left the lamplight on. Her eyes fluttered several times and she drifted off.

The *King George* stayed on its uninterrupted course for England. The captain ordered the sub to surface. He spied calmly out over the English Channel through the telescope, front side and back. "All is clear," he said triumphantly to a warm reception of hoots and hollers of approval from his crew.

Kurt's mind raced in a panic. Hitler had a plan for personal revenge that had every chance of succeeding. The only hope as he saw it was to disembark at

Calais, follow the bombs to the air base and do what he could to prevent the mission from taking place. In the hallway, immediately behind the galley, he spotted a door labeled in German. It was a supply room. He opened it to find a dark and deep hall closet. Inside were emergency equipment, flares, fire extinguishes and a bevy of other items he could barely make out.

Behind him he heard footsteps. He closed the door and kept quiet. Two members of the crew talked anxiously about arriving at Calais. He cocked open the door a tad and watched them as they passed. He reached for a flaregun and shoved it in the small of his back, along with several flares, which he put inside his pants pocket. He pulled out his lengthy top shirt to conceal it. Making his way to the galley, he planned out his next move.

Hundreds of miles away in the rolling countryside near Paderborn in West Phalia mist-shrouded peaks rose like ziggurats into the night sky, foreboding in appearance. A reconstructed medieval castle had been adapted to serve as an SS retreat. Here a secret chapter of the order assembled on only the most special of circumstances. Each member had his own armchair with an engraved, silver nameplate. The overseer was Reichführer Himmler himself, the supreme head of the SS.

He had assembled twelve of his most trusted SS leaders in the main meeting room. The only light came from the torches that sprang out from the walls. It was a large and airy room and ornate. They sat at a circular table, all in deep concentration. Moments later Hitler opened his eyes and arose.

"Our Führer will be avenged tonight. We'll bring great tribulation to the English crown and her government."

The men sat in total silence, all eyes affixed on Himmler. Their ceremonial daggers rested in front of them on the highly polished wood table.

"The occupation of the island will necessitate extreme measures," he said. "Each and everyone of you has a specific objective once England falls, to implement party policy efficiently and at all costs."

This night held great import in Himmler's heart. Himmler, like Hitler, was a great believer in the occult and he looked upon that night's meeting in as much a spiritual context as a political one. He slowly raised his arm smartly and gave the party salute. All rose to meet it with the thunderous cry of "Heil Hitler!"

Himmler reached for his danger in front of him. "This, gentlemen, will be the night our destiny will be realized."

Each man took up his own dagger respectfully, holding it out in front of him, all in a perfect circle around the table and in total silence. The men were bonding in mind and spirit. Not one man present there that night could defy feeling the mystic powers emitting from the circle of the brotherhood.

Kurt spotted the captain on the way to his quarters and realized they must be close to Calais, for the captain was stashing his bottle of schnapps inside. Remaining quiet in the dark corridor behind the partially opened doorway, Kurt observed the captain sealing up his private quarters and heading back to the wheelhouse. The boat was abuzz as the crew prepared to dock. Men raced from stern to bow in anticipation of their final run to harbor.

Several men dressed in dull gray headed toward the steps leading down to the engine room. More men marched on the top deck, where the heavy weapons were stored. He got an idea. He disappeared into the darkened corridor. Topside, waves were heaving and the thick lines that held the bombs in place creaked as the ship pitched.

Calais was becoming visible along the coastline. There was a moment of ease as one of the Germans lit up a cigarette. Kurt stood there over the foredeck and gazed at the harbor in the distance. There was some mist at sea level though the winds kept blowing it along.

"It was a good run, ja?"

Kurt turned. It was the captain.

"Tonight," the captain said, "I will dock and unload, then head out with the men to town. The women, you know...wunderbar, like no where else except Berlin. You will join us?"

Kurt managed a wide grin. "Jawohl, Herr Kapitän, it will be a pleasure."

The captain asked slyly, "Are you married?"

"Me? No, I haven't the time."

"I understand. The bachelor life is lonely sometimes, but it gives great freedom. Take tonight for instance. I already know which ladies I will visit. They always wait for me. I take a few gifts, stockings, cigarettes, maybe some chocolate, yes, and of course the schnapps. They treat me like a king."

Kurt eyed the entryway to Calais harbor, ignoring the captain. He noticed the German U-boats on either side, guns at the ready. There were eight large crates top deck, and it would not take them long to unload. He wondered whether to sabotage them on board or blow it all up as they entered port, or wait and slip away with the crew to the airstrip, which would be far riskier. He could be sure to get back to the coast either way.

The captain said gleefully, "She's a stupendous, buxom brunette. I could introduce you to her if you wish. She's as beautiful as an angel with lips like cherries. I'm sure she could warm you up after tonight's trip."

"Herr Kapitän," Duran replied, "I'm honored and it will be a pleasure to accompany you and meet this woman."

The horn blew as the ship approached the stationed U-boats. Germans on either side waved at the *Valhalla* from their decks as she glided toward the docks. The mist was clearing and Kurt saw the awesome spectacle assembled before him. There was military hardware stationed along the dock.

"I must see to something." The captain stepped lively down to the deck below and shouted orders in German.

Duran observed several crewmen cutting the restraining ropes to ready the crates for unloading. He in turn worked his way down, took out a small knife and began to cut into the thick weaves as fast as he could. Waves were crashing into the jagged rocks at the sides, and the ship rolled a bit as it turned slightly to meet the dock. There was a snap, followed by a thud, as Kurt cut the line and a large wave caused the crate to crash into two of the hands, catching one on the leg and knocking the other overboard.

Panic ensued as the captain raced to the scene. "What has happened here? My God." He saw the man's leg wedged between two crates. "Mach schnell!" Quickly!" he cried out as he ordered his men to free him. He raced to the starboard side to toss over a line. Up came the German through the murky green sea water, gasping, looking around in a kind of bewilderment, lunging for the line that dangled before him. The captain asked Kurt to help pull him up. "You're down two men for the night," Kurt said. "Perhaps I could postpone your generous invitation for another time and help with the unloading and delivery?"

"Good idea. The last thing I need is my superiors to be cross with me on a mission like this." The man came up and was gasping. He had been taken by complete surprise when he was flung overboard and had gulped down a great deal of sea water. The captain ordered a crewman to take him down to sick bay, along with the other wounded sailor. The captain made it across the gangplank to meet Lieutenant Hoffmyer, who was walking up to the *Valhalla*.

"Guten abend, Herr Kapitän," the lieutenant said. "You made good time." He was dressed smartly in a leather overcoat and highly polished boots.

"Good to see you again," the captain replied. "Well, then let us unload the cargo, shall we?" The captain shouted orders to his men as they scrambled about. The harbor crane started to creek as it began moving its long arm over the ship, its metal hook and chain swinging as it went.

"Come here," the captain said to Kurt. "You will make sure each line is secured before they hoist, understood?"

"Jawohl Herr Kapitän." Kurt could see off the starboard side the convoy trucks parked on the dock below with a small army of soldiers armed with machine pistols. They waited in stony silence to receive the cargo.

Jacqueline had arrived back in London but her heart was still with Kurt. She desperately hoped and prayed there would be word of him, but there was none. She had left the OSS building and was assigned a driver who would take her home. She had insisted on being taken to the place she had agreed upon with Kurt and sat in the backseat of a black Mercedes Benz. She took out a small piece of paper with the directions to Kurt's home written on them.

She handed it to the driver. "Take me there as fast as possible." Her eyes grew misty; war had no rules. She had lost a family and now possibly the love of her life. "No," she told herself. Kurt had asked her to wait for him there and that was what she intended to do. She tried to remain in a positive state of mind and was in fact looking forward to seeing how he lived and to be in the isolation of the countryside. She wanted no part of the war. She needed time to recover and to reconnect with the simple pleasures: The scent of her lover, the feel of his caress, the warmth of his embrace.

She tried to light herself a cigarette but her hands trembled too much. She sighed, took in a deep breath and tried again. After a quick smoke she looked down in reflective silence. Indifferent to her surroundings, consumed by her hopes and fears, she prayed. She maintained her quiet demeanor until the driver informed her they had arrived.

"Thank you so much."

"Will there be anything else, my lady?"

"No."

The place looked deserted. "Is someone waiting for you?" the driver inquired.

She looked at the dark exterior of the house and saw how the moonlight cast its shadow over the front door. She envisioned Kurt standing there and smiled. "Why yes, there is."

"Very well, have a good night." The driver backed up, turned and sped away.

She was lonelier than she had ever felt in her life. She reached in her purse and pulled out a gold chain. On it dangled the Star of David, something she dared not wear in occupied Europe. She had received it on her seventeenth birthday from her mother. It sparkled beautifully. She kissed it and placed it around her neck. Looking up at heaven she said softly, "Dear God, watch over my love tonight and deliver him to me."

He had told her where he kept the spare key, between the third and fourth stone on the right side by the front door. She reached down and felt it, brought it out and unlocked the front door. She stepped inside. Turning on the lights she saw that the rooms were clean, everything in its place. She was starting to feel a bit more at ease now, feeling she actually had come home.

The winds were quite strong and she was cold, too tired to eat. She felt a good night's sleep was in order.

Fate had dropped him onto the cargo ship, Duran thought to himself. His hands were sweating profusely. The amassed firepower along the docks was staggering; this was a very special place indeed, he thought. He stood on the loading dock while the last of the crates found safe haven among the convoy of trucks.

Kurt watched intently as the Germans swarmed around him like locusts. The captain of the *Valhalla* had done his part and was sitting regally in the jeep with the staff sergeant at the wheel.

"I'll say hello to Angelina for you."

Kurt smiled and waved at the captain. "Have a good night, Herr Kapitän."

"I will, my boy, that I will."

The vehicle raced past him, exited off the dock and into the night. SS troops stepped smartly in front of him as they got into the trucks to accompany them back to the airstrip.

"Well don't just stand there, get in the truck," an SS major shouted at Kurt.

He saluted and followed orders. The canvas canopy hung low, the seats were all hardwood, and the SS were like robots, silent, an air of brutish vulgarity to them. There sat a total of six men with him, all in one truck, weapons in front. Kurt said nothing, just observed. He checked his watch and he realized the SS were in parade uniform. That meant dignitaries would be present wherever it was they were going.

One of the Germans spoke. "How long have you sailed with *Valhalla*?"

Duran was at a loss momentarily. "All of eight months," he said.

"Ah! You're the lucky one, always on the sea. My father was a seaman in the first world war. But for me, I like the land more," he laughed. The other SS men joined in. Kurt offered a tense smile.

The truck rumbled along the dirt road as it hit an occasional dip. Kurt peered over his shoulder as the vehicles behind them slowed to a halt. Their truck stopped as well. It was a ride of no more than ten minutes. He was the first to jump out, and as he looked around his heart started to race. Before him lay an airstrip with makeshift hangars. The sight of it was truly awesome. The field was cleverly concealed from reconnaissance. Specially constructed camouflage prevented any close scrutiny.

There were in all two hundred planes hidden from aerial view. Along the side of the strip was a concrete bunker. There were dozens of specialists to ensure a smooth attack that evening, and there was a certain tension in the air as the weapons were unloaded and moved out. In no time Duran found himself entering the concrete bunker along with the SS as he wheeled in one of the bombs. The interior was stark and foreboding. The men inside all wore white.

"Halt," someone shouted.

Another shouted out from a corner. "Nein. This way, quickly," the SS started to push the bomb along on a transporter. A man stepped out from the shadows. He was tall, in his late forties, with a thick beard and spectacles. His arms were folded across his massive chest. "Very good. You're just on time."

"Quickly!" an SS officer called out, and the bombs were wheeled away in an adjacent tunnel. There were lightbulbs overhead every ten meters. An iron door opened by itself as they neared the end. Outside stood huge German bombers, the swastika painted on the end tail of each plane. The bomber doors lay open. Inside each cockpit pilots sat patiently waiting to receive their cargo. The SS stopped directly under the belly of each aircraft and secured their loads. Powerful metal clamps bore down to hoist the bombs into the underbelly of each aircraft.

Kurt saw attack aircraft off to his right, aligned in rows across the airstrip. This armada would be the Luftwaffe shock wave before the bombs were to be dropped. The other bombs containing high explosives were already loaded. In the distance he could see troops moving toward the planes, ten thousand in all.

An SS lieutenant beamed with pride as he told the corporal of the guard, "After our bombs wipe out the British government, our SS storm troops will parachute down behind enemy lines and a guerilla war will be waged, the likes of which the English have never seen. The ruling class will suffer sabotage and murder."

This was Hitler's real operation Sea Lion. A quick airborne assault, aided by incredible firepower to rain terror and destruction on London. This airborne operation was to spearhead the assault.

He watched heavily armed storm troopers climb aboard the aircrafts. The Germans would use the night fighters as decoys to take the brunt of the RAF defensive measures, and the main body would then fly on to London and beyond. There, ten thousand storm troopers would parachute into the countryside.

It would be another twenty minutes before take off. Cloud cover was minimal and the wind was favorable.

Kurt looked around and saw that security was lax as the lieutenant chatted away. Kurt disappeared from view. He found himself on the edge of the airstrip all alone in the darkness. He moved in great haste along the freshly cut grass to a fuel truck. The driver sat in wait behind the wheel. There was no one else around.

"Un moment, bitte," Kurt said in perfect German as he strolled by the side of the vehicle.

The driver looked down at him. "Good evening, what is it?"

"I'm afraid there's a gas leak in the back of your truck."

"That's impossible," the older man said straightening up as he opened the door and got out. "Where? Show me." As the man walked behind Kurt he in turn took out his knife and punctured the gas tank. Then stepping aside Kurt led him around. As the man watched in surprise the leaking gasoline, with a swift chop to the neck, the German fell down and Duran pulled him out of sight. Kurt donned the driver's cap, jumped behind the wheel, turned on the engine and gave it some gas. He slowly began to drive along the airstrip, gas spilling out on the roadway near the edges of the planes. He came to the end of the strip and stopped, turned off the engine, exited the passenger side, and made his way back under the cover of trees.

He noticed a large commotion at the beginning of the runway. The German elite were there among the crew, scientists and dignitaries to watch the beginning of the assault. Duran stopped fifty yards from the fuel truck and took out the flare gun and loaded a flare in its barrel. As he cocked it to fire he took careful aim and squeezed the trigger. A bright flash shot out as the projectile found its target and a brilliant explosion ensued, lifting the truck off the ground, the trail of gasoline whipping out into a frenzy of shooting flames.

Plane after plane exploded, row upon row all across the field. Pandemonium struck as frightened storm troopers tried to jump, only to be blown away before they reached the ground. The wave of fire and explosion began heading directly to the main planes and all at once a series of explosions shot up, spewing red and yellow flames into the night sky, the bombs detonating and taking with them the Nazi entourage. Debris rained down on the bunker, which started to melt into the ground.

Hiding behind rocks along the side of the hill, Kurt patiently waited as explosion after explosion rocked the compound, his face aglow in the intense red light of the flames. He watched in stunned disbelief at how close England came that night. As the smoke started to clear he could make out huge craters populating the field where moments ago stood a deadly armada. The twisted wrecks were engulfed in flames, pieces still falling out of the sky in places.

Kurt wasted no time in running for the coast. As he raced through the terrain he felt a certain exhilaration overtake him. He had averted disaster and the anticipation of seeing his beloved Jacqueline was now all-consuming.

Out from nowhere shots rang out and he dropped. An SS patrol that had not been hit by the explosion started moving and opened fire. He lay motionless, face down, hands in front of him. In the distance he could hear a rumbling through the brush. He inched his way to a cluster of bushes and hid behind them, out of sight. It was difficult for him to get a clear view of the surrounding area.

Not too far ahead two silhouettes popped out, carrying machine pistols. They strode silently past as he stared at them behind the flickering leaves and branches. There was no way he could know how many more there might be, so he waited. He wanted to be sure. A moment later one more soldier walked up and stopped directly in front of Kurt. The German looked around and down toward Kurt's locale, and spotted one of his feet sticking out.

Before the German had a chance to call out to his comrades, a knife blade was wedged into his abdomen. The German dropped his weapon, gasped and fell over dead. Picking up his machine pistol, Kurt took off.

The other two SS were twenty yards ahead when a voice called out from behind him, warning the Germans. A fourth soldier appeared to his left. Kurt opened fire, cutting him down immediately. Before the other two could return fire, Kurt hit them as well. All was silent. He could not see any more movement.

Alexander Presniakov

He ran to the road, where there was a jeep. He got in and drove; the coast was only a few minutes away.

Chapter Eighteen

First came the flashes of lightning, then thunder crackled overhead. It started to rain. Kurt stopped the vehicle and directly below him he saw a small French fishing boat leaning out from behind the cliffs. He knew this was his last chance.

He started to make his way down the beach, tossing his jacket aside. His face was pelleted by raindrops as he ran on down to the shoreline and dove into the sea. The surf was going out and swept him along toward the vessel. The ship had its netting out over its starboard side and he grabbed hold, hanging firm. Water smacked his face now and again as he took deep breaths in between. The sky was growing dark gray and the waves were breaking into whitecaps, creating a very difficult ride.

He shot up for a fresh gulp of air. As he came out spouting a mouthful of water, a hand took hold of his shoulder. He flinched and stared straight up. There a man with a kind face, red whiskers on his chin, and captain's hat greeted him. His stubby fingers bore deep into Kurt's shoulders.

"You know I can't hold you all day. Climb aboard."

Kurt leaned against the railing coughing. "Are you all right?"

"Yes," he said, "I suppose. Please, sir, let me explain."

"No need," the captain replied. "Ian Richards radioed me and said to keep an eye out. You are Kurt Duran, are you not?"

His face lit up. "Why, yes. Then you are—"

"We're with the French Resistance. No self-respecting seaman would be fishing in this type of weather but we need to keep up appearances so the German U-boats don't bother us. We can get you to the coast of England."

"That would be perfect," Kurt smiled hesitantly as he looked over his drenched clothes.

"Come, my boy, let's take you inside. I'm sure you could use some hot coffee." In his cabin the captain asked, "Ian mentioned a woman."

"Yes, she was picked up by the English, but the Germans surprised us and the submarine had to disengage. I was left behind."

Kurt grew hesitant then asked, "How is Charles von Krongt?"

The captain lowered his head. "He's a good man you know, unfortunately the Nazis didn't think so. We've got word that he was imprisoned and interrogated but I'm sure he'll say nothing. That explosion we saw, was that you?"

"Yes. The Luftwaffe was about to launch a retaliatory strike over London. It would have been quite messy."

The captain let out a heartfelt laugh. "Instead you left a mess with the Germans, right?" The captain positioned himself by the wheel as Kurt sat in a rather uncomfortable armchair sipping his coffee. A cabin boy ran in, "Captain, we are clear."

"Good. Now it is full steam ahead. We have to make sure no Krauts were in the area before we gave her the juice," the captain explained. "Sit back and relax, we'll be in England in no time."

"One question for you, Captain. How did Richards know I'd be needing your help? After all the English sub was there."

"Yes, but Ian felt it best to put out a general alert throughout the French Resistance and through good fortune we happened to spot you in the nick of time," the captain said, smiling.

In London, Ian Richards sat behind his desk in his drab office. He was quite weary from the day's events and the captain of the English submarine the *King George* was there with him. Richards had just had words with him. He was extremely distressed over the decision to leave Duran behind. "We must make arrangements for another run," he said. "He'll have sense to stay put and wait. Dammit, our best agent left in that Nazi-infested coastline."

There was a knock at the door. His secretary stepped in. "This just in, sir." She handed him a piece of paper which read:

Kurt Duran picked up by a farmer
in Norfolk, by the coast.

"Thank God," Richards exclaimed. "Captain, return to your duties, your services will not be needed." Richards stormed out of his office. "Get my driver ready."

As the secretary called ahead he put on his coat and raced through the doors.

"Well you're a sight for sore eyes," Kurt said, as he sat on a tree stump in front of the farmhouse smoking a cigarette.

Richards stuck his head through the back window of his Mercedes. "Speak of the devil."

The driver came to a halt and the sun came out. The winds swept across the meadows as rows of poppy seed and grass swayed below.

"I'm glad to see you're all right." Richards stepped across the dirt road, hand extended.

Kurt stood up, his cigarette dangling between his lips.

"How's Jacqueline?" he asked.

"I haven't heard from her," Richards replied. "I believe the captain of the *King George* said something about her promising to meet you at your country house."

"Kiel Holmby is a spy."

"What?"

"It's true."

"Well, he has disappeared since you left."

"That's not surprising."

Richards looked around. "You couldn't have picked a better place to wash up. The prime minister is at his country estate not far from here this week, and expressed an interest in seeing you."

"I see. Well, I'm honored to say the least. By the way, old man, I've got a bit of good news for you."

"Save it. The prime minister doesn't like to be kept waiting, and you can't very well go to him looking like that. Put on this." Richards removed his overcoat and helped Kurt into it. "Now let's get moving."

Churchill was only fifteen minutes away at his favorite retreat, his Norfolk country house, which provided him with a much needed escape. He strolled out onto his balcony, puffing on his cigar, and looked out to sea. The Channel had a particular peace to it that day.

His valet stepped in behind him. "Sir."

"My boy, what is it?"

"Mr. Ian Richards is here to see you, and he's brought someone with him, a Mr. Kurt Duran."

Churchill energetically turned around. "Let me pass," he warned, as his intense eyes stared straight ahead.

Churchill was ecstatic at the sight of his guests.

"Welcome," he said. "Please, come inside."

Both men approached him. "Please, sit down," Churchill said, as he made his way to a large armchair in the corner by the window. He sat down, his feet extended out on the floor in front, puffing rings of smoke. He was extremely content. "Nothing quite like a good cigar," he said. Both men sat quietly at the edge of the couch. "Now then, I was told you did a very brave thing recently, Mr. Duran, and I'm not one to overlook heroism. Rest assured, your message from Europe was received. We in turn have taken all necessary security precautions."

Kurt shifted in his seat. "But, Prime Minister, the information was false, it was a trap."

Churchill smiled, "Yes, I know."

Kurt looked surprised. "We have our own double agents in Berlin," Churchill said. There was a pause as Churchill sat there, his eyes downcast. "My sincere apologies for that fiasco regarding your rescue. You see, naval intelligence is a world all its own. They have certain procedures that only make sense to them."

Richards stepped in. "Mr. Prime Minister, I believe Duran has some rather pressing information he wanted to share with us."

Kurt cleared his throat a bit. "Well, sir, you see, after the *King George* submarine departed I sought out other means of rescue. After my message was sent I fled Gestapo pursuers and managed to come across a ship that in turn led me to Calais. It had on board a very dangerous cargo of bombs to be used as a retaliatory strike by Hitler against London."

Churchill listened intently.

"There was a makeshift airfield with troops and planes, and fortunately I was able to sabotage their efforts and the base was destroyed." Kurt waited in anticipation as Churchill eyed both men.

"Sir, the kind of bombs they had were incendiary and high explosive. It did not take much on my part to get the fireworks started."

Churchill beamed with delight. "You did quite well, and for this I must reward you."

Kurt nodded. "Well, Mr. Prime Minister, there is something. You see, there is a very special lady in my life and quite frankly my furlough was cut short so I could ready myself for this mission."

"Think nothing of it, my boy." He turned to Richards. "How much time does Duran have coming?"

"One week, sir."

"Make it two," Churchill said. There was a call as the prime minster's valet informed him dinner guests were due to arrive shortly. The prime minister arose. "My heavens, I've lost complete track of time."

Richards and Kurt stood up as well. Churchill thanked them for coming and excused himself.

Once outside, Kurt cracked a smile. "Two weeks," he said.

Richards rolled his eyes. "I heard."

The Mercedes pulled up to OSS headquarters in London. Both men got out. "Well I suppose you'll be needing a ride to your house. Take the car," Richards said. "It will be all right."

"But I won't be needing the driver."

"So be it. Say hello to Jacqueline for me."

"My pleasure."

He got in and drove for what seemed hours. It was dusk and on a lonely stretch of road he came upon a convertible with its hood up. It was directly in the roadway. Kurt had stopped off at his London apartment and changed some time before, and was now in his civvies, leather sports jacket and slacks.

Kurt got out and asked, "What seems to be the matter?"

The man behind the hood said, "I'm no mechanic but I think it's the ignition."

As Kurt walked up he received the shock of his life.

Kiel Holmby stood there, holding a Mauser with silencer.

156

"Good to see you again, old man."

"I can't say the same thing for you," Kurt replied. "How did you know where I'd be?"

"I'm with OSS, remember?"

"You mean you were."

"Little matter. You'll no longer be with anybody. I had high hopes for you. Training you for the Eagle's Nest. The plan seemed foolproof. You deliver false invasion plans to Churchill and the real attack would have caught the British off guard. But I suppose every plan has its risks."

"How could you—"

"How could I be a spy? I work for what I believe in, as you do, only our ideologies are different. So invasion won't come this month, or maybe not even next, but sooner or later England will fall."

"I won't bet on that." Duran stood there, carefully staring at the Mauser, both hands in his pockets. "And I had the greatest regard for your instructions."

Holmby snapped back, "Get off it. We had a mission and it almost worked."

Kurt frowned a bit. "So, Kiel, or whatever your real name is, where do you go from here?"

"Berlin. To be reassigned. They obviously can't use me in OSS anymore, but Europe is a big place. Enough of this stalling. I've got to finish this today. Step over to the side." He pointed with the tip of his gun, gesturing sternly.

Kurt waited by the side of the road for what was to come next.

"Have any last words?"

"Well, just these. The wars not over 'til it's over."

Holmby looked confused and asked, "What's that suppose to mean?"

A shot rang out. Both men stood perfectly still. The Mauser in Holmby's hand slipped and fell to the ground. A small stream of blood ran down the corner of his mouth as he looked down at his chest. "I forgot to frisk you," he moaned.

"That you did," Kurt replied.

Holmby fell backward into the brush, dead.

Kurt took out the smoking, snub-nosed, six-shot revolver, walked over to his car and tossed it into the passenger seat.

By the time he drove up to his home it was dark. He could see the curtains moving; Jacqueline had seen somebody pull up. The front door flung open, she ran outside in her nightdress and stopped. His headlights were turned off.

"Kurt, is that you?" she called out anxiously.

A figure got out and walked up to her. "What did your mother tell you?"

She smiled, her eyes danced with joy as she leaped up to him, her arms extended, embracing him passionately. They kissed, and he looked lovingly at her as she answered him.

"That love will always survive."

157

That evening there were no interruptions. As they lay in bed she told him, "Not knowing if you were alive or dead was the hardest thing." She paused a bit and asked, "What of invasion, when will Sea Lion happen?"

"It won't," Kurt said gently. "Hitler missed his chance. He'll bomb us now and again to be sure, but there won't be an invasion." He reached down to his pants on the floor and with his right hand removed a dark object.

"What's that?" she asked inquisitively.

"That, my dear, is all that's left of a German night bomber. I found this in Calais." He tossed it aside as he leaned closer to her and asked, "Now shouldn't we have that champagne while it is still chilled.

The End

About The Author

Alexander Presniakov is a painter, sculptor and inventor. He is published by *Who's Who in International Art* in Switzerland. His website is http://www.whoswhoart.presniakov.ch Mr. Presniakov lives in San Francisco.